TUSKS

A ***Just Cause Universe*** Novel

Ian Thomas Healy

Local Hero Press Edition

Tusks
A *Just Cause Universe* Novel
Published by Local Hero Press, LLC

1st Printing
Local Hero Press: trade paperback, May 1, 2016
Printed in the United States of America

http://www.ianthealy.com

ISBN-13: 9781971445090

Cover art by Jeff Hebert
Book design by Local Hero Press, LLC

Books by Local Hero Press

The *Just Cause Universe*

Just Cause
The Archmage
Day of the Destroyer
Deep Six
Jackrabbit
Champion
Castles
The Lion and the Five Deadly Serpents
Tusks
The Neighborhood Watch
Jackrabbit: Big In Japan
Arena
Hero Academy
The Path
Cinco de Mayo
Search and Rescue
Rooftops
Plague
Soldiers of Fortune
Just Cause Universe Compendium
Destroyer of Earth
Flint and Steel
The Club
Jackrabbit: Rinse and Repeat
Posse
Extinction Event
Rain Must Fall

Pariah of Verigo

Pariah's Moon
Pariah's War

Three Flavors of Tacos

The Guitarist
Making the Cut
The Scene Stealers

Collections

Airship Lies
High Contrast
The Good Fight
The Good Fight 3: Sidekicks
The Good Fight 4: Homefront
The Good Fight 5: The Golden Age
Muddy Creek Tales
Caped

Other Novels

Assassin
Blood on the Ice
Funeral Games
Hope and Undead Elvis
Horde
The Murder Squad (2026)
Roast Wyvern (and Other Recipes)
*Starf*cker*
Strings
The Oilman's Daughter
Troubleshooters

Nonfiction

Action! Writing Better Action Using Cinematic Techniques

DREAMERS

Here we are again. This is the ninth time I've written one of these and it still feels awkward. As it takes a village to raise a child, so does it take one to create a book, and I have several folks without which this book would not exist. First and foremost I must thank my dear friend and editor Allison M. Dickson, who knows more about the *Just Cause Universe* than any living person besides me. I'm also grateful to Jeff Hebert for yet another fantastic cover. Many thanks to the people who've developed the internet and application tools I use to bring books to you. I support a free and open internet and open-source software, and so should you. Special thanks to my dear friend and partner-in-crime Alicia Howie, who keeps me going through good times and bad. Much gratitude for my family, who's pretty well resigned to the fact that I'm never going to give up this writing thing. And last but not least, thank you to my fans, without whom there would be no *Just Cause Universe.*

—Ian Thomas Healy
April, 2016

All people are tools. Some are sharper than others.

August, 2009
New York City

As hard as it was to lead a superhero team during the times of conflict and crisis, Sally learned it was even harder to do so during the lulls in action. After the initial turbulence surrounding the opening of Just Cause New York died down, the political drama and the scandal drifted further and further away from the front page, top-of-the-website headlines, Sally had found being in charge was a lot like being the Residence Assistant for a dorm full of particularly difficult students.

Take Snapdragon and Snowball, for example. The two heroes couldn't be more different. His powers were based in fire, while hers focused upon ice. He was the child of ethnic Albanian immigrants, while her ancestry was Scandinavian within spitting distance of the Arctic Circle. He was tall and lanky. She was a dwarf. And yet, the two of them had connected early on, even before JCNY had officially opened. More than once Sally had rounded a corner to find steam billowing through the halls—a side effect of their passion throes. She had to bring the two of them into her office to have the same talk that Juice had once given to her and Jason. Don't let it interfere with duties. Keep things professional in public. She'd felt funny saying those things to her younger charges, knowing full well that she and Jason and been in the same place years before. Nabil and Sara made such a great couple that Sally really enjoyed watching their relationship blossom from the sidelines.

When they broke up, it was loud, ugly, and messy.

Their arguing had echoed up and down the halls of Fort Justice, to the point that even Jason had looked up from his laptop and asked Sally if she was going to do something about it. If it had been loud enough for him to notice, it must have been bad.

"We broke up once. We got over it." Sally was wearing a strip in the carpet of her office, pacing back and forth at super-speed as she often did when struggling with a problem. Her assistant Davey had suggested replacing it with a treadmill generator to help offset the power requirements of the base. Sally had chuckled, but she'd also seen the item come up for her approval on budgetary forms. She hadn't rubber-stamped it.

"And as I recall, babe, it took someone trying to take over the world to get us back together." Jason closed his laptop. He'd been experimenting with some composition software, thinking about getting into the production side of music. Ever since getting nailed in the head with a powerful sonic attack several months prior, he'd been dealing with some minor hearing loss. It wasn't enough to affect his daily job or ability to toss cars around like they were frisbees when the time called for it, but it meant he had a hard time playing his guitar the way he'd used to. Sally could tell it hurt him in ways she, someone who couldn't carry a tune, would never understand.

"We'd have worked it out, eventually."

"And we weren't having our knockdown drag-out in a rebuilt floating oil rig or shooting fireballs or ice streams at each other. I know it's high summer, and it's miserable out there, but I really don't feel like going for an unplanned swim in the Bay, and neither do you." As if to illustrate his point, the entire base shuddered and Sally overheard techs in the Command Center ordering pumps to adjust ballast to one of Fort Justice's legs.

"Fine, I'll go talk to them. What do I say?"

"You're the boss. Be the boss." Jason grinned. "Bring down the Gavel of Swift Kicks in the Ass Justice."

Sally smiled back. "Oh, I can definitely bring that. I'll be right back." She left her office at what was for her a gentle trot, but to Jason she would have vanished in a blur of crimson and gold.

She found half of the residence level coated in a thick sheet of ice, already melting into puddles on the carpet that would have the cleaning crew working overtime. A whooshing sound and flash of heat suggested Snapdragon wasn't taking the argument any better than Snowball. The door to Sara's room was frozen solid with multiple layers of ice, but the sounds of the couple's anger carried clearly through it. Sally knew from experience how to deal with ice walls. She placed her hands against the sheet and started quivering them at super-speed, setting up a sympathetic vibration in the ice that shattered it into snow. She didn't have the brawn to kick open the door like Jason could have, but she could still make an entrance, and proceeded to at top speed.

Snapdragon got doused with a fire extinguisher before he knew what hit him. Snowball got a super-speed-redirected jet of water from the kitchenette faucet to the face that froze in place. A moment later, both heroes stood stupidly in their dripping, steaming clothing while Sally gave them the kind of dressing down that would have been a legendary scene in a movie if anyone had thought to film it. She suspended them both for a week and ordered them off the base. "I don't care where you go, but you better not go there together. I find out you're anywhere near each other for the next week and your next duty assignment is cleaning toilets in Deep Six!"

Thoroughly cowed by their boss' righteous anger over their behavior, Snapdragon and Snowball departed, one flying toward Manhattan on wings of flame and the other jetting off toward the mainland atop an icy ribbon.

Sally turned to leave and found Davey standing in the hallway with a woman she didn't know personally but about whom had heard many good things. "Was it too much? I don't think it was too much."

Davey shook her head. Her mass of curls was pinned up atop her head in an artful stack. "No, I think you showed remarkable restraint, and it will help our newest member here know that you're one not to trifle with."

Sally smiled at the newcomer. "Yeah. No trifling, like she said. You must be Penelope. Do you prefer Penny?"

The woman cracked a smile. "Please." She was a minor telekinetic with a law enforcement background and a real success story for the Parahuman Resources Agency, as she was the first Champion ever promoted up to regular membership with Just Cause. Sally had specifically requested Penny Lane for New York for her non-parahuman talents. She had spent seven years in the NYPD, was a member of the Emergency Services Unit, and a top-rated sniper. Her ability to fling weights of less than one ounce with deadly accuracy was a bonus. She might not replace Sally's former second-in-command Crackerjack, but she would certainly fill the tactician spot on her team that had been lacking since his retirement. Penny was only a couple inches taller than Sally, but probably had fifty pounds on her, all rock hard muscle. Sally knew women had a harder time in police departments, and those who went into SWAT training had to fight against years of discrimination and sexism. From the scar decorating one eyebrow to the nose that had been broken a couple times, it looked like Penny had fought every step of the way.

"Your folks are Beatles fans, huh?"

Penny rolled her eyes. "Never heard that one before."

"My husband likes the Beatles, but he's a musician. Personally, I can't stand them." Sally spotted Yunbao at the end of the hall, looking at the melting ice chunks with curious interest. "Yunbao, are you busy right now?"

The Chinese woman trotted down the hall, her paws making no sound on the floor. She was one of the rare parahumans who'd developed actual physical mutations—in her case, the appearance and abilities of a humanoid leopard. She was the daughter of former Just Cause member Lionheart and a formidable martial artist. "I am free."

"Yunbao, this is Penelope Lane, our newest member. Would you show her around Fort Justice and help her get settled in?"

Yunbao bowed. "I would be honored."

Penny looked up at the lithe felinoid. "I hear you're quite the bad-ass. I hope you've got time to teach me some nifty moves."

Yunbao bowed again. "I have some talent in close-quarters fighting I would be pleased to share."

The two women headed down the hall, their conversation rapidly turning to discussion of various techniques and applications of hand-to-hand combat. Sally and Davey watched them go. "She's more like Jack than I thought. Punching and guns on the brain."

Davey chuckled. "Wait until you see her costume."

"What is it?"

"She doesn't have one. It's a SWAT jumpsuit and combat boots."

Sally laughed. "My God, she *is* Jack. We better make sure they never meet. They might accidentally blow the base up on purpose."

"So what are you going to do about the more immediate problem of Snapdragon and Snowball?"

"Let them cool off. A little time apart will do some good. Then when they come back, if they're still in a mood to fight, we can all head down to the Tank and go a few rounds."

"Combat therapy?"

"It has its place."

"That it does, boss. That it does."

* * *

"Are you going to spend all night doing paperwork or are you coming to bed?" Jason was lying on his stomach on the bed with his head where his feet would normally be, his feet kicking up behind him and his chin resting on his clasped hands. He was putting maximum effort into being cute and sexy at the same time, and Sally loved him dearly for it.

"You think you're annoyed? Try running a superhero team for the government sometime." Sally grimaced at her computer. "This system runs so slow that every time I start exceeding normal human words-per-minute, the buffers crash and burn and I have to call a Command Center techie to replace processors and memory and stuff."

"Government cheese at its finest." Jason yawned. "Maybe you should hire your friend Vanitha to come redo our systems."

"I've asked her to. She's not interested. She's got some big time corporate clients that are keeping her in hardware without her having to worry about the PRA breathing down her neck."

"I thought everyone wanted a big fat government contract." He batted his eyelashes at her.

"Not everyone, babycakes."

He patted the bed. "Come on over here, beautiful. Don't make me go all Tarzan on you."

"Oooh, are you going to knock me in the head, drag me back to your cave by my hair, and have your way with me?"

"I'm thinking about it."

"I always heard that the sex dried up after marriage." Sally put her computer into standby mode and stretched her arms over her head. "Somehow I don't think we got the memo."

Jason grinned and let his native Georgia drawl shine. "I ain't never thought highly of book-learnin'."

"Stay right there, lover. I'm just going to brush my teeth and take my pill. Be there before you can say *the sixth sheik's sixth sheep's sick*."

"I can't say that and you know it." He rolled over onto his back and looked at her upside down. "You ever think maybe about skipping your pills? You'd make a beautiful mother, you know."

Sally sighed. It seemed like the topic of starting a family came up more and more frequently. She knew Jason loved kids. He'd grown up with a couple of younger brothers, in a tightly-knit neighborhood where everyone's kids knew everyone else's and they all looked after each other with the kind of care that can only happen in the South. As long as she'd known him, he was involved with volunteering for disadvantaged kids. Their first date had been to an inner-city children's center. She'd enjoyed it more because of the time she got to spend with Jason than the kids. Sally's opinion of kids was they were walking germ and snot factories, forever handing you things that were inexplicably sticky and crawling with filth. "I don't have to be a mother to be beautiful, silly boy."

"No, but then I could call you my MILF."

Sally looked down at the wheel of her birth control pills. She had never seriously considered not taking them. The idea of being pregnant had about as much appeal as a strong bout of the stomach flu. She popped the next pill out of the foil and swallowed it. "I hate that term."

"Sorry, babe. I know you're not really into us having kids."

Sally brushed her hair in swift, vicious strokes, making it snap with static electricity. "Then why do you keep bringing it up?"

"I can't help it. I know this is something we probably should have talked about before we got married. I can't force you to have kids. I really hope you'll want them someday. I'm just afraid of something happening to one of us before that point." He sighed. "Also, my mom keeps asking about it."

Sally felt like stamping her foot as if she were a petulant child. She held back her temper, knowing it wouldn't make either of them feel better. Instead she pulled off her sweats and t-shirt and laid down beside Jason, nuzzling his neck. "Someday my clock will go off, and that's the day I flush the rest of my pills for good."

"Yeah?" He kissed her forehead.

She let her hands wander down his torso. "Until then, all we can do is keep practicing."

* * *

An odd buzzing sound woke Sally from her post-coital slumber. She listened to Jason's stentorian snores, a sound which might have disturbed someone else but which she found to be as soothing as a white noise generator. The sound repeated itself and she sat bolt upright in bed. Unexplained sounds had no place in a secure paramilitary facility. A flashing drew her eyes toward her computer. It was no longer in standby mode. A swirling maelstrom of colors danced across the screen to coalesce into the terrifying visage of the goddess Kali. The fanged, blue-skinned woman's tongue lolled from her mouth like a serpent as the necklace of shrunken heads dripped realistic blood down the face of Sally's computer screen.

Normally the sight of such an unexpected image could be interpreted as the beginning of a dream or a nightmare, but this was someone familiar. "Vanitha? What are you doing here?"

Vanitha Bhat, or Kali, as she called herself, was a freelance parahuman operative with the ability to physically enter computers and control them from the inside, making her the perfect hacker. She had been instrumental in helping Sally several times in the past couple of years, and Sally trusted her—at least as much as one could trust a reliable and honest mercenary. “I’m fulfilling a contract.” The Kali-figure spoke with a lisp, probably due to the flopping tongue. It wasn’t necessary; Vanitha could have simply used her own voice, but she prided herself on realism in her hacks. “An interested third party wants to speak with you.”

“What about Jason?” Sally glanced over at her husband. Unlike her, he was a notoriously light sleeper, and she was surprised he hadn’t already awakened.

“He’ll stay asleep. I’m broadcasting a subsonic carrier wave designed to keep him in delta wave sleep. Just like that signal I used to awaken you was broadcast on a frequency that he can’t hear due to his auditory damage.”

“How do you know that? Did you hack into his medical records?”

“You make it sound like I used a blunt axe, Sally. Please. It was much more finessed than that.”

“Dammit, Vanitha!”

“Hush. It’s still possible for Jason to wake up if you keep stomping around there like an angry elephant. Now get up, get a drink of water, and pick up your phone.”

“My phone?” Sally looked at the smartphone on her bedside table.

Kali’s image appeared on the small touchscreen. “Incoming call in ten . . . nine . . . eight . . .”

Sally didn’t know what else to do, so she went and took a drink of water like Vanitha suggested. It helped wake her up and cleared some of the sleep taste from her mouth. She returned to her phone and a chill ran down her spine. There were very few people in the world who could afford Vanitha’s services and then use them solely to reach out to Sally. She couldn’t see how anything good could come from such an arrangement.

“ . . . three . . . two . . . one. Go ahead, sir.” The Kali image vanished from Sally’s phone to be replaced with the standard screen for phone calls.

“Hello, Sally.” The voice sounded oddly familiar, yet incomplete, like it needed something more for her to identify. That very thought was the nudge her brain needed to realize to whom she was speaking.

"Harlan Washington." Of course it would be him. The man who murdered several heroes at Tornado's funeral in 1985. The man who took away any chance for Sally ever to know her own father two months before she was born. The man who had time and time again been a nasty thorn in the side of Just Cause, and who'd taken his grudge to deadly levels.

The man to whom she owed a favor.

When a nanotech plague had threatened to eliminate human life on the Earth in favor of solely parahumans, Sally had swallowed her pride and approached the most brilliant and devious man she knew, and he had delivered. His ability to understand, build, and control machinery was as primal as a god shaping life from the mud of a river bed. His counter-plague had saved the world, and nobody but Sally ever knew how much a debt he was owed. All he had asked for in return was a favor, to be called in at a time of his choosing, which she was bound to accept. Sure, she could refuse it, but then the world would know she had made a treaty with one of America's most-wanted criminals. It would mean the end of her career in Just Cause.

"It's time, Sally. I'm calling in the favor you owe me."

Sally grimaced and swallowed against the acidic bile threatening to rise up her throat. "What is it?"

"I need you and your teammate Minerva to assist me for a period not longer than one week. You won't be doing anything illegal or immoral. I promise."

Sally shook her head even though Washington couldn't see her through the phone. Or maybe he could. Maybe he'd paid Vanitha enough money to be spying upon her through her computer's camera even while talking to her. "No. Minerva's not part of this. She owes you nothing."

"But you do, and the favor I'm calling in requires her as well."

"No deal. Pick something else." Why was he asking for Minerva? Something about her teammate's powers, certainly, which were at best undefined. Was she the real goal? Was Sally only a stepping stone to Minerva?

"This is the favor. I'm calling it in. Or perhaps you'd like me to start contacting the media? There's nothing Americans like better than to see a hero taken down a peg or two. Your association with me will ruin you."

"Dammit, Washington! I don't have an association with you!"

"That doesn't matter once the press gets hold of it. You will be ruined and we both know it. It doesn't have to go that way. Fulfill my request and we're quits."

"How do I know you're not just doing this to get me and Minerva out where you can attack us?" Sally didn't say *kill us*, even though it was precisely what she was thinking.

Harlan snorted. "Please. If I wanted you dead, you'd have been feeding the worms a long time ago. No, you're far more useful to me alive."

"Useful." Sally's tone was bitter. "I'm just a tool to you, aren't I?"

"All people are tools. Some are sharper than others."

Sally sighed. She was going to have to accede to his request, and couldn't do anything to back out. He was holding all the cards and they both knew it. "Minerva's my second-in-command. The two of us can't just leave the team together for some unknown location or an indeterminate amount of time."

"You leave that to me."

"Why am I not surprised?" But the phone beeped to let her know Harlan had already disconnected the call.

Almost immediately, her computer pinged with the arrival of a new email. Sally didn't want to look. She wanted to go get a cup of hot chocolate and then cuddle up in Jason's arms and never leave. But she looked anyway. It was from Davey, who never seemed to sleep. Apparently, Sally and Minerva had both been assigned by Juice, Sally's friend and Director of the Parahuman Resources Agency, to attend a leadership seminar in Philadelphia. Just Cause Richmond second-in-command Icebreaker would assume temporary command of JCNY until they returned.

And that, as they said, was that.

Two

I never said it was a good idea. I said it didn't feel like a trap.

When Sally got to the lounge, Minerva was already there, waiting for her, a mug of tea warming her hands. The smell of smoked leaves filled the lounge, reminding Sally of the desert camping she and Jason had done on their honeymoon. Without her Roman-style armor and flowing cape, Minerva seemed more like an average twentysomething girl dressed for a comfortable sleepover. Her thick black curls were caught up in a topknot and her lavender pajamas were nearly too large for her. She had her feet curled up beneath her in a chair and she sat unmoving, not checking her phone or watching TV or doing anything at all, really. She looked at Sally and raised an eyebrow like she was a Vulcan.

"Leadership seminar?"

Those two words carried more accusatory tones than if Sally had gotten a full-on shouting lecture. Sally dropped into the chair opposite Minerva and hugged her knees. "I need to tell you something, Minerva, and I need you to trust me."

"I've always trusted you, Sally. I don't intend to stop. What is it?"

Sally licked her lips. "We do have to go away for a few days. You and me."

"Where?"

"Philadelphia, I think. Beyond that I'm not sure."

"Why?"

"I owe someone a favor, and you're part of it."

"Who?"

"Uh . . . Harlan Washington."

"You owe Destroyer a favor? That's a story I would like to hear sometime."

"He helped me stop Champion's nanotech plague."

"I see." Minerva sipped at her tea. One of the things Sally appreciated about her second-in-command was her intuition and innate understanding of the way things connected to each other in the world. Minerva could understand more from a single sentence than Sally could by sitting down and reading a dissertation. Minerva's senses were so finely-tuned that the smallest sound was like a full symphony, the barest swatch of color was an epic mural, and a few stray molecules could tell her an entire novel in the language of scents. "What does this favor entail?"

"I don't know. I suppose he'll tell us when we get there. He promised me it was neither illegal nor immoral."

"You believe him." It wasn't a question, and Sally was surprised to discover she actually did believe what Harlan Washington had told her.

"Yeah, I guess I do. Like he told me, if he wanted me or the rest of us dead, we'd be dead. Maybe he could pull it off and maybe he couldn't. We're a pretty stout bunch and hard to kill, but he's really good at it. Either way, I don't think that's his game."

"I think you're right."

"Are you mad?"

"No. Anger is a fruitless emotion."

"You sound like Yoda. *Anger leads to hate. Hate leads to suffering.*"

"I did finally watch those movies, you know."

"Did you like them?"

Minerva sipped her tea again. By not answering immediately, Sally knew her teammate was working on something tactful. "Some of them. The Campbellian Hero's Journey was done well. I can see why you like them."

"You know I'm just a big nerd." Sally sighed. "Listen, you can't tell anyone anything about what's going on with us. Not even Ment." She paused. "He, uh, he doesn't read your mind, does he?"

"Not without permission. I would know if he was trying to do so, and that would mean the end of our relationship. He knows that too, so he behaves himself."

"Good." Sally paused to think about what Minerva had just said. "Wait, so you let him read your mind sometimes?"

Minerva offered a rare smile. "It does heighten intimacy at times." She sniffed the air. "He's up now. I should go tell him I have to leave. And you should tell Jason."

"He's not going to be happy. Neither of them will be."

"We're women. We have to have secrets from our men."

"I guess you're right."

"I usually am." From anyone else, it would have sounded insufferably conceited, but Minerva was only stating the truth.

* * *

Sally had only been to Philadelphia once before in her life, and that was to meet Harlan Washington. Returning there was leaving a bad taste in her mouth. She and Minerva had said their goodbyes to their teammates and loved ones and taken the ferry to Manhattan. They'd packed their costumes. At least, Sally had packed hers in a messenger bag, which was the only thing that would hold her boots. Minerva only had a small purse slung over her shoulder. It wouldn't have held her helmet, much less her breastplate, skirt, lace-up sandals, spear, and cape. And yet, Sally knew when the moment came for Minerva to gear up, her costume would be readily available. It was part of the mystique of her abilities which even Minerva admitted she couldn't easily explain or define.

Sally enjoyed the trip on the ferry as much as she could, considering the nature of their end destination.

The sun was bright on the water and the normal wreath of smog and haze seemed to have taken the day off, leaving the New York skyline a sparkling cavalcade of towers against an azure sky. "Maybe I can get a tan. I've been pale as a ghost since we moved out here." Sally rubbed her arms. Born and bred in Phoenix, Arizona, she considered anything less than a pure Polynesian brown to be an unhealthy pallor. She regarded Minerva's natural tan with jealousy.

"I can't help my ancestry." Minerva shrugged. "That guy over there is checking you out."

"Are you sure? Eek!" Sally whispered. "I can't look. I don't want him to know."

"You're not missing anything. He smells like clove cigarettes and five dollar wine."

"Yuck."

Eventually they had to leave the bright sunshine for the confines of a train station and shortly boarded one for Philly. Minerva asked Sally to give her as many details as she could remember about her conversation with Harlan Washington, both when they made the deal for her to owe him a favor in return for him saving the world from Champion's nanotech plague and when he called it in. Sally scrunched up her face as she tried to drag every stubborn detail from the morass of her memory. The conversation filled the trip and before Sally realized it, the train was slowing down to pull into a station in Philadelphia.

"We're here." Minerva looked through the window. "Weather's not as nice here."

"That sucks. I wonder if we have time to go get a cheese steak and run up the steps of the Art Museum like Rocky. That's what you're supposed to do in Philadelphia, right?"

"I've never been here before either." Minerva sniffed the air. "I wouldn't buy any food from any nearby street vendors. Their ingredients and sanitation are . . . questionable."

"You're convenient to have around. It's like having my own personal food taster."

Minerva grimaced. "You should experience it from my perspective. I'll have nightmares about our train car. Some days there isn't enough soap in the world."

The two women caught a cab to the destination for their so-called *leadership workshop*. Sally felt her heart starting to hammer with urgent anticipation as the cab pulled up in front of the building where the workshop was supposed to take place. It was in a fairly busy section of downtown Philly, with people in business attire hurrying to and fro while tourists wandered at a more lackadaisical pace like colorful butterflies amid a sea of monochrome beetles. Minerva nodded her head toward a young black man in a hoodie and jeans who was leaning against a support pillar for the building. "That guy is waiting for us."

Sally didn't ask if Minerva was sure or how she knew. "That's not Washington. Maybe a lackey or henchman."

Minerva chuckled. "Henchman. I didn't know that was a real thing. He's a blood relative. Too many similarities in facial structure to be a coincidence."

"God, you're telling me Harlan Washington has a son? Now that's a woman with a serious lapse in good taste."

Minerva shrugged. "Anyone can fall in love. Look at me and Ment."

"He's a superhero."

"His father was a supervillain."

"His father was pathetic."

"You're talking about a man who could be my future father-in-law."

"That's . . . wait, are you and Ment going to get married? This is new."

"Let's just say that we've opened discussions on it and leave it at that." Minerva cocked her head toward the young man who was openly staring at them. "Come on, boss. We're expected."

They crossed the plaza to meet the young man. As they drew closer to him, Sally thought she could see some of the facial similarities Minerva had mentioned, although they were far more subtle in her eyes. His hair was divided into short dreadlocks that gave his head a mop-like appearance. He shuffled his feet a lot and once he saw the women heading his way, spent more time looking at those feet instead of Sally and Minerva. "He's nervous. I can see that even without having powers like yours."

"He's meeting two powerful superheroes. That might be a big deal for him. Sometimes we forget what that must be like for people who don't travel in our circles."

Sally nodded. She'd spent her entire life surrounded by superheroes. Before Just Cause was her time with the Lucky Seven team in Chicago. Before that was the Hero Academy. And before that, she was raised by her mother, who'd been a member of Just Cause. With the exception of Davey, her assistant, virtually everyone Sally knew was a superhero.

They reached the young man. Sally accelerated her perceptions briefly to get a good long look at him without overtly staring. He was only a bit taller than Minerva and slender like a runner, but without the associated muscle definition. Now that she could see his face clearly, she thought perhaps he did look enough like Washington to be a relative. His clothes looked funny and it took her a second and third glance before she figured out why. They had no seams, no fabric texture. They were colored like regular clothes, and they had surface details that suggested seams and fasteners, but upon closer inspection they were merely patterns on the surface. The clothing looked more like it had been manufactured as complete items instead of put together from pieces.

"H-hello. Are you Minerva and S-Sally?"

"I'm Sally, and this is Minerva. Who are you?"

"My n-name is March. March W-Washington."

At first Sally thought he was terrified to meet them, and indeed, he did look somewhat intimidated, but she quickly realized he had a stutter. "Nice to meet you, March. Harlan was too busy to come meet us himself, I take it?"

March nodded. "I'm to take you t-to him."

Sally glanced at Minerva, who nodded back. "It's fine."

Those two words did more to put Sally at ease than anything. If Minerva couldn't sense a deception or a trap, the odds were it was as safe as anything involving a powerful supervillain could be. "Is he here in Philadelphia?"

"N-no. I have a . . . a car."

Somewhere close, then, Sally thought. Well, once she fulfilled her role in whatever twisted plot Harlan Washington was after, all bets were off and she'd take him down once and for all. Her father's death would finally be avenged and she'd go to sleep with a smile on her face the night afterward. "Fine, let's go."

March led them across the plaza to a parking structure and they took the elevator to the rooftop. The doors slid open to a completely empty level except for a single vehicle parked several yards away. Sally looked over toward the exit and saw the gates down and orange cones blocking off the level, a simple and effective barricade to almost anyone. March headed straight for the vehicle, some kind of low-slung van with dark tinted windows and flat, featureless hubcaps like Sally had seen in pictures of old hot rods. The van looked like it was sheathed in stainless steel or brushed aluminum and Sally immediately thought of the DeLorian from the *Back to the Future* movies. "What's this, a time machine?"

Minerva hesitated. "No, it's something else."

"Dangerous?" Sally felt her perceptions about to accelerate in preparation for combat.

"I . . . I actually don't know. I've never encountered this before."

March raised a remote and the side door of the van slid open, operating on smooth, silent electric motors or hydraulics. "Ladies, if you p-please." He entered the side door as well and slipped into the front seat."

Sally looked at him, then at Minerva. "You still think this is a good idea?"

"I never said it was a good idea. I said it didn't feel like a trap."

"Want to forget this and go get a cheese steak instead?"

Minerva thought about it for a moment. "I'm curious."

Sally hated to admit it, but she was as well. "All right, then. Let's get this over with. We're superheroes. We can handle anything that comes our way, right?"

They climbed into the van. Instead of a couple rows of bench seats, there were two seats where the middle row would be, each one looking more like something from a jet fighter. The interior of the van was all black plastic and rubber bumpers, with a dark carpet lining the floor and walls. The cabin ended right behind the passenger seats, sealing off the entire rear of the van.

"B-buckle up." March wiped his hand across the van's center console and it shifted and flowed, folding and unfolding until it resembled something that belonged in a futuristic concept vehicle.

"It's not a time machine. What is it, a flying car? Do you know how many people have spent their entire lives wanting flying cars?" Sally fussed with the seat belts until she figured out the complicated locking mechanism. "Washington could build these and sell them and make billions. Who needs to be a supervillain when you have a dream patent? I've dealt with corporations who put to shame a single guy with a battlesuit and a bad attitude." Even despite her flippant attitude, being inside the van was pushing all of Sally's science-fiction-nerd buttons, and she couldn't help but be a little excited at the idea. She'd flown in the arms of other heroes, in the cabin of the high-tech Just Cause VTOL jets, and even ridden on Destroyer's battlesuit high into the skies over Guatemala once, but a flying car? That was the stuff of which dreams were made.

March touched a control on the center console that made the entire van seem to shimmer momentarily, like some kind of Hollywood special effect. "Stealth mode eng . . . gaged. Repulsors online." The van lurched upward a few inches, making it feel to Sally like she was in a small boat. March looked back at her and smiled. "Watch this."

The van shot into the sky like a rocket.

THREE

You could have said no.
And then you could have dealt with the consequences of that choice.

Sally had grown up watching *Doctor Who* and *Star Trek* reruns on TV, and had never missed a first-run episode of shows like *Babylon 5*, *Andromeda*, or *Farscape*. She considered herself an authority on all things *Star Wars*, had a long brown overcoat for Halloweens when she wanted to be Zoë Washburne from *Firefly*, and could hold her own in discussions of all things related to geek culture and space for hours and hours without getting bored, which was a major accomplishment for someone with her kind of super-speed.

She'd never thought about actually going into space herself, and when it became apparent that's where March was taking his flying van, she couldn't help but start squirming with excitement like a child the night before Christmas.

The flying car would have been cool enough all on its own. The stealth modifications that made it invisible to radar and visual scanning were like the frosting on a cake. Then March took it on a slow but steady climb, heading east over the Atlantic Ocean, climbing higher and higher until the sky was more black than blue and the clouds looked like tiny bits of cottonwood fluff floating on the expanse of the ocean. The curve of the Earth made a magnificent sweep across the sky. At first,

Sally thought the windows were misting over, but then she sniffled and realized she was crying just a little.

"Are you all right?" Minerva reached over from her seat and touched Sally's hand.

Sally smiled back at her. "Yes. This is . . . amazing." She turned back to the window, wiping her eyes, and stared out at the Earth as it fell away below her. "Does Washington live on a secret satellite? Maybe that's why we couldn't ever find him."

March didn't look back at her, busy flying the . . . Sally couldn't very well call it a flying van any longer. It was a spaceship, plain and simple. "No. Well, n-not exactly. It's a secret."

"How does this vessel fly? What is its power source? It seems too small to use standard rocket fuel." Minerva slipped her purse off her shoulder, held it at arm's length, and let go. It floated in midair, tumbling gently in the microgravity.

"It's t-t-t . . ." March took a deep breath.

"Technical?" asked Sally.

He nodded. "Yeah."

Sally shrugged. "It's probably some kind of reactionless thruster that violates physics as we know it. Kind of like the parahuman ability to fly, except recreated by that overcooked lump of charcoal Washington calls a brain."

"Sally . . . Let's not forget that March is the man's nephew." Minerva retrieved her purse.

"Minerva, let's not forget the man killed my father. And Forcestar. And Glimmer. And a whole lot of other people." Sally felt a stab of anger poking into her excitement. "I don't have to like him. I just owe him an . . . *ohhhh!*" She gasped in wonder as the spaceship swept far enough around the Earth for her to see a false sunset behind them. It was the most beautiful thing she'd ever seen, and fresh tears came to her eyes, except instead of rolling down her cheeks, they stayed stuck in her eyes like she was looking through chopped-up clear Jell-o. She scrubbed the backs of her hands at them until she was able to see once more. Tiny droplets spun away from her knuckles like diamonds.

"St-stand by for acceleration . . ." March turned back to look at them. "Seatb-b-b . . ."

"They're fastened." Sally felt bad about his stutter. She hoped it wasn't because she made him nervous. She tried to remind herself that he couldn't help who he was related to, and she shouldn't judge him just because of that. "It may be my first time in a spaceship, but I didn't just fall off a turnip truck yesterday."

Minerva looked at her with a raised eyebrow.

"It's something my grandma used to say."

"My grandma used to say that too. I wonder who picked it up from whom." Minerva smiled. "I would say we're going farther than either of us expected." She nodded toward the front window of the van. A brilliant white circle gleamed in its center, blocking out the light of the stars around it.

For a moment Sally didn't understand what she was seeing, and then it came to her and she laughed. "That's no space station, it's a Moon. *The* Moon. Are you telling me we're going to the Moon?"

Minerva nodded. "So it would seem."

Sally squealed in barely-restrained excitement. "But I didn't pack for the Moon." Then her giddiness subsided and the gravity of the situation settled in around her. "We're going to the Moon. Harlan Washington has a secret Moonbase. How the hell did he manage that?"

"Nuh . . . nuh . . . nano . . ." March pulled back on a lever and sudden acceleration pushed all of them back in their seats. A roaring howl came from somewhere behind Sally and she wondered what kind of amazing and mysterious engine Washington had invented to propel them through space. She wondered if this was how it felt to fly in the *Millennium Falcon.*

"Nanotech. He built his base using nanotech." Minerva nodded her head. "That's why this vessel smelled so odd to me. Moon dust and it wasn't manufactured so much as it was grown. That's . . . *Amazing* doesn't even begin to cover it. I'm impressed."

Sally nodded. "He's one devious son of a bitch, that's for sure." She looked ahead at the Moon, already growing larger in the windshield as the engines howled behind him. "I hope this doesn't turn out to be a one-way trip."

"Don't w-worry. I'll b-bring you home safe." March locked down the controls and turned the seat around to face them. "I p-promised."

"Was it ever in doubt?" Sally folded her arms. "I mean, was the original plan to use us up and then throw us away? That sounds right in line with his M.O."

March's lip curled out and he spoke through gritted teeth, slowly enough to avoid stuttering. "He. Is. Not. Like. That."

"Maybe not all the time. But then, you're family. You know he killed my dad, right? He told you that, right?"

"Sally, now is not the time." Minerva's voice was gentle but insistent.

Sally knew Minerva was right. She wasn't behaving like the leader of the world's premier superhero team. She was being, well, a petulant bitch. March spun around in his seat again to face front. From the way his shoulders hunched, Sally could see he was upset. She felt bad about making him feel that way.

But only a little.

* * *

It took several hours of flight time for them to cover the distance between the upper reaches of the Earth's atmosphere and the long shadows of the mountains of the Moon, filled mainly by the stony silence between Sally and March. Sally had waited for him to say something to her, to respond to her last attack upon him, but he'd kept his own counsel. Then she'd wondered if Minerva would perhaps chastise her for being so callous, but her friend and second-in-command had seemed content to sit in quiet contemplation of their journey.

The Moon drew closer, filling the windows with its stark gray and white beauty. The reflection of sunlight off the Moon's surface bathed all of them like they'd been fixed in the wash of a floodlight. Very little of the Moonbase existed above the surface, which Sally thought was probably to better protect the facility and its inhabitants from solar radiation. The idea of inhabitants worried her. How many people lived down there with Harlan Washington? Could he actually convince others to stay under his protection? His past record showed his willingness to work alongside others so long as they were working toward helping him achieve one of his goals, but the minute they were no longer of help, he would cast them aside like a crumpled receipt. Was it possible he lived there by himself? Sally was betting on it. Washington hated people, and he'd just as soon kick someone out of the airlock than have to listen to them or deal with them. The fact that he'd gone to such great lengths to retreat from the world, and had gone to equally great lengths to bring one of his greatest enemies to his very doorstep meant whatever he had in mind was of the utmost importance to him.

Sally wondered what it could be.

Harlan Washington's Moonbase was set into the side of a crater on the Moon's north pole, out of view of the Earth altogether. The spaceship dipped down into the crater, making for a pair of large metal doors built into the side of a hill. The doors slid aside, showing a tunnel or ancient lava tube descending at a forty-five degree angle. Lunar dust swirled around the tunnel mouth for a moment before the doors closed, shutting out the perpetual twilight of the Moon's north pole and leaving the spaceship to settle upon a landing pad. It touched down with the slightest of bumps, which was still enough to elicit a squeak of delight from Sally. "I'm on the Moon. Holy shit, Minerva."

March engaged the vehicle's wheels and it became a van once more as he drove it from the landing pad into an airlock. Doors shut, pressure equalized, and the van's vents opened, letting in air that resembled the smell of chalk dust when blackboard erasers were pounded together. The van rolled through the opposite side of the airlock to halt upon a circle on the floor. As soon as it came to a stop, the circle moved, rotating the craft around to face the airlock door once again in preparation for its next departure. Autonomous machines rolled or floated up to the van, connecting themselves to ports and inlets and sockets, performing what Sally figured were restocking and recharging tasks.

March slipped out of his seat through the driver's side door, shutting it behind him while Sally was transfixed by the intricate mechanical ballet outside the windows. "Hey!" she yelled after him. "Where do you think you're going?"

"It's all right, Sally." Minerva took a slow, deep breath, feeling the air with all her senses, forcing it to give up its secrets to her. "He's not doing anything untoward."

"He better not be."

The side door of the van slid open with the barest whisper of hydraulics, and in doing so, it revealed the man to whom Sally had hated since she was old enough to understand what it meant. Harlan Washington stood alone in a pool of overhead light, his eyes hidden in the shadow of his brow. He wore a simple black one-piece jumpsuit made without seam or stitch, zipped up to his sternum, over a plain white t-shirt. He was not a large man, in fact only a few inches taller than Sally. He *seemed* larger, though, mostly because Sally had seen his colossal battlesuits firsthand, and she always had to remember that *they* were only vehicles for the small man within. *He* was Destroyer. His battlesuits were just costumes, like Sally's own crimson and gold outfit. His hands rested at his sides, as cold and unmoving as the rest of him. He was the sort of man for whom extraneous movement was a distraction, a sign of weakness. His skin had a slightly shiny appearance, giving it the color of deeply-burnished bronze. Sally knew it was because his body teemed with nanotech of his own design.

Ever since he'd been a child, Harlan Washington had been fascinated by machinery and the myriad ways in which he could force it to do his bidding. As he grew older, his mastery over it had grown more and more exacting until now at this stage of his life, Sally knew he'd achieved one of his heart's dreams—to become fully melded with machinery until it was no longer simple to determine where *Harlan* ended and where *Destroyer* began. She knew he could sheath himself in impregnable armor with a simple thought, or fly like any number of superheroes, or cast forth deadly streams of energy, all thanks to the nanites permeating his body.

She wondered if he even had a battlesuit anymore.

"Welcome to The Preserve," said Harlan. "Thank you for coming."

Sally snorted in disgust. "*The Preserve*? That's an awfully pretentious name, even for you, Washington. And I didn't have a choice, did I?"

The corners of Harlan's mouth twisted up into the most unnatural, forced smile Sally had ever seen. "Of course you did. You could have said no. And then you could have dealt with the consequences of that choice."

"Well, I said yes, and now I'm dealing with the consequences of *that* choice. So tell me, Washington, why am I here?"

"All in good time. March, will you please take our guests to the lounge and see that they get some refreshments and time to acclimate to the lunar gravity?"

March reappeared from a side passage. "Yes, uncle."

"I will join you in an hour and explain my purpose for bringing you here." Harlan turned away from Sally and Minerva and floated into the air like he naturally had the parahuman ability to fly instead of one founded in nanotechnology.

"Why not now? Hey, I'm talking to you, Washington. Why not now?" Sally took an angry step forward and felt herself bounce in an awkward fashion. It occurred to her that at the reduced gravity of the Moon, she only weighed about the same as a bag of charcoal.

Harlan didn't look back. "Because I'm not ready, and neither are you." He flitted on down the corridor until he was swallowed up by the shadows.

Sally felt like punching someone. She would have chased after him, and caught him in between heartbeats, if only she felt like the first super-speed step she took wasn't going to catapult her into the roof. Clever of Washington to pick someplace like the Moon, where her powers were much less of a factor. "Sally, calm down." Minerva's soft voice spread over Sally's flaring temper like oil on a hot pan. "Remember we're here to fulfill a favor to the best of our ability. The least we can do is be pleasant guests."

Sally took a deep breath, trying to shed her deep-seated hatred. "I'm trying. Maybe you need to treat me like you do Ment, keeping me on an even keel."

Minerva nodded. "That's what I'm doing. And right now, I can tell your blood sugar is low and you're dehydrated. I believe there was a mention of refreshments, March? Now would be an excellent time."

March indicated another corridor. "If you would b-both follow me."

Sally resolved to try to be a better guest, like Minerva had suggested in her typically untactful way. At the very least, March didn't deserve her wrath. He was likely as much a pawn in Harlan Washington's devious games as she was. "March, I'm sorry I'm being such a bitch. I'm still trying to wrap my head around this whole secret-base-on-the-Moon thing. Can you forgive me for my hurtful words and, I don't know, throw a rock at me or something if I start up again?"

Minerva snickered into her sleeve, something she rarely did. Sally always felt it a victory when she elicited an emotional response from her normally cool and collected second-in-command.

March smiled back at Sally. "It's ok-kay. I'm not mad. Come sit and I'll b-bring you suh . . . suh . . ."

Sally worked up a smile of her own. "That's fine, March. Thank . . ." She lost her train of words as the corridor ended in a broad room with tall, wide windows that seemed to be set into the side of a crater wall, for a great grayscale landscape spread out before her, punctuated by long shadows from the sun and the sparkles of what must have been ice crystals on the crater floor. Overhead, stars shone steadily, showing none of their characteristic twinkles. A large couch sat in the center of the room with a couple of convenient end tables nearby, facing out into the void. "God, that's beautiful."

Minerva drifted across the room and sat upon the couch. "Very peaceful. And comfortable. Come sit down, Sally."

Sally joined Minerva and for a few minutes they sat in silence, looking out at the universe. March loped back into the lounge with a tray of cookies, crackers, and unmarked bottles of brown liquid. "C-cola and snacks. Please enjoy them." He hesitated. "They're safe."

Sally felt her face grow hot. "I wasn't going to . . . I mean, I'm sure they are." She glanced at Minerva, who said nothing but helped herself to the items on the tray, which was as much an indication of their safety as anything. Sally took a handful of snacks herself and nibbled on them. They had an odd texture and flavor. She wondered if her sense of taste was being affected by the lighter gravity. She'd heard astronauts often craved items like hot sauce because their sense of taste diminished over time. Or maybe the food was manufactured by Washington's nanotech as a completed product instead of prepared conventionally. That wouldn't have surprised her in the least.

Washington rejoined them after a while, flying into the lounge and then walking over to the couch where the two young women sat. "I trust you're feeling more comfortable now."

Sally's ire rose like a fire fed fresh oxygen, but she forced herself to keep her cool. She was a *guest*, dammit, and she'd behave like one until she was given a real reason not to. "Yes, thank you." She paused. "Look, I know this isn't easy for any of us, Washington, but I'm really trying, okay?"

He nodded. "I understand. If there had been any other way to do this, you must believe I would have tried it first."

"Tried what? What is it you want from us?"

"I want . . . I *need* your help to heal my sister."

FOUR

You've already been dead to us for years.

"I thought your sister was dead. Didn't she die in the Twin Towers on 9/11?" asked Sally.

Harlan clasped his hands behind his back. "Perhaps you're not as familiar with my blood relations as you think. My older sister Irlene died along with her rat of a husband, but I'm speaking of my younger sister Reggie."

Sally gasped, and then felt guilty. She'd forgotten he had two sisters. She'd read through his file dozens of times in Just Cause headquarters, trying to glean any bit of information or understanding about Harlan Washington the man, so she'd have an advantage the next time she had to face him. "I'm sorry. I guess I just always assumed that she died at the same time. I mean, didn't they all live together? Irlene and Javier were raising her, right? I remember that much about it."

"That's one way of looking at it." Harlan stayed where he was in the lounge and pulled his legs up into a sitting position while floating over the floor. "Let me tell you all a story, beginning in 1977 after Just Cause decided I was too much of a danger to be left alone."

"That's one way of looking at it." Sally sniffed. "Some would say it was because you torched half of Harlem."

"You say *tomato*." Harlan smiled unexpectedly, and it was unnerving enough to drive any further interruptions from Sally's mind. "While I spent a couple years as a guest of the state of New York, my older sister gained legal custody of Reggie, as our mother was . . . killed during the Blackout rioting." He paused, as if expecting his version of the tale to be challenged, but when neither Sally nor Minerva interjected, he continued.

"I've never had friends. Not the way normal people do. I've had acquaintances, and even allies over the years, but nobody who was ever close to me. I suppose in a way that's my fault. My sociopathic tendencies are easily diagnosed, and because of that I see others as a means to an end, not as an opportunity to make an emotional connection. Oh yes, I've read my own file. It's surprisingly thorough, given how hard I've made it for others to learn about me over the years. I commend your investigatory teams for that.

"Reggie, though, she was as close to a friend as I've ever had. She and I . . . we always had an unspoken understanding between us. When I was in trouble with our mother, Reggie would find ways to come to my defense. I did not put her up to that. She did so because I think she cared about me." His face broke into a wry smile. "I honestly cannot imagine what she saw in me."

"You were her older brother. She looked up to you." Sally sipped at her cola.

"Perhaps, but there's no accounting for some tastes. Regardless, after the events of the Blackout, Reggie lived with Irlene in Just Cause Headquarters, surrounded by all manner of jackasses. She and I fell out of touch, thanks largely to my incarceration and Irlene's efforts to insulate Reggie from me however she could. The best I could manage after my escape was to drop an occasional blank postcard in the mail. To this day, I don't know if Reggie ever got them. I like to think she did, though, and that she knew in some way her brother was still thinking of her."

"I imagine she did." Minerva tucked her legs beneath her on the couch. "Please continue."

A tic developed in one of Harlan's cheeks and Sally noticed his voice had developed an edge that hadn't been there previously, and he spoke through clenched teeth. "Fast forward to 1985. I was back in New York City after spending a few years honing my skills in Philadelphia."

"Running a gang, you mean." Sally shrugged. "What? Why call it something it wasn't?"

"As you wish. I was in the process of building the Mark II suit. I put down that so-called Subway Vigilante myself. Swift justice, as I see it. On the surface, the law didn't approve, but I bet the average man on the street would have said I'd done the world a favor by ridding it of Bernard Goetz. I spent every day designing, building, testing. The Mark II was growing like a living thing in my hands. You can't imagine what it's like, seeing your creation come alive. It's like being a god. But even gods can't be everywhere at once, and I wasn't where I needed to be on the evening of June 7th, 1985."

The temperature in the room seemed to drop several degrees with the utterance of that date. Sally wasn't sure why; it meant nothing to her. It was terribly important to Harlan, though—she could see it in the way he seemed to curl himself up even tighter.

"Reggie went to visit some friends and was walking home through Central Park late in the afternoon. She was dragged into some bushes and attacked. Brutally. By several men. They held her down. They took turns raping her and beating her. It took more than an hour. Not one person admitted to witnessing the event."

The snacks Sally had eaten swirled uncomfortably in her stomach. "Jesus," she whispered.

Harlan's voice grew even harder. "It was at least two more hours before anyone found her. By that time, she'd lost a tremendous amount of blood. Her skull was fractured in multiple places. Her wrists and ankles and several ribs were broken. Her organs were hemorrhaging. She was more dead than alive." A tic appeared in the corner of Harlan's jaw. It was the most emotion Sally had ever seen him display and it terrified her. He was seething with barely-repressed rage, and in that moment she had no problems seeing him as the Destroyer, whose list of crimes against humanity both as a whole and as individuals would have stretched all the way back to Earth.

"Doctors had to induce a coma to prevent further brain degradation. She couldn't safely be moved from the intensive care unit and so that's where she stayed while Irlene and Javier went hunting for the men who'd attacked her. As did I. They found some of them, eventually. They never found the ones I got to first. They were charged, convicted, sent to prison, and I used my contacts to make sure none of them lived out their first year."

"I can't say I blame you for that." Sally hugged her knees. It was perhaps the most disturbing thing she'd heard in many years, especially when delivered by Harlan Washington's grim monotone.

"Months passed. It became apparent that Reggie had been . . . impregnated . . . during her attack. I don't know what Irlene and Javier said to each other about it, but I had worked up some careful fake identities and was able to get into the hospital to see Reggie often. I used my financial resources to guide her treatment, making donations to the hospital, to the coma ward. Ensuring sympathetic administrators put sympathetic doctors in charge. I kept a close eye on her records through my fake identities and that's how I learned about her pregnancy, and how long it was taking her injuries to heal. Her prognosis for surviving a full-term pregnancy was grim, and then there was the question of the disposition of the baby if it survived the full term and delivery."

"I'd think Irlene and Javier would have taken charge, since Irlene was Reggie's sister." Sally looked over at March. He must have been Reggie's son. It was the only explanation that made sense given what she'd learned so far from Harlan's story.

Harlan snorted. "You'd think that, but you're failing to take into account the weakness that plagued that part of my family. Irlene had no stomach for motherhood. And to raise a child that wasn't her own? One who was conceived from a violent rape? No, she signed a document remanding custody of the baby to the state, where it would be placed up for adoption. She also decided to have Reggie moved to long-term hospice care. She gave up on her sister. Wrote her off, the way she wrote off everything else except that fucking Puerto Rican drug addict Javier." He clenched his fists. "I broke my silence. I contacted Irlene. Offered to help. She turned me down. She said *you've already been dead to us for years.* It was October when I found out."

Sally gasped. "October . . . You mean Tornado's funeral?"

"I took the news about Reggie's future poorly."

Sally jumped to her feet, awkwardly flailing in the lunar gravity before she got herself planted back upon the floor. "Poorly? *Poorly?* You threw an airplane onto Tornado's graveside service! You killed my father!"

"Sally . . ." Minerva's voice was soft, albeit heavy with warning tones.

"Your father was collateral damage."

Sally took a step toward him and suddenly Minerva's spear was in front of her, the blade dangerously close to her throat. "Sally, stop."

Tears trickled down Sally's cheeks in slow motion. She sat back down on the couch, feeling helpless and put upon.

"Were you going to say *it's not fair*? Life isn't fair. It wasn't fair that my sister was raped. It wasn't fair that Irlene wasn't willing to provide the care she needed. It wasn't fair that she wouldn't adopt her own nephew when she had both the resources and ability to do so. You don't get to argue what's fair when it comes to my life, my sister's life."

Sally wiped away her angry tears. "So what did you do, steal the baby?"

"In a manner of speaking. It was easier for me to get into the hospice and alter records. Reggie was still in her coma. She was moved, then moved again, and then she didn't get to where her records said she should have gone. I intercepted her and moved her to a facility of my own choosing. A private one, where she got nothing but the best care. I found an obstetrician who'd been suspended for prescribing drugs illegally. I paid him a handsome sum to deliver my nephew safely, and then bought his silence after he successfully did so."

"You killed him. Like you kill everyone." Sally glared at Harlan.

He shrugged. "It's the most permanent solution I've found to any problem."

"Why didn't you let someone else adopt March?" Minerva asked. "You don't strike me as parent material."

Harlan chuckled. "Nobody adopted black children in the Eighties. If I didn't raise him, he'd have been guaranteed a life of hardship, bouncing from foster home to foster home, probably getting killed or arrested by the time he was eighteen. That's the way of the world."

Sally shook her head. She couldn't believe Harlan Washington as a parent. What must it have been like, having a supervillain like that for a father? Going to parent-teacher conferences? Cheering on the sidelines during sporting events and taking pictures from the audience during concerts? No, he couldn't have been like that. However he'd raised March, he'd probably messed up that poor young man well beyond anyone's ability to fix without many years of therapy. "So you bit the bullet and took on the role of father. Good for you. That doesn't explain why we're here."

Harlan studied his fingers. A cloud of tendrils like smoke wafted from the fingertips, swirling around before disappearing back inside his hand once more. "Parahuman abilities run in my family. Irlene had the ability to control the size of objects. I have the ability to control technology. Reggie may or may not have an ability, but March most definitely does."

"And what's that?"

"He can control dreams."

Sally snorted. "Is that even a thing?"

"It's t-true." March looked uncomfortable at being put on the spot. "I can see the dreams of others. G-guide them even."

"That's a weird power. It doesn't seem very useful. What can you do with it?" Sally felt bad for him again. He'd gotten the short end of the stick seemingly in every aspect of his life.

"It's not what he can do, it's what he can do when his abilities are boosted by Minerva." Harlan folded his arms. "Reggie is still in her coma and has been for the past twenty-four years. I've dosed her with nanomachines to repair the damage in her brain at a cellular level. Physiologically, there's nothing wrong with her anymore. There's no reason she should still be comatose, but we can't wake her up. Nothing I've tried has been successful. I've mapped her brain activity and it reads like someone who's in a deep dream state. March has caught flashes of it, but his powers aren't strong enough to overcome whatever block is in her mind. That's where the two of you come in."

"I don't understand. How can seeing her dreams help her?"

"It can't. At least, not as I understand what's going on with her. Between March and Minerva, I intend to have you enter her dreams and try to break down the barrier keeping her comatose from the inside."

Sally blinked, and for several long seconds she couldn't think of a single word to say. At last she managed to come up with something. "You want me to *what?*"

"Enter her dreams. Find the key to her prison, whatever that is, and release her. Bring my sister back to me. Bring March's mother back to him."

Minerva rose to her feet. "I see. Yes, I believe I can do what you are asking of us."

Sally stood as well, more in a show of solidarity than any sense of understanding. "Well, I don't get it. I can accept a lot of weird things. Hell, I'm a superhero. I've *done* a lot of weird things already in my life. But why me? You're her brother, Harlan. Why don't you do it? You already said the two of you had a connection growing up."

Harlan turned away from Sally to stare out at the unending universe beyond the glass. "I can't. I've tried. She's got some kind of powerful mental block that's keeping me from doing the same thing I'm asking of you. I can't override it."

"Okay, so why not use a psi like Ment instead? That seems more like something a psionicist would be able to perform."

"I've had three psis perform deep scans over the years. The mental block is not psionic in nature. The part of the brain that psis can access is inert in Reggie. As far as they can tell, she's completely vegetative. March is the only reason we know that her mind is still alive and functioning."

"Then why me, of all people? She doesn't know me. Wouldn't she be more alarmed by a stranger than someone familiar?"

"You will seem familiar to her. She . . . knew your mother and father during the years she lived in Just Cause Headquarters with Irlene and Javier. She actually had more time in their company than she did in our mother's. Also . . ." Harlan turned back to face Sally, and she saw a battle raging behind his eyes as he struggled to find the right words to explain the unfamiliar concepts of emotional connection. "You're a good person, and I'm not. Reggie was a good person too. I'm . . . hopeful she will let you in."

"What if it doesn't work?"

Harlan clenched his fists. "I don't know. I've spent more than twenty years trying to break through her barricades. All I can do is keep trying. Everything I've done has been to help her in some way. I brought her to the Moon because there's less strain on her body in a lower gravity field. Every crime I committed, every unsavory deal I made, I did so because it could help me in some way to further my research into bringing back my sister."

Sally felt a sudden, unexpected lump in her throat. Here she'd spent her entire life seeing Harlan Washington as nothing but a monster, the technological boogeyman who turned up sowing death and destruction in his wake. Now he was telling her the reason for his existence was something . . . honorable. It didn't justify the heinous acts he'd committed, but at least it gave her new insight into what drove him.

Even an inhumane monster could care about something.

Sally cleared her throat. "I'll, uh, I need some time to think this over."

Harlan nodded. "Take a day if you want, but this is what you owe me. I won't take no for an answer. Not when the two of you are here at last and there might be a chance for Reggie to come back from her dream world."

FIVE

He fixes things, not people.

March showed Sally to what he called the guest quarters, a cozy but sparse room where she would be staying during her visit to the Moon. He asked if she needed anything but she declined. "Just some space," she said. "I know, bad joke."

March smiled, and it made her feel a bit better about herself. "If you need me, just p-push the button by the door. I'll come t-to you."

"Am I going to be locked in?"

"No. You're a guest, n-not a p . . . p . . ."

"I understand." Sally gave him as warm a smile as she felt she could manage. "I promise, I won't go opening any strange doors and accidentally venting the whole place to vacuum. Trust me, I'm a geek. My other car is an X-Wing."

He nodded and turned away. Sally shut the door behind him and turned to face the tiny room. It had a cot that was surprisingly soft and springy. She suspected it was built by Harlan's nanomachines, like everything else on the Preserve. Silly name for a Moonbase, that. *Preserve* sounded more like some place in Africa, or one of the big open-air zoos where animals roamed free and guests drove around and marveled as baboons threw stuff at their cars. Or ate them. "It's like Jurassic Park, but in space," she said aloud. "And I'm the adorable moppet. Well, me and Minerva." Any second now, she was sure, a gigantic space tyrannosaur would begin rampaging, followed by a gang of lunar velociraptors. At least she could outrun something like that, even in one-sixth gravity. She sat on the cot and bounced up and down for a few minutes. She thought best in motion, and she was finding the gravity to be a real challenge.

Deep down, she knew she should agree to Harlan's proposal and just run with it. She'd learned a lot about him over the years, whether from reading his file, talking to those who'd survived encounters with him, or from personal experience. He was a lot of things: a murderer, a villain, a petty revenge-driven child, but she had never come across anything or anyone labeling him a liar. She didn't feel like he'd been dishonest with her about his needs either. Maybe she wasn't a human lie detector like Minerva, who could taste a lie in the air by the pheromones that accompanied its dispersal, but she thought she had a pretty good handle on reading people.

Say Harlan was lying to her. Say he had some ulterior motive for her coming to the Moon. Like he'd said, if he wanted to kill her, he'd had ample opportunities over the years, and she hardly believed he would build an entire Moonbase and go to the expense of bringing her and Minerva across thousands of miles of empty space just to kill her. That would be an extreme waste of his resources, and she just didn't buy it.

So what else could he want? Maybe he wanted to get into Sally's mind, somehow. Maybe she had information locked up in her brain that he couldn't access any other way. Again, she didn't see that as a viable option. Harlan was the very definition of an evil genius. He had the knowledge and the resources to obtain, infer, or uncover whatever information he needed. And what secrets did she possess anyway? Email passwords were no problem for someone like her friend Vanitha, and Harlan had hired her before. Most of the sensitive data that Sally could access in her position as commander of Just Cause was stored either in digital mediums, paper files, or both, and Harlan could gain access to those as easily as he could anything else.

The only real reason Sally could come up with to explain why she was sitting in a room on the Moon was that Harlan had told her the truth.

Sally bounced up from the cot. She needed to move. She thought better on her feet. Indeed, she'd rather be running. She wondered if there was a gym or someplace on the Preserve where she could go exercise a bit. It would be weird doing so in the low gravity, but she needed the physical activity to loosen up her brain. The door was unlocked, as March had told her, and it slid aside without so much as even a *Star Trek* hydraulic hiss. She went back into the corridor, which was surprisingly mundane for such a science fiction setting. It could have been a corridor in any office building under construction: unadorned walls, plain doors with labels and bar codes upon them. The only concession at all to what Sally like to think of as The Future in vague, uncertain terms, was the recessed LED lighting that bathed everything in a smooth, antiseptic white light. At least she could pretend she was on the space station from *2001: A Space Odyssey.*

Then she realized she was being an idiot. *She was already on the Moon.* She didn't have to pretend anything. She skipped down the corridor, lighter than ever on her feet, until she came to the lounge once more. There she found March, sitting on the couch and staring out across the barren landscape of the Moon's north pole while listening to a refreshingly mundane iPod. At first she felt like she was intruding upon his quiet time, his personal space. His head bobbed in time to whatever music was playing, his short dreadlocks twitching with each motion like the tendrils of a sea anemone. She'd just decided to turn and leave him when he noticed her presence. He dug the earbuds out of his ears and hung them over the back of his neck. "Hey. D-do you need something?"

"No. Well, kind of. I guess I just needed to move around. It's tough for me to be cooped up in a small room for any amount of time. I'm used to running for hundred mile stretches at a time."

"Down Route 66 in Arizona. I r-read the article in *Rolling St-stone*."

Sally blushed. It had been a few years since she'd been profiled in the magazine. That was before Just Cause New York. Before Champion. Before she'd been married. "It always surprises me when someone brings that up. I always forget about it. I guess it wasn't that important to me in the grand scheme of the world."

"You always seem t-to have bigger things on your mind."

"Yeah, kind of like now. It's hard to wrap my mind around the idea that I can and should help my oldest enemy."

March stood and wandered over toward the windows. "I know my uncle has d-done some terrible things over the years. When I was younger, I didn't r . . . r . . ." He clenched his fists and took a deep breath. "Realize. How bad he'd b-been. More recently I've been tr-trying to help him. To k-keep him fr . . . r . . ." He bowed his head. "Sorry."

Sally moved to stand beside him. "It's okay. I get what you're saying. Have you had it all your life?"

"Long as I can remember."

"Did Harlan try to fix it?"

March snorted. "He fixes things, not people. That's why he needs help with my, with my, with my mom." He looked down at her. Starlight reflected off his dark eyes like they were a continuation of the black velvet sky beyond the windows. "Your help."

"He fixed your mom's brain damage. Isn't that fixing people?"

"His n-nanotech fixed the physical damage, but that's not fixing *her*. It's like building a house. You could make the m-most beautiful palace in the world, but it doesn't mean anything unless someone luh . . . lives in it."

Sally sighed. "I know, I should do it. It's the right thing to do. You've never even met your mom as a person. Only through the stories of other people who've known her."

"I've seen her dreams. Th-they're really well-formed."

"Does she dream about you?"

March shrugged. "I d-don't know. Dreams aren't like, like, like movies. They're not always linear. T-time isn't steady in them. Everything is symbols instead, instead of literal."

"What does she dream about, then? What kind of symbols are they?"

"What d-does it feel like in your mind wh-when you slow your sense of per-perception?"

"Well, it's . . ." Sally stopped, taken aback. "Oh. I see what you're getting at. I don't know how to explain something like that to you, and it's just as hard for you to explain seeing dreams to me."

March nodded.

"Well, darn. I was hoping to maybe get the Cliff's Notes from you. Guess I'll have to pay attention to the lectures anyway." Sally looked around the lounge. "Listen, March . . . Do you guys have a gym or a track or anything here? I need to do something physical. I think better that way."

March shook his head. "No track. Uncle Harlan's n-nanos keep our bodies in shape."

"You have them too? I thought it was just him."

"No. Me too. And m-my mom. It's to monitor and pro . . . protect us."

"From what? Moon monsters?"

"Radiation. Pressure loss. B-bone degrad . . . gradation."

"Well, maybe there's a place I can run and get up some speed?"

March looked at her, and then out the window. "We could go outside."

"Outside? You mean out there? Like in space suits?" Sally's heart skipped a beat. Being on the Moon was one thing, but getting to walk on its surface—its *real* surface—that was the kind of thing she'd dreamed of since she was a kid. "Are you serious? He lets you do that?"

"Sure. He knows I won't go far. Where is there to g-go?"

"I'd love to. I mean it, March. I don't even care if I can't run in a space suit. Can we really?"

"Sure. Follow me." March led Sally down another corridor to an antechamber with an airlock at one end. Hanging from a rack along one wall were something like a dozen sky blue space suits. They looked nothing like the ones worn by the Apollo astronauts, or even the contemporary ones worn by those on the International Space Station. Where those were bulky, awkward designs, those on the rack seemed more like wetsuits. Like every other thing Sally had encountered on the Preserve, they appeared to have been manufactured by nanomachines.

She wasn't unfamiliar with the process of rebuilding matter. The Combat Simulation Chambers in the various Just Cause bases around the country used similar technology, albeit far less advanced or refined. The training rooms were reconfigured using nanomachines to represent various environments where superheroes might be called upon to use their abilities. A combination of uniquely-powered parahumans mixed with some of the finest minds from Silicon Valley had developed the technique, and it had become one of Just Cause's most closely-guarded secrets.

Harlan Washington, of course, was undaunted by security measures, and it was discovered well after the fact that he'd spent several months masquerading as a CSC technician in Denver, during which time he'd acquired samples of all the various nanomachines for his personal experimentation. The mere presence of the Preserve around Sally was evidence of his perfection of the technology. Nobody else could have managed what he had in such a short time. She wondered what he could have accomplished in his life had he chosen to apply his mind and abilities toward the betterment of mankind instead of destruction.

She realized she hadn't been paying attention to March's briefing at all. "I'm sorry, can you say that again?" He sighed, and Sally felt terrible. For March to repeat himself was much more difficult than for someone else. "Never mind, I'll figure it out as I go along. It can't be that hard, right?"

"Right. The m-most important thing to remember is not to . . . to . . . to let your helmet crack."

"It would be bad."

"Yes."

Sally looked at the rack. "Why are there so many suits? Isn't it just the three of you here? Well, and me and Minerva. Still, why so many?"

"Uncle Harlan is a c-c-contingency planner. He never throws anyth-thing away." March motioned to a small room off to one side. "You can change in there. I'll wait. You, uh, have to be completely n . . . n . . ."

"Naked?" Sally grimaced. "Okay, I guess if that's what it takes." She took a suit into the changing room with her. There was a small shelf upon which she put her clothing, neatly folded the way Jason would have done it instead of thrown on the floor, which was her preferred technique of undressing. She had to climb into the suit through the neck hole, which wasn't as difficult as she would have thought. The material was stretchy without being constricting, and the inside was coated with a layer that kept her skin from sticking to the rubbery surface. She slipped her toes all the way down and pulled the suit up over her. As she slipped her arms into the sleeves and adjusted it over her shoulders, the suit seemed to flow around her, constricting in places like it was alive. As it settled in around her, she marveled how it felt more like a second layer of skin than something she was wearing. Her

Mustang Sally costume was more of a burden than the space suit. She ran her hand down her arm and was amazed to discover she could feel it both in her fingers and along her arm. It was like the suit had made her nerve endings stretch all the way to its exterior.

She stepped out of the changing room to discover March had also put on a suit. He stood, garbed in a blue body suit like her. The skintight covering highlighted his slender form, so different from Jason's thick muscles when he wore his own Mastiff costume. "You look good." He smiled.

Sally smiled back, suddenly feeling shy and uncomfortable. She was used to being ogled when in costume. It was something superheroes had to get used to when they wore their colorful skintight outfits. The space suit covered as much of her body as did her Mustang Sally costume, but it felt like she was naked. "This feels so funky. It's like I'm not wearing anything at all. How does that even work?"

"Tech." March handed her a pair of low-cut boots with Velcro straps and a thick, studded tread upon their soles.

Sally pulled them over her the feet of her skintight suit, feeling like she was strapping on running shoes. "Why are the suits blue? Every space suit I've ever seen was white."

"Blue shows up w-well on the surface. Also it's his f-favorite color." March pulled a helmet -backpack combination from the rack.

"I guess it would be. His suits have always been blue." Sally took the helmet-backpack. "So I just put this on? It's got air and power and everything?"

"Yes. It will merge with the suit for a per-per-perfect seal."

Sally pulled the helmet over her head, not sure what to expect. She knew she should have been thinking about what to do with Harlan's request for her help, but she needed the distraction of walking on the Moon. Doing so would give her subconscious a chance to really chew on the problem and help her make a decision. The helmet made a hissing sound as the shoulder supports tightened over and around her, giving her the distinct impression that a friendly octopus was entwining itself over her head. "This is so weird. And cool. But mostly weird."

March opened the airlock door. "Can you hear me?" His voice came through a pair of small speakers set up high and back in the helmet where they wouldn't be in Sally's line of sight.

"Yes. Oh my God, we're really going to do this, aren't we?"

"We don't have to."

"No, I want to." Sally shook her hands, feeling like jumping up and down as the butterflies in her stomach really got going. "Someday I'll be able to tell my grandkids about this." She immediately felt guilty. She'd have to have kids if she was ever going to have grandkids, and that was the ongoing conflict between her and Jason.

"Say *H-U-D*."

"H-U-D." Sally gasped in surprise and delight as a digital display appeared around the edge of her helmet. At first she was afraid it would be complex and hard to understand, but after studying it for a few seconds, she realized it was laid out the way a video game would have done it. There was a GPS with map overlay, directional arrow, a green bracket over March, and two columns of vital stats. One showed Sally's own body temperature, respiration, blood pressure, pulse, and oxygenation, just like she would have in a medical facility. The other column tracked the suit's power, pressure level, and the amount of consumable air and water remaining. She noticed one column that was blank and as she focused upon it, the helmet detected her interest and brought it up into a larger view so she could see it. It was the capacity of the waste reservoir. "Oh. Hey, uh, am I supposed to pee in this if I have to? I mean, I didn't put on any kind of, you know, catheter or anything."

March chuckled. "If you have t-to go, just go. The suit will take c-c-care of it." He reached for the airlock controls. "Are you ready?"

"You've done this before, right? I mean, you're allowed? This isn't like you sneaking out and taking the car when you're supposed to be studying, is it?"

"Yes, many times. I like to go to the top of the . . . the crater. You can see the Earth from there."

"Ohhh, I'd like that. Can we do that?"

"Sure."

Sally felt herself wanting to pace at super-speed but she forced herself to hold still. Mostly. She wrapped her arms around herself in a nervous hug. "Okay, do it."

March closed the airlock door. "D-depressurizing."

An indicator on the airlock door showed pressure dropping. Sally's suit became a little more taut than it had been. A gauge on her helmet showed external pressure reducing while suit pressure remained stable. She wished she could chew on her fingernails as the airlock pressure reached zero. She knew it was dangerous, what they were doing, but she and danger were old friends. One didn't become a superhero without being willing to accept certain risks.

But when the external airlock door opened, she found herself clutching at March's hand like a nervous child nevertheless. The airlock extended out to a metallic patio stained with smudges of dust. Beyond the edge of that apron was speckled gray rock, and a slope descending gently toward the bottom of the crater. Sally took a hesitant step forward, then another, shuffling out in the low gravity until she was standing with March on the patio, looking down the crater slope. Her helmet beeped at her and highlighted her physiological readout in red. According to the monitor, her heart rate and respiration were dangerously high. She forced herself to relax a little, knowing she didn't need to be super-speedy here.

She turned around to look up toward the crater lip. A bright glow lit up the entire horizon. It had to be Earth's light. "Where do we go? Is there a way up?"

"Follow me."

March started up the side of the crater, following an actual path he must have made over multiple journeys. The climb might have been tiring under Earth gravity but to Sally it wasn't any more strenuous than a walk around a lake. As they climbed, the arc of the Earth's atmosphere appeared as a blue aura, and then the curve of the mother planet itself. Every step closer to the top brought new features of Sally's homeworld into view, until she and March stood at the top of the crater, staring out at the great blue semicircle crouched just beyond the horizon. Without any atmosphere to blur her focus, it was so clear she felt like she could have reached out and touched it. She couldn't make out any landmasses thanks to some clouds over what she thought might have been the Atlantic seaboard. The black terminator of nightfall was creeping across the planet. "I . . . I can see my house from here." Sally's joke came out as only a whisper. It might have been the most gorgeous vision she'd ever had.

"It's b-beautiful. Uncle Harlan doesn't ever come up here, b-but I like to make sure I never forget where . . . where . . . where I came from."

Sally turned to look at March. He was staring across the lunar plain toward the Earth. "I don't see how anybody could ever forget that once they saw it. March, you came from your mom, and she's trapped inside her own head and it's terrible that she's never gotten to hold you or tell you she loves you. I'm going to do it. I'm going to go in there and help her find her way home."

SIX

She was the Universe, and the Universe was her.

Reggie Washington seemed little more than a skeleton with skin drawn tightly over it. Her form hovered over a cot on a cushion of air warmed to body temperature. Harlan said the design was to keep her from developing bedsores, something he'd spent a long time battling as part of her care. She wore a soft cotton singlet that kept her comfortable and dry without being overly clingy, binding, or chafing. Sally could see all her ribs through it, and the woman's limbs were as skinny as a starvation victim's. Nevertheless, her skin had a healthy glow to it and she seemed more like she was asleep than comatose. Her face still retained a youthful quality to it, making her seem younger than Sally even though Reggie was a good dozen years older.

Her scalp was bald, not from any side effect of the coma but because of the tech Harlan was using to monitor his sister's brain. A fine metallic mesh wrapped all around Reggie's scalp, with individual wires reaching down her face and a ribbon of them running down her neck and disappearing beneath her singlet. A thick trunk of wires emerged from the mesh to connect to a machine that monitored every bit of physiological information, putting special effort into brain activity.

"Mom, th-this is Sally and Minerva. This is my mother." March stood by Reggie's side and held one of her limp hands in his own.

Sally cleared her throat. "Hello, Ms. Washington. Reggie. Your brother asked us to come and see if we can help you wake up. Your family misses you very much." She glanced at Harlan, who stood off to one side with his arms folded as he gazed at the technical information on the readouts.

He shook his head. "Nothing."

Minerva and Sally were dressed like Reggie in simple singlets, as was March. Harlan had prepared three cots for them. Each had an air cushion design like Reggie's bed, and banks of monitors surrounded them. "So how is this going to work?" Sally asked.

Harlan touched his fingertips together and then spread them apart. A membrane stretched between them, displaying information upon it like a biological screen. Sally knew it was something the nanotech in his system did, and even though she'd seen it before, she still found it unnerving. "I need to inject both of you with a few milliliters of nanites so I can monitor you effectively both internally and externally. Nothing malicious, I promise you."

"Hey, now wait a minute, you didn't say anything about filling us up with your little bugs." Sally held up her hands in protest, but felt like her argument was weak in the face of what she'd already seen Harlan could accomplish with them. Once again, she knew if he really wanted to harm her in some way, he'd already had ample opportunity to do so. It really seemed like his sole focus was upon helping his sister, and Sally knew she needed to approach it the same way.

"It won't hurt. They're just there to monitor your vitals and help facilitate the connection between the four of you."

"Are you going to be able to see into my thoughts?" Sally asked. The idea was enough to make her feel queasy.

"No. I'll be able to see your brain activity, but it won't be any different than if a neurologist had you inside of a scanner. You won't even notice the nanites."

Harlan closed his membrane screen and opened a cabinet to withdraw a tray with two small silver spheres upon them the size of quail eggs. "When the journey is complete, all I need to do is issue a command and the nanites will become inert material, at which point your body will eliminate them through the normal methods."

"What do I do?" Minerva sounded relaxed, which helped to put Sally at ease.

"Make yourself comfortable on your cot. Relax and I'll take care of the rest." Harlan picked up one of the silver spheres with a pair of plastic tongs.

Minerva floated herself up onto the cot. The warm air cushion made her hair float around her face like an ebony wreath. "This is very comfortable. I might have to ask you make one for me for back home."

"It wouldn't be very relaxing in Earth's gravity. The air pressure needed to accomplish this would be very loud."

"If anyone could get past that obstacle, I'm sure you could, Harlan."

Harlan paused and Sally saw his brow wrinkle as he considered how to solve such a problem. She waved at him. "Hey, stay on task here, huh? One problem at a time."

"Of course. Minerva, your hand, please. You will feel a slight tingling sensation as the nanites enter your body, and then nothing. They will anchor themselves at predetermined locations around your brain and organs to provide me with real-time information about your physiological state and brain activity."

"Fascinating. Would you prefer me to remain awake or sleep?"

"Whatever will best facilitate your communication between Sally, March, and Reggie." Harlan placed the sphere on Minerva's upraised hand. It quivered for a moment and then melted into her skin like smoke into a breeze.

"This is remarkable." Minerva closed her eyes. "Go ahead, Sally. It's fine."

Sally hopped onto her own cot. "Be good, Harlan. Minerva will know if you try anything, and believe me, she's the worst person in the world to make an enemy of."

Harlan snorted. "That's up for debate." He raised the second silver sphere. "If you've ever been under anesthesia, you'll fall asleep that quickly as the nanites situate themselves. Then I'll attune all the signals together and leave you, Minerva, and March to find your way in Reggie's mind."

"How will I know what to do? How to wake her?"

"I have no idea." Harlan placed the sphere on the back of Sally's hand.

She was going to ask something else but her consciousness fled with the speed of a thought.

* * *

She was the Universe, and the Universe was her.

Awareness first came to Sally like a gradual lightening of the darkness, the graylight of pre-dawn after a Moonless night. She felt the stuff of the cosmos rushing past her as she rose through the murk, like a bubble seeking the surface of the ocean. The formless void began to take shape around her, shadows coalescing into the seeds of ideas. She floated through it like a dust mote in a sunbeam, vaguely aware of other motes around her but not knowing what or whom they might represent. As the Universe flowed past her, she recognized galaxies as they swirled like eddies in a stream. She must have been traveling at an unimaginable velocity, far beyond anything so pedestrian as the speed of light. This was the speed of Dreaming, and the only laws it followed were subject to the whim of the dreamer.

A galaxy raced in upon Sally, growing in size until it was too big for her to see, or even to comprehend. Stars shot past in blurs as she tore through nebulae and left black holes spinning away into nothingness in her wake. Star-stuff filled her body, leaking in like water into a sponge, and she felt it tingling like a symphony orchestra performing in each of her cells.

She dove in toward a single star, growing from a brilliant pinprick amid the others of the galaxy to a great blinding furnace of blistering fury and coronas. She skirted the surface of the star, letting its radiance bake away her fear as she skated through prominences, threading the needles of their towering arches like a surfer shooting a perfect Hawaiian barrel.

As she left the sun behind, she flew onward toward a gleaming azure dot that became the Earth. Before she had a chance to gasp in surprise and delight, she was tearing through the clouds, ever slowing in her headlong descent, as an entire continent spread out beneath her until it grew beyond the edges of her vision. Wind whistled in her ears as she fluttered like a leaf, twisting and spiraling on the capricious breezes. A golden plain laid out, grasses swaying like cilia of some gargantuan creature, dotted with the copper of rocky outcroppings, verdant trees, cerulean pools.

And then, with a puff of dust, her journey came to a sudden end at the foot of a strange tree that looked as if it were growing upside-down.

For a long moment, Sally lay on the soft green and gold prairie, feeling the sun warming her back, inhaling deeply of the scents of clean, sweet earth and listening to the footsteps of beetles as they explored the towering blades of grass. Her descent had been exhilarating, and yet her memory of it was already fading into the background as was the way of dreams. This savannah was her new reality. A gentle breeze drifted across her back, making her skin twitch in an unfamiliar but not unpleasant way. It was like when wind blew through her hair, but all over instead of being confined only to her head. She started to roll over and caught sight of the forelimb of some tawny-furred beast beside her. She jumped back, suddenly afraid of what monsters might reside within the dreams of Reggie Washington, and the arm followed her.

She realized it belonged to her and froze as her eyes roved up her arm, then down her body all the way to her toes. She was covered in a thick golden fur, like that of her teammate Yunbao back in Just Cause New York. The fur of her belly lightened from the rich gold of her arms and legs to a creamy color reminiscent of hard-pack vanilla custard. Her fingers and toes were tipped with claws, and she had pads like those of a cat. She was nude, but didn't feel naked with her coating of fur. She reached up to explore her face with her fingertips and discovered it had transformed as well. She had a muzzle, and she could see it if she crossed her eyes. Her nose felt large, and she could feel long, sharp teeth inside her mouth with a long tongue. Whiskers sprouted from her cheeks and her ears had risen toward the top of her head and were tipped with fine tufts of fur.

"I'm a cat." She said the words aloud and they seemed to solidify her self-image. Perhaps not a cat so much as a lion, although she had no mane. Did female lions have manes? She didn't think so. She wasn't a tiger or a leopard. Maybe a cheetah, although she didn't have any spots. Why a lion, of all things? She didn't dwell on the question. It wasn't her dream; if it had been, she might have instead envisioned herself as a horse of some sort. After all, horsey imagery ran in her family for three generations. As she examined herself, she found she was in possession of a *tail*, which made her giggle. She tightened muscles in her ass and discovered, to her great amusement, that she could make it twitch.

"Okay, so I'm a lioness. Now what?" Her voice sounded odd to her, perhaps because of the unusual shape of her mouth and teeth. She took a few minutes to look around her immediate surroundings. She had arrived—or perhaps *landed* was a better term—in the middle of a grassy savannah, filled to brimming with a lush, fragrant sward that swayed in the gentle hot breeze wafting from the south. Insects hummed and chirped all around her. Some marched along the dry ground in the shade of the stalks, seeking their fortune amongst the fallen seeds and scattered remnants of long-dead animals. Others sought richer fare, braving the tall grass to find the best seeds and pollen clutched at their summits. Those insects provided easy snacks for small birds that flitted about, lunging for beetles and then perching among the branches of the upside-down tree to enjoy their meals.

The tree itself was like something out of a nightmare. It had a thick, bulbous trunk with odd swellings like tumors, while its branches bifurcated at unexpected intervals and seemed like the gnarled hands of ancient crones. The sparse leaves and generally-unbalanced appearance convinced Sally it was a baobab, something she'd heard of but never seen in person. She was pretty sure baobabs were African. That knowledge, mixed with the hot, dry air and the shimmering sward of green and gold, led her to one conclusion. "I'm in Africa. Why am I in Africa? Why's Reggie dreaming of Africa?"

She looked around as if expecting the dream itself to provide an answer and convenient directions what to do and where to go, but the world gave her nothing but the thrumming drone of cicadas. Sally gazed up into the sky, from where she'd come, and saw nothing but faint wisps of clouds and a blazing sun. "What am I supposed to do?"

Sally walked all around the isolated baobab tree, causing the small birds to scold her from the twisted branches. She didn't find any clues regarding her next move. It would have been too much to hope for a signpost, or a path, or even some kind of sigil on the ground or a distant landmark. Then it occurred to her there was a mark, after a fashion. She trotted back around the tree to find the spot where she'd first struck the earth. There it was, a body-shaped depression marked by bent and broken blades. Her feet had pointed toward the baobab and her arms in a straight line away from it. That was as much of an indication as she was likely to get.

She shook out her fur, enjoying the rustling feel of it against her skin, pointed her face squarely away from the baobab, and started walking.

After a while of trudging through the hot grass, her innate desire for speed grew, and she broke into a trot. Her odd, feline muscles tried to protest at the unfamiliar activity of jogging. She could tell she was built for short bursts instead of sustained distance running. And to think, she'd once run all the way up Central America in one night. Her new body couldn't have achieved such an effort, but perhaps she could catch a gazelle or zebra, if there were any gazelles or zebras to be caught. It was a dream world, so why should she need to eat to survive? Nevertheless, it wasn't her dream, and as a guest in Reggie's world, apparently certain laws and needs remained in place, and she was getting thirsty.

Surely there would be a watering hole somewhere eventually. She sniffed the air, noting the myriad unfamiliar scents, and wondering which one might lead her to water. She paused at the top of a hill and looked back toward the baobab where she'd landed. It was far enough away that it looked like a dead man's hand reaching out of the ground, reminding Sally of too many horror movies. She shivered, hoping she wouldn't inadvertently turn Reggie's dream into a nightmare. The realism of the dream-world was palpable—she could touch things, feel their texture; smells danced around her head; the sounds of wind, of insects, of her own feet thudding against the dry ground . . . all these things seemed more real than the pale landscape of the Moon she'd recently explored. It was as if someone had taken a knob controlling sensory input and turned it all the way up until colors were brighter, scents were sharper, and sounds were clearer.

If the dream changed to something more sinister, Sally was pretty sure it would be utterly terrifying.

She put her back to the distant baobab once more and ran, climbing a hill, then descending into a shallow valley, then finding another small hill. The sun crawled across the sky, making Sally's shadow grow long against the grass, which transformed from green and gold to bronze and red as the sun descended toward the western horizon. She wondered if she'd need to sleep in the dream-world. She was certainly feeling other needs such as hunger and thirst, and incipient exhaustion from the running her feline body wasn't built to perform.

A squat, umbrella-shaped object on the horizon appeared after she crested another hill. It looked like a tree, although she'd never seen one with limbs spread so broad. Like the baobab, it seemed terribly unbalanced, but in its case she didn't see how its spindly trunk could support its spread-out branches. Nevertheless, she reached it as the sun had become a red fireball low in the west. A tall mound sat underneath the northernmost tree limbs. Even though the waning light of day hid most of the details, she could still see—and smell—the fat, white termites crawling to and fro across the mound, busy in whatever their chores might have been.

She was hungry, and she was in a dream, so she told herself it wasn't the worst thing to do. She picked a termite off the mount, crushed it between her claws, and sniffed at the residue. It didn't smell terrible. She rolled her long, feline tongue out and licked the bits off her fingers. It was only a dream, she told herself. It wouldn't make her sick. The taste rolled around her mouth for awhile, and she decided it tasted good enough for her to start picking the insects off the mound like berries from a bush. They had a slightly sweet, tangy flavor that reminded her of pineapple. She ate termites until the sun was gone. They took enough of the edge off her hunger for her to consider her nighttime plans. Safety was a consideration. Whether or not she was actually at any risk inside Reggie's dream, she felt it better not to take chances. Using her finger and toe claws for purchase, she climbed up into the branches of the tree beside the termite mound, careful to avoid the surprisingly sharp thorns until she found a nook of reasonable comfort. She curled up into it, wrapping her tail around herself, and went to sleep.

SEVEN

*The elephant turned his one good eye toward her.
His voice rumbled like thunder. "Flee."*

Awakening while still being asleep in someone else's dream was a completely new process to Sally. In her normal life, it took her many long minutes to drag herself from the morass of her own sleep. She had always told Jason her powers took a great toll on her, which is why she slept as often and long as possible. Then he would joke and call her names like *lazybones* and *sleepyhead* and as often as not they would find a mutually enjoyable way to wake up—even though it made them both crave even more sleep afterward. Still, when Sally absolutely had to wake up, even with the aid of an alarm, there was a lot of tossing and turning, complaining and groaning, slothful crawling and trudging, and whining like a toddler. If Sally could get away with throwing a tantrum instead of getting up, she might consider it.

There was none of that reticence in Reggie's dream-world. One moment Sally was asleep, with a hint of a dream inside of a dream that she couldn't remember no matter how hard she tried, and the next she was crouched on her feet, her back to the trunk of the acacia tree, claws digging into the wood as she checked her bearings. It was as if she'd always been awake and alert, and there was some sort of massive battle just over the next rise. A great cloud of dust swirled in the sparkling morning air. The caterwauling and trumpeting of warring beasts rang in her ears. She'd have been afraid under different circumstances, but now instead she was curious.

"It killed the cat, Sally, don't forget." She reminded herself of the trope aloud, twitching her tail for emphasis. "Don't get involved. Don't go look and see what it is. It has nothing to do with you."

A thud shook the entire landscape, like a great stone falling over.

"Shit." Sally sprang from the branches, landing softly upon the dust beneath the tree limbs. She trotted past the termite mound and up the side of the hill. As she climbed, she dropped to all fours and discovered it wasn't nearly as uncomfortable a way of moving in her new feline form as it would have been with fully human limbs. By the time she reached the crest of the hill, she was crawling on her belly, her face pulled into an unconscious snarl at the thought of how dirty she was making her pretty white fur. She wondered if she'd have to clean it with her tongue. She hoped not. And then all thoughts of herself vanished as she crossed the top of the hill and saw the tableau laid out at the base of the hill before her.

An elephant was under full attack by several felinoids like Sally. They leaped, snarling, using their claws to rake furrows in the elephant's sides and belly, worrying at its feet. Blood ran down the elephant's wrinkled hide like rain down shingles. The ground beneath the elephant's feet had grown muddy with gore. One of the noble beast's eyes was a bloody ruin, having been torn away along with half of one cheek in a vicious slash. The elephant's sides heaved as it struggled to draw breath, clearly exhausted from the battle. Nor was this the first it had ever fought, for white scars decorated its sides and legs. This was no young bull, wandered away from its tribe. No, this was a grizzled veteran warrior, and two of the cat-men had paid their ultimate respects to him and his station, trampled beneath his mighty feet.

Sally's first instinct was to rush down the hill to defend the elephant, even though she was outnumbered seven to one. Her second instinct, coming from a far more bestial place, was to join in the joyful killing, to tear out the elephant's soft organs, to bathe in its blood beneath the all-seeing sun.

One of the felinoids was careless and slow getting away after a slashing attack, and the elephant tripped him with his trunk and then stomped down upon the hapless man's head, splattering blood and brains in all directions. The impact shook the land, dislodging beetles from their grass ladders and launching startled birds skyward. Another cat-man misjudged a leap and the elephant caught him midair, squeezed him until his spine shattered, and then flung the grisly missile away. The dead felinoid crashed to the side of the hill just beneath Sally's vantage point, and she squeaked in surprise and dismay.

The five remaining cat-men looked up in her direction as they circled the elephant warily, seeking their opening for a final, fatal blow. "Join us!" cried one. "Come and share in our kill and feed. It's a beautiful morning for the end of a hunt, and elephant is the greatest delicacy of all."

"N-no!" Sally arched her back like a cat when confronting a threat. "I don't want to."

The elephant turned his one good eye toward her. His voice rumbled like thunder. "Flee." He trumpeted a warning and tried to spin around, but the cat-men were faster. "Their kill-lust is strong. You are not safe here."

"No!" Sally clenched her fists. She didn't know which was the right side, or if she should even be involved in this battle of the dream-world, but she did know one thing. The cat-men had invited her to join them. The elephant warned her away. Only one had her safety in mind.

She would defend the elephant, even at the risk to her own life. Could she be killed in a dream? She'd had dreams about death before. All people did, surely. But this was different. If she died in Reggie's dream, would it affect her? Was it like *The Matrix*, where virtual death was equivalent to real death? Or would she simply awaken? She hadn't awakened in the real world when she'd slept in the dream-world. What did it mean to die in a dream?

Sally raced down the hill, splaying her claws, charging toward the battle. Her approach seemed terribly slow to her, as if she were running in slow motion. That was a familiar sensation to her as a speedster, but in the dream-world she didn't seem to have super-powers. The dream slowed things down around her, like when she accelerated her own perceptions in combat. The difference was now she was moving every bit as slow as those she prepared to fight. She had the perceptions of a speedster, but she was trapped in a helpless and pathetic unpowered body. It was agonizing to watch as she lunged at the first cat-man, who didn't seem to believe she was actually attacking, and misjudged her angle so badly that she didn't catch more than a few strands of fur.

"Sister, what are you doing?" The cat-man was aghast at her brazen attack.

"Kill her," said a second. "Kill them both. Take their livers. Eat your fill."

Sally slashed at the first man, surprised at her own ferocity. The lioness in her was taking charge, subsuming her humanity beneath the pure hunting and fighting instincts of the unquestioned Queen of the Jungle. Her claws tore deep furrows across the flesh of his chest—not a killing blow by any stretch of the imagination, but he shrieked from the pain of it nevertheless.

All the cat-men froze for a moment, stunned by the sudden assault by one who should have been an ally.

The elephant was wounded and exhausted, but he hadn't lived to an old age by being a poor tactician. The momentary lapse of attacks was all he needed to grab one of the remaining five by a leg and smash him into the ground. A pillar of a foot put an end to that particular cat-man's screams.

Sally found herself beset by the other four felinoids. They encircled her, lashing out with their hands, trying to force her to commit to one direction so they could overwhelm her from the sides and behind. She'd fought multiple opponents many times over the years, both in Combat Simulation training and against real live foes, but in those battles she'd always had her super-speed to draw upon. Now that it was denied to her, she realized how much she'd grown to depend upon it instead of what her old friend Jack had called *combat smarts.* His philosophy, one he'd tried to impress upon Sally many times, was to always assume that an opponent was better-armed, better-skilled, better-equipped, and generally better at everything. Doing so kept one on one's toes and forced one to think like a warrior instead of like a superhero. Sometimes warriors had to cut their losses and retreat. Honor was a fools' concept, he'd said. It's wiser to flee when you're outmatched than to stay and fight and get cut down for your trouble. That kind of thing only works in the movies.

If he could see her now, he'd be shaking his head in disappointment because she hadn't learned a damn thing.

She needed a superior tactical position when facing too many opponents. The obvious high ground was cut off, so she needed to find a spot where one side was protected. Without a wall or convenient building, she chose the most solid thing in the area as her best defensible position. She ducked beneath a lunging swipe and retaliated with a double-punch to the cat-man's torso. He fell back, coughing and gasping from her blow having knocked the wind out of him. She dove headlong, rolling in a tight somersault past the staggered cat-man, and came right up against one of the elephant's forelegs.

"Flee . . . little one." The elephant's voice was ragged and his breathing labored. The bloodied mud beneath him was ankle-deep and stank of copper and iron.

Sally jumped to her feet, taking a combat crouch with her back to the elephant. Mud dripped from her hands and tail and she snarled at the encroaching cat-men. "No. They should flee." She inhaled deeply, letting the scent of blood fill the wild parts of her brain, and let loose with a challenging roar that shook the savannah. She was a lioness and by every god in the pantheon, they would fear her or know the reason why.

The largest of the cat-men leaped at her and she rose up to meet him. They wrestled, arms locked over each others' shoulders, snarling and biting at each other's faces. Sally slashed at his face with her fangs, moving faster than he, and opened up the side of his face. He yelped in pain and his own teeth ceased worrying at her ears. The opportunity was there, so she twisted her head around and clamped her teeth across his throat. She couldn't tell him to surrender or his friends to give up, and she didn't believe he would have done so even if she could.

He slashed at her, opening cuts in her side. They hurt more than she imagined possible. How could dream pain be so real? But real it was, and she knew if she released the cat-man, he'd have the advantage to attack while she was regrouping. She did the only thing she could think of in the heat of the moment, and clenched her teeth together over his throat until they met through his windpipe. Hot blood jetted across her face and down her throat, and she would have gagged were she not full of the fire and fury of battle. She tore herself away from the man and he fell without a sound, clawing feebly at his own face.

The other three felinoids hesitated in their attack. Seeing their leader go down under Sally's insistent jaws was enough to make them re-evaluate their choices. Sally pressed her advantage and charged toward them, spitting and snarling like a rabid housecat. One of them tripped over a rock jutting from the hillside and fell onto his back. Sally was on him in an instant, digging into his hips with her toe claws and ripping her fingers across his face, sending splatters of gore across the savannah grass.

A cat-man tackled her, knocking her sideways. They rolled down the hillside back toward the bloody mud pit beneath the elephant. The male was stronger, and she wound up on her back with his paws over her wrists, straddling her hips in the grotesque pose of a would-be rapist. Sally strained against him, thrashing and kicking up a cloud of dust. As the male bent down, jaws gaping wide to tear out her own throat, she lunged up with the desperation of a cornered animal and closed her teeth upon his jaw, tearing through sinew and skin like paper until she grasped hold of the bony mandible. He made a surprised mewling sound. His blood rained down upon Sally's face and she shut her eyes against the torrent. His grip upon her wrists relaxed as she squeezed tighter, feeling bone crackle beneath her muzzle.

She freed one hand and dug it into his midsection, like punching into a bucket full of chum, and twisted. The cat-man died suddenly, violently, in an explosion of ruined organs and fleshy tatters. She flung aside the corpse and rolled over to get onto her feet.

The final cat-man threw himself atop her, driving her face into the ground. He shoved harder, pushing down until the blood-scented mud filled her mouth and nose and she couldn't breathe. He was shouting something but all she could hear was the roaring in her ears as her body struggled to find air where none was to be had. A rock poked hard into her cheek, sending a stabbing pain all the way down to her tail, like a single beam of clarity on a foggy night. She flailed her arms and legs with rapidly-diminishing strength, trying to find the right move to achieve freedom. Then all she could hear was the blood in her ears, a drumbeat growing slower and fainter.

And then the weight was lifted from her back and she pushed herself from the mud, coughing and spitting and gasping for huge inhalations of sweet air. She wiped muck from her eyes just in time to see the elephant squeeze his trunk around the cat-man's head until his pinched-off neck separated from the rest of him and his body fell, adding more blood to the already slick, stinking mire.

Sally coughed and wheezed, combing mud from her whiskers as she looked up at the elephant. "Thanks."

The elephant groaned, swaying on his feet. Sally saw how badly his belly had been torn and gasped.

He toppled, splashing into the bloody mud with a thud that might have shook the entire world. For a long moment Sally thought he'd died, but then he took a slow, shuddering breath, laboring under the weight of his own body with muscles starved for blood and oxygen. She could tell his death was inevitable and wondered if she should speed it along, like putting down a dog who was stricken with cancer. But he'd spoken to her, the elephant, and she didn't know if she could do it.

The way he'd fallen, his good eye was submerged in the mud, and his ruined eye wouldn't have seen her anyway, so she trotted around his bulk until she was near his trunk. She knew that was a dangerous place to be after seeing how easily he'd dispatched a couple of the cat-men with it, but perhaps his sense of smell would let him know it was her and not one of the hunters. "H-hi." She felt stupid, not knowing how to address such a majestic beast. Her simple greeting seemed far too pedestrian, but she didn't have a grasp of the sort of flowery court language one should use on such an occasion.

"Little one." The elephant's voice rumbled and bubbled as he spoke around a mouthful of mud. His trunk gave his voice a strange, resonant quality, like a trombone or a middle-range pipe organ. "You should have fled."

"I couldn't let them kill you."

"But they have, little one. I am dying."

Sally bowed her head. "I'm sorry. I wasn't fast enough. I'm not used to that. I've always been fast."

"Death is part of the circle of life. You are wounded, and weakened by your wounds." The elephant took another deep breath. Sally could hear the rattling of fluid in his lungs. "If you do not regain your strength, you will die here. After I die, feed upon my flesh. It will strengthen and sustain you."

"No! I couldn't do that!"

"But you must, little one . . . You have . . . important work to do here." The elephant coughed, splattering bloody mud across the hillside.

"I don't even know what I'm supposed to do here. What do I do? Where do I go?" Sally had never felt as lost in her life as she did at that moment.

The elephant curled his trunk around one of his own tusks and flexed it hard over the tip, breaking off a piece half the size of Sally's hand. She gasped at the unexpected self-mutilation, and shrank back when the elephant offered the piece to her. "Take it . . . it is . . . a totem. It will . . . guide you."

Sally reached out and took the piece of ivory. The tip was smooth and polished from many years of use, while the back side was jagged and irregular. "I hope you're right, because I could use some directions about now."

"You must . . . rescue the . . . Elephant Queen. She is . . . prisoner of . . . the Ticking Lord."

The elephant stopped speaking, and didn't take another breath.

Sally sighed. She'd been given some vague words of wisdom she didn't understand, a mysterious totem of questionable usefulness, and an opportunity to sample fresh, raw elephant—something she'd never considered might ever be a part of her diet. Nevertheless, her stomach growled at the scent of fresh blood and the dark wetness of the elephant's open flank had a strangely inviting quality to it. Maybe if she didn't think about it too much, she could manage to eat. It was just a dream, she told herself. She wasn't eating real elephant.

And yet, as she tore away the first strip of flesh for sampling, one ludicrous thought nearly overwhelmed her, like a comedian who didn't know when the crowd had turned hostile. "I'm Mario," she said, chewing on her first bite of elephant and trying to decide if it was as terrible as she thought it should be or if it was just an acquired taste. "That princess better be in the first castle."

EIGHT

The dream was fleeing her mind as fast as if it were running away from her at super speed.

Sally awakened with a start, as if something had fallen over in her bedroom. She sat up and nearly catapulted herself off her bed in the weak lunar gravity. Her singlet was soaked with sweat. The lights were too bright. Harlan Washington stood near her, regarding her with the dispassion of a man looking at an insect pinned to a display case.

Her mind caught up with her a moment later and she froze. Her stomach twisted and rumbled with hunger, filling the back of her throat with its acidic cry. She grimaced and pushed her damp hair out of her face. Minerva lay on her side on a bed nearby, watching Sally as she rested her head on one folded arm. March was sprawled on another, still asleep.

"How do you feel?" asked Harlan.

"I . . ." Sally didn't really know how she felt. Being asked to self-analyze only seconds after being dragged from a sound sleep was more difficult a task than she could normally manage first thing in the morning. "Okay, I guess. How long was I asleep? A couple of hours?"

Harlan shook his head. "Two days." He pulled up the strange membrane-based display he could create from the nanites embedded within his body. "I was getting worried about your physiological status. You need nutrients. I'm not going to keep you unconscious and feed you intravenously if I don't have to."

Sally looked down and noticed a tube emerging from the inside of her elbow. "What is this?"

"It's how I kept you hydrated."

A chill ran down Sally's spine. Harlan could have injected any kind of drug into her blood through an IV. Then she realized she already had his nanotech inside of her. Who knew what they were doing? She looked at Minerva. "Are we okay? He didn't do anything to us?"

"No. Nothing he didn't already clear with us." Minerva smiled. "I'm glad you're awake. I need a break."

March twitched on his cot, redirecting a stray jet of compressed air toward Sally's face and making her hair float aside. "How's March?"

"He's exhausted. I'm monitoring his status. He'll need a break as well, but he's not ready to be awakened yet." Harlan paused, turning his membrane scanner toward Reggie. "No change in Reggie's physiological status either, but there was definitely some activity in a previously dormant part of her brain." He looked back at Sally. "I'm not sure if you accomplished anything, but that's something new. What did you see?"

"I saw . . ." Sally stopped. The dream was fleeing her mind as fast as if it were running away from her at super speed. All she had left was a general sense of incompleteness. "There was grass . . . and it was hot . . . and I had a tail. I remember that much." She rubbed her temples. "I think I was fighting. It's hard to remember any details. I'm not good at remembering my dreams. Never have been."

"Your brain activity suggested you were indeed in some kind of combat." Harlan made his membrane scanner vanish once more. "Who or what were you fighting?"

"I don't know." Sally swung her legs off the cot to stand beside it. The lunar gravity made standing easier, but she still felt dizzy and weak.

"Why were you fighting?"

"I don't know!" She glared at Harlan. "I need a bathroom and a toothbrush and a burrito as big as my head. Maybe then I can remember some of this stuff."

He nodded. "Of course. Take several hours. We'll resume after you've bathed and eaten and done whatever else you need to."

Minerva floated off her own bed to hover beside Sally. "How long do you intend to keep us here?"

Harlan folded his arms. "Not long. Either you'll fail or you'll be successful in reaching Reggie's conscious mind. If you're not making any more progress, I'll know and I'll have to come up with yet another plan." He turned away from the young women to regard his comatose sister.

Sally and Minerva left the medical wing without saying another word to him. "What do you think?" Sally asked Minerva as they headed back to the part of the Preserve where their temporary quarters were.

"He's disappointed. And he's worried about his sister." Minerva turned to face Sally as they stopped outside her door. "He's also worried about you."

Sally snorted. "I'm like his worst enemy. Why would he care?"

"I don't know, but if I were to make a guess, it's because he feels like you've got the best chance of succeeding where he's failed for so long. If something happens to you, he's back at square one again."

Sally rolled her eyes. "He's only thinking of himself. The man isn't capable of caring about anyone or anything." Even as she said it, she knew it was a lie. She'd seen glimpses of his deeply-repressed emotions when talking about Reggie, the way he'd brush the back of her hand as he walked past her in the medical bay. There was a tenderness beneath his iron skin, buried deep in his core.

Minerva said nothing further about Harlan, for which Sally was profoundly grateful. She didn't need to be reminded of her self-dishonesty. "I'm going to see what taking a bath is like on the Moon."

"That's not a bad idea." Sally felt the still-damp singlet clinging to her skin. "Think I'll do that too."

As it turned out, bathing on the Moon wasn't too terribly different from bathing on the Earth. Harlan, always a great believer in form over function, had designed the bathroom like a utilitarian version of a Japanese-style bath. It was a small, tall tub barely big enough for Sally, full of pleasantly warm water. The tub was contained within a slightly larger room with a drain in the floor and a shower head attached to a hose. A couple of pump nozzles emerged from the wall beneath the shower and Sally guessed they held body wash and shampoo. Probably no conditioner, because the Moon was primarily a Boys' Club. She'd had to educate Jason in the ways of conditioner, face wash, and how one didn't wash one's hair with body wash no matter what the advertisements said. It appeared the same lack of knowledge was rampant among the Washingtons. She tested each nozzle and decided, pretty much arbitrarily, the one on the left was shampoo and the one on the right was soap. If she woke up from her next sleep session with hair matted like a rug and dry, itchy patches all over her skin, she'd know she'd gotten them reversed.

She washed herself off in the tiny shower cubicle, wishing she had anything like a washcloth or loofah. Soap bubbles were still soap bubbles on the Moon, and they drifted pretty much the same way as on Earth, but water fell slower, and Sally enjoyed watching the droplets wobble and twist as they spun toward the floor. At last, she shut off the shower and decided to take the bath she'd promised herself. Climbing into the tub on Earth might have required a step, but in the lunar gravity she had no problem hopping over the tall side of the tub and lowering herself into the warm water. Some of it slopped over the side and but there was already a drain in the floor so she didn't feel guilty about it. The process was similar to sitting in a hot tub, something Sally truly enjoyed on account of it was the only time she ever truly felt warm outside of her home state of Arizona. She wished she could stretch out her legs, but the tub design forced her to keep her knees up by her chest. At least the water came all the way up to her chin.

Nevertheless, it was comfortable enough that she could close her eyes and almost imagine she was in a spa back home. Steam wafted off the water. She splashed her fingers upward and watched the sparkling drops as they spun back down to the water again. She wasn't sleepy, but the persistent warmth was forcing her to relax, to let her mind unwind.

She'd eaten elephant.

Sally blinked. She'd had a sudden flash of her dream journey. She'd eaten . . . *elephant*? What kind of horrible thing was that to cross her mind? It had to be part of the dream. That kind of random thought didn't float into her head without some kind of trigger. She leaned her head back, letting the water caress her scalp just below her ears, and focused on the elusive memories of the Dream-world.

Many years ago, when she'd first become part of Just Cause, a telepath named Glimmer had installed what he'd called *recording architecture* in her mind, ostensibly so she could be used as a human camcorder, recording every sound, sight, smell, and touch she experienced, which could later be disseminated to a group for intelligence purposes. The architecture was still there, something her teammate Ment had confirmed. She wondered if she could somehow access it to recapture her experiences in the dream to become easier to remember. She'd never been particularly good at remembering her dreams, but she knew it was the sort of thing some people could do. Perhaps she could train herself to do it too. She shut her eyes, letting the warmth of the water soak into her, bathing on the Moon.

It had been a brutal battle. None survived it but her.

Her stomach twisted itself in knots. She knew she'd been in a fight, but she wasn't sure why. And she'd been the only one to survive it. That was a terrible thing to dream. She'd fought them tooth and claw to . . . *tooth and claw.* She'd had claws. And teeth. She hadn't been herself. What had she been in the dream? She couldn't quite reach it, like being slightly too far away from someone to overhear their conversation except for the inflection and cadences. She could get bits and pieces, flashes of the dream, but the main content, the important part—that kept eluding her.

At last, relaxed and surprisingly, wide awake, she emerged dripping from the tub and discovered to her delight there was a powerful heat lamp built into the ceiling. By the time she emerged from the tiny bathroom, her hair was dry and already frizzing up, and her skin was a healthy pink glow. There was no mirror in her quarters, and why would there be? Boys' Club, she reminded herself. Still, she could feel her hair becoming a rats' nest and grimaced at the damage she'd do to it if she stayed too long on the Moon. Then she giggled, because she *was* on the Moon.

She wrapped herself up in one of Jason's oversized sweatshirts and some leggings and went off in search of something to eat. She found Minerva in the lounge, eating something that looked suspiciously like a Hot Pocket. Minerva looked and smelled like she'd also bathed, and of course, her hair was perfect. Sally sat down beside her. "Hey. Remember how you transformed my entire body when I infiltrated Champion's organization?"

Minerva swallowed a mouthful and smiled. "Of course."

"Think you could fix my hair? I'd hate to have to shave it all off."

"Of course. Are you hungry? There's quite a selection of frozen snacks and TV dinners right back there. And a microwave." Minerva pointed toward one wall that held a small kitchenette.

"I'm hungry enough to give them consideration. I take it there's no fresh alternatives."

Minerva looked down at her meal. "Nothing that I could detect, but my senses aren't working quite right here. They have the means to come back to Earth. They must get fresh food occasionally. Perhaps there's a greenhouse." She sniffed the air. She sounded a bit congested to Sally. "If so, I can't tell."

"What's the matter with your senses?" Sally walked over the the freezer, rummaged through the boxes until she found something that looked remotely appetizing. "You think Harlan's nanites are messing with you?"

"No. They're inert right now." Sally didn't ask how Minerva could know that. Of *course* she could. "Perhaps my powers are tied to the Earth. After all, what are the chances that I would ever not be there?"

Sally watched the box of her pot pie spin around in the microwave. "*Never tell me the odds.*"

"Han Solo. *The Empire Strikes Back*. I told you I watched them."

"Very good." Sally removed her pot pie from the microwave, careful not to burn herself on the bubbling yellow gravy that might have been chicken. "Listen, Minerva, did anything, you know, happen while we were asleep?"

Minerva smiled at her. "I was asleep. How do you think I would know?"

Sally sniffed at the pot pie, wondering if it had ever been even within spitting distance of a chicken. "Because you're you. You'd know."

"That's true. And no, nothing happened. I may have made a slightly veiled threat to Mr. Washington before I fell asleep."

Sally shivered a little. She'd heard one of Minerva's threats before. The young woman's abilities were mysterious, powerful, and enough to give anyone nightmares if she turned those powers to the aim of causing grievous, lasting harm to someone. She dug into the pot pie, let the greasy, flaky crust wash around her mouth some, and decided it wasn't half bad. Maybe food tasted better on the Moon, like when one was camping. "Did you see anything? In the dream, I mean?"

"Not at first. I started to figure out the right kinds of connections towards the end of the second day. I saw things like they were at a great distance, blurred through a smeared lens."

"But no details?"

"No, not really. I need to have a talk with March. See if I can feel around his mind better. Maybe I can work out a way to actually enter the dream myself."

"That would be nice. I can barely remember more than a few flashes of it. If you were there, it might be easier to put the pieces together." Sally looked down at her rapidly-disappearing pot pie. "This is a lot better than it has any right to be."

"First solid food you've had in two days." Minerva wiped grease from her fingers.

Sally ate in silence for a few minutes, finally scraping out the last crumbs and debating whether or not she was hungry enough to go make another one. At last, she decided she didn't have enough self-loathing to risk it. "I can't believe I did that. I need to go work out now."

"I thought they didn't have a gym here."

"They don't, but I'll figure something out. I'm not going to break all my routines just because I'm on the Moon." Sally grinned. "You know, I don't think I'll ever get tired of saying that. I bet Neil Armstrong and Buzz Aldrin and all the other guys who landed here smiled every time they mentioned it."

"Some day you can tell your children you ate a pot pie on the Moon."

Sally snorted. "And you can tell yours you watched me do it after you ate a Hot Pocket."

Minerva nodded. "*Touché.*"

Sally found a trash receptacle. Given the cloudiness of the air within it, she suspected it was full of nanites that would break down the cardboard tray into its component molecules for use in other projects. If nothing else, Harlan had constructed a technological marvel. She hoped someday he might share that knowledge with the rest of the world. If he wanted to, he could make the Earth an amazing place.

She wasn't going to hold her breath over him changing his mind about humanity, though.

Sally wasn't much of a weightlifter. She left the heavy muscle work to her husband as much as possible. She didn't like lifting, or strength and resistance training. She'd much rather run. Unfortunately, she could almost hear her friend and trainer Hector berating her about it. *You can already run, chica,* he would say. *You need to work on the shit you're bad at. The shit you hate. You ain't gonna get any better otherwise.* And then maybe he'd try to blindside her with a table leg. But that was just Hector, and she respected him like few other people she'd met in the world. He was right, of course.

Lifting wouldn't work well in lunar gravity, but she could still do isometrics, because that didn't depend upon gravity. She found an empty storeroom and set to it, straining her muscles against each other in intervals the way Jason had taught her. Soon she was warm enough to strip out of her sweatshirt and just work in her sports bra and tights. After a good solid hour of isometrics, followed by a bout of shadow boxing, she'd worked up a sweat and was ready for a change of pace.

She'd had an idea about running in the lower gravity, and the empty storeroom would give her the chance to try it. If it didn't work, she'd probably smash her face into a wall, give herself another concussion, and force an early retirement. But what was life without risks? If she'd wanted to play it safe, she wouldn't have been a superhero in the first place. She put her back to one wall, took a deep breath, and bounded across the room like a gazelle. Three steps and she was nearly to the far wall. She put her foot on the wall and pushed herself up. Her momentum and the light gravity carried her three steps up the wall, still accelerating. She felt centrifugal force pressing her against the ceiling as she took three steps across it. Gravity started to take hold of her once more as she dashed down the wall and turned her path back to the floor. Grinning at her success, she poured on the speed, turning the storeroom into an endless racetrack. The faster she went, the harder it became to keep her legs beneath her. The centrifugal force was like she was growing heavier with every step. She'd never thought to train like she was inside a giant hamster wheel before. She'd have to try it back home on Earth. It had some challenges and introduced some difficulty to her running she hadn't encountered before.

She was so lost in her thoughts as she encircled the room time and time again that she nearly shrieked in surprise when she saw March peek his head into the storeroom and say "Whoa!"

NINE

You should be grateful.
Before this, my hobby was destroying Just Cause.

Sally had spent so much of her life around other parahumans, she occasionally forgot how astonishing their abilities could be to mundanes. Even someone who couldn't do anything more than fly, like her friend Surfboy, was still a wonder to behold. And when it came to Sally, who didn't like to admit she was one of the most powerful parahumans on the planet when it came to things she could accomplish strictly on her own, it was sometimes like regarding an earthbound goddess. Or Moonbound, she thought. Either way, the look of pure amazement on March's face was one she wouldn't soon forget.

"Sorry. I was just trying to do something physical. I love sleeping as much as the next person. It's kind of my hobby, actually. But I can't just sit around and do nothing. Unless maybe it's binge watching one of my favorite shows." Sally realized she was babbling and tried to slow herself down.

March nodded. "I've w-watched a lot of shows here. I might have . . . have them in my library."

"Is that what you do when you're not taking care of your mom?"

"I don't have . . . have a lot of people t-to talk to."

"No Facebook?"

March shrugged. "No friends."

Sally's face fell. "That's terrible. I'm sorry."

"It's not so b-bad. I have chatbots. They play games. They're s-smart enough to be entertaining."

"But what about social interaction? I realize you can't just have friends over to the Moon whenever you want, because it's your supervillain uncle's secret base and all, but you've got a space van. Don't you ever go down to Earth and, I don't know, go clubbing or something?"

March shook his head. "I'm kind of shy."

"Because of your, uh stutter?"

"No. I just am."

Sally hadn't ever spent much time alone in her life, even though she'd grown up an only child. Her mother and grandmother, both former superheroes, had spent much of her childhood taking her around to visit other superheroes, enrolling her in special training classes, and generally doing everything they could to prepare her for a lifelong career as a superhero. It was similar to how some parents invested everything they could to train their children to become professional athletes, or musicians, or scientists. March had spent a lifetime undergoing a different sort of training, she supposed. *How to Be A Supervillain in Ten Easy Steps.*

"I guess it must have been tough growing up in your situation."

"It wasn't as b-bad as you think. Maybe Uncle Harlan isn't the nicest p-person in the world, but he . . . he cares. In his own way." March spread his arms wide as if to encompass the entire Preserve. "He b-built all this for my mom. To t-take care of her. He took money to do bad things so he could f-fund his research."

"The ends don't always justify the means." Sally frowned. "But I guess I see your perspective. It's just hard for me to wrap my mind around the idea of Harlan exhibiting any kind of concern for his fellow man. He killed friends of mine. He killed my father. He would have killed me if I hadn't gotten away."

"He hasn't killed anyone in a long time. And he saved the human race from ext . . . extinction."

Sally sighed. There it was, the trump card that had brought her to the Moon in the first place. She hadn't known where else to turn to prevent a nanotech plague from sterilizing all non-parahumans on the planet. Harlan Washington had cured it as easily as a doctor prescribing medication for a cold. And what had he asked for in return? He could have held the world hostage. He could have insisted upon virtually any payment, for what price was too much to pay for salvation? Instead, all he asked was for Sally and Minerva to come to the Moon to try to rescue his sister's mind.

One woman's life against the weight of the entire human race was staggering. Sally couldn't even say she'd done as much when she struck down the Archmage. She'd taken a life to potentially save the world. Harlan had saved the world and in return was working to return a life not yet lived.

It was staggering when she really thought about it, so much so that she had to sit down against a wall.

March crouched beside her. "Are you okay?"

Sally nodded. "Just a little light-headed. Sometimes it's a lot to take in. All this." She waved her hands. "I mean, you're used to it. It's your everyday life. I'm having to reinvent my ideas about a lot of things."

"Can I bring you anything? Some w-water?"

"That would be great."

March disappeared into a side corridor and returned a minute later with a water bottle. Sally accepted it and drank half of it before holding the cool plastic against her temple.

"March, it's been a strange couple of days."

His smile was honest and charming. "I bet. Listen, Uncle Harlan wants t-to start another session in a few hours. I've got a big film library if you . . . you want to watch something."

Sally smiled back. "Yeah, I think I'd like that. Something campy and fun."

"I know just the thing. Meet me b-back in the lounge? I'll wait for you."

"Sure, that sounds good. I'm just going to sit here and finish my water and try to remember my dreams."

March looked back over his shoulder as he left the storage room. "They're not your dreams. They're my mom's."

Sally sat against the wall and drank her water, wondering what was going on back home. Jason would have figured she was still at her conference, but he'd be wondering why she hadn't even texted him yet. Their duties as both superheroes and representatives of the world's premiere superhero organization often required them to be in different places, but rarely did a day pass without at least a quick *I love you* message. Maybe Harlan had already planned for that. He could have hired Vanitha to spoof Sally's phone number, make it look like she was sending messages to Jason.

And then she felt guilty. She'd been on the Moon for a couple of days and it was the first time she'd really thought about her husband. When she returned, she would have to be especially nice to him. She wasn't ready to have that long-awaited discussion about children, but maybe she'd buy some surprising, interesting underwear to model for him.

She didn't see a place to recycle her bottle in the storage room, so she carried it with her and planned to take it back to the lounge. When she stepped out into the corridor, she realized she didn't remember which way she'd come to find the room. Oh well, she thought. The Preserve couldn't be that big. She'd find her way back to the lounge on her own. She picked a direction and started off.

Almost immediately, she decided she'd taken a wrong turn from the start, but her curiosity got the better of her, so she continued on, wondering if the Preserve was shaped like a ring and she'd eventually find herself in familiar territory again or if the corridors led off to dead ends. If she learned the latter was true, what would be Harlan's purpose in separating parts of the base from each other? She theorized it was a safety measure; if one part of the base lost air pressure, the rest could be sealed off. That was Living in Space-101 stuff, right?

Then she wandered into a laboratory, and stopped dead in her tracks at what she saw.

A robot stared back at her with cold, dead eyes from where it hung from a rack, connected to dozens of machines by a thick mass of gleaming fiber-optic cables. The lights on the machines flashed like the LEDs on a modem, performing their intricate luminal dance. It was only partially-constructed, a skeletal framework with the robotic equivalent of internal organs and muscles filling its structure. Only a few dangling wires and tubes hung down beneath the torso. A partially-built leg sat on a workbench underneath a broad magnifying scanner. As Sally looked around the room, she saw other components clearly part of the robotic creation: a hand sitting upright on a frame with each finger bent at a slightly different angle; pieces of sheet metal bent into shapes that could only be skin or armor.

"What are you supposed to be? The next Destroyer?" Sally reached out to touch the robot. She was more curious than afraid, even though she'd seen more movies with evil space robots than she could count on both hands. The device was unfinished, and even if it was somehow awake and alert, it was still only a robot. Sally had never seen anything like it before, and yet it seemed familiar to her.

"What are you doing in there?"

Sally spun around to see Harlan approaching down the corridor, a thunderous expression plastered across his face. "Nothing. Honest. I took a wrong turn."

Harlan reached her. His teeth were clenched so tightly behind his cheeks that his ears quivered. He raised a slow, deliberate hand and pointed. "It's. That. Way."

"Oh, sure. Glad you told me. Otherwise I'd have had to ask the robot for directions." Sally waved at the partially-finished device over her shoulder. "What's that, your new lackey?"

For a moment, she thought her jibe was going to get her in real trouble as anger and embarrassment both vied for control of Harlan's face. "It's a hobby. I needed something to do to keep myself occupied when I wasn't working on helping Reggie." He glared at Sally. "You should be grateful. Before this, my hobby was destroying Just Cause."

His words triggered an unexpected memory and shivers ran down Sally's spine. "Is it . . . Are you recreating the Steel Soldier? I saw pictures of it in the Just Cause archives. You destroyed it in '85. When you killed my father. Why are you rebuilding it?"

"I'm not rebuilding anything. I started from scratch."

"Why the Soldier?"

Harlan's fury subsided a bit as he realized Sally's interest was genuine. "I first encountered the Soldier in '77. It was an astonishing piece of technology. I'd never seen anything like it. Javelin made me repair it. I learned so much then. Without that opportunity, I'd never have built the Mark II."

"You got into the guts of the Soldier all those years ago, and then you stuck a bomb in it and blew it up at Tornado's funeral, and now you're rebuilding it? What kind of twisted circular logic is that?

"Everybody needs a hobby."

Sally thought about protesting, but she had to admit Harlan was right. There were far worse things he could do with his spare time than rebuild the robot that was a former member of Just Cause. "What are you going to do with it when it's done?"

Harlan shrugged. "Maybe nothing. Art for art's sake. Not everything has to have a purpose."

"The original Soldier was a combat android. You better not turn this one loose on the world. I'll stop it."

"I know you will. I've already destroyed one masterpiece of technology when I was a foolish young man. I don't repeat my mistakes. Now get out of my workshop. Go watch your movie with March." Harlan pushed past her and began shutting down equipment in the lab.

Sally didn't move. "So what's his deal? How'd you mess him up?"

"Mess him up?" Harlan kept his back to her. Somehow she figured he could see her clearly nevertheless.

"His stutter. Did you give it to him? Experiment on him? Maybe you tested out your nanites on him?"

Harlan paused in his work. "Of course I didn't. I don't deny I'm a monster, but I've never tested anything on him. Why would I do that?" He looked back over his shoulder. "Things work when I build them. They don't need testing."

Sally snorted. "Aren't we full of ourselves?"

"It's the truth, and you're well aware of that fact." Harlan spread his fingers across one arm and another membrane screen appeared across his skin. His fingers flew across touchscreen controls upon it. Lights shut down in the workshop. "His stutter is due to abnormalities in his brain function."

"You haven't tried to fix it?"

"No, and I'll tell you why. I'm selfish. If I tried to fix it and somehow ended up damaging his ability to enter dreams, I might never reach my sister again."

"Or maybe you just didn't want to risk harming March in some way. You raised him from a baby. You must have some kind of feelings for him. You can't be that hard, Harlan." Sally stepped back into the corridor. Harlan followed her out and the door to the workshop slid shut with an angry hiss.

"Don't ever presume to tell me what I can or can't be."

TEN

Then, of course, she remembered she was in someone else's dream, and that was reason enough.

The journey into Reggie's dream was truncated the second time around, almost as if Sally's mind had edited out the travel time, as sometimes happened in dreams. She became aware of her surroundings and noted that she was no longer crouched down in the shade of the elephant's corpse with his blood streaking her fur as she ate. Instead, she was curled into a ball at the base of a towering mountain that seemed to have risen straight out of the flat savannah. It reminded her of the magical peak created by the Archmage several years ago. She'd had to climb that one to reach the supervillain at the top and she knew instinctively she would have to climb this one as well. Something was calling to her from the summit.

Although she'd awakened in a different place when entering the dream, she discovered she still had the piece of ivory clutched in one paw. On the heels of that realization came the confirmation she was once again wrapped in fur and built more like the felinoids she'd dispatched in the previous incarnation of the dream. She wondered what was the significance of her appearance. She was pretty sure she'd read somewhere everything in dreams had some kind of deeper meaning, because the subconscious was working its way through problems experienced in the waking world. What problem could cause her to manifest as a humanoid cat?

Ultimately it didn't matter, she decided. What was more pressing was her lack of pockets. She didn't want to just abandon the piece of elephant tusk. The elephant had given it to her before he died, and she still had it. It was capital-*I* Important, and she wasn't going to let it go no matter what. She gazed up the steep slope of the mountain. There was no obvious path—at least where she stood. It was steep enough that she was going to need both her hands for the climb, which meant the tusk would have to go somewhere else. At first, she wondered if she could carry it in her mouth, but in practice it felt awkward and made it difficult for her to breathe. Admittedly, breathing in a dream might not be the most important part of it, but it felt real enough to Sally and she didn't want to take any chances. Maybe she could wear it? But she wasn't exactly MacGyver, and didn't know how to fashion any kind of crude tools.

And then it came to her. She popped out her claws and examined them. They were plenty sharp. She'd used them to shred the catmen in the prior incarnation of the Dream-world. Picking at the rough end of the ivory, where it had snapped off from the elephant's tusk her claw dug right into it and with a bit of effort, she managed to work a hole all the way through the bottom. If she had a cord, she could hang it around her neck like the shark's tooth her friend Surfboy wore around his. String seemed to be in short supply in the African savannah, though. At first she entertained the idea of trying to do something with her own fur, but then realized the long prairie grasses might provide a suitable alternative.

She'd had long hair for most of her life, only cutting it to a short and super-speed-practical bob when she first took command of Just Cause New York. As such, she was accomplished at braiding, and it only took a few false starts before she managed to make a sturdy cord out of multiple layers of grass. She hung the ivory totem around her neck and gave it a few experimental tugs to see if the cord would hold in place. When it didn't break with the initial tugs, she pulled harder, and then really yanked on it. It held. Sally looked at her cable of simple braided grass in wonder. "Why aren't we making armor out of this stuff?"

Then, of course, she remembered she was in someone else's dream, and that was reason enough.

The sun had politely waited until she'd finished fashioning her new necklace, but now it was tearing across the sky as if trying to make up for lost time. Sally knew she couldn't tarry any longer. The mountain's summit beckoned to her as she looked up its flanks. "All right," she whispered to it. "Bring it on."

And with that, she reached up to the first rock and scrambled up its side until she was perched atop it. One yard down. The next rock was taller but had enough rough spots for her to dig her toes into. She reached the top of it and looked back only to discover she was barely ten feet up. How tall was that mountain, anyway?

She proceeded up the broad lower slope. Sometimes she had to climb up broken rock faces, hanging onto crumbling and uncertain stone with her fingertips, wedging her toes into crevices in the absence of any actual crampons. Other times, the slope was gentle enough for her to pick and choose her path around the rocks, moving back and forth across the mountainside like a rock-crawling four-wheeler. The sun marked her progress on its blazing trail against the azure sky. The changing shadows made her journey tricky. Sometimes they would hide the loose rock, where other times the light would illuminate a previously-hidden crack into which she could dig her claws.

Eventually the sun slipped too far around the mountain for Sally to continue her climb safely, and she found a small cave in the side, stinking of bat guano and sulfur, with a warm breeze emerging from its mouth. She might have been skittish about caves in the mountains in real life, but in the Dream-world, she felt like it might not be a terrible thing. She sat down, cross-legged, and watched the shadow of night spread across the savannah below. If she squinted, she could see animals moving about far below, like a herd of what she thought were probably zebras, and farther off, barely visible in the growing darkness, impossibly tall and slender giraffes, like wide-screen images compressed onto an old television.

Sally wondered if she would sleep within the dream, like she had before, but although her muscles ached from her exertion, she found herself alert and content to watch the stars winking into existence over her head. A glow on the distant horizon suggested moonrise wasn't far off, and that gave her an odd sense of double-vision in her mind. As the pale orange crescent appeared above the curve of the horizon, Sally felt almost like she was looking up at herself, deep asleep and exploring someone else's dream, so many thousands of miles away.

That's when she noticed the glow on the rocks around her. At first, she thought they were lit up from within with a faint orange photoluminescence like the slowly rising Moon. Then she realized the light wasn't coming from the rocks, but from the depths of the cave behind her. When she turned to look, she saw a ruddy glow coming from within it. It was lava, of course. It had to be. Why wouldn't she be climbing an active volcano? Maybe the mysterious Ticking Lord was like a supervillain, hiding out in a volcano fortress. Maybe she was a lot closer to the end of her journey than she thought.

"Don't go into the creepy volcano, Sally," she said aloud. "Bad things always happen, right?"

Nevertheless, she stood, brushed sand and pebbles from her fur, and twitched her tail in nervous anticipation. She knew she shouldn't go down the hole.

Every movie she'd ever seen with this scenario ended with someone falling into a pit of lava, or getting captured by denizens of the underground, or perishing from any number of fatal incidents. Spelunking was dangerous enough in real life without the added complication of potential dream monsters awaiting her. She still didn't know what would happen if she died while inside Reggie's mind, but her plan was not to need to find out.

"Maybe just a few feet. That's probably okay." She said so ostensibly to convince herself as she stepped beyond the threshold of the cave mouth.

The floor was irregular in elevation, but smooth and polished, like she was walking over an ice-cream sundae. The cave walls were close, more like a New York Sewer, which she'd had the unfortunate opportunity to traverse in her superheroic duties. Why couldn't it have been like the broad, beautiful caves in her home state of Arizona?

Not that this cave wasn't beautiful. White crystals in the walls picked up and amplified the faint orange light from below, giving her enough to see by with her cat-like vision. She didn't see any stalactites or stalagmites, but wouldn't expect to in a volcanic cave. She reached what she first thought was the end of the cave, but light and heat streamed upward from a hole in the floor. The air carried a distinct tinge of sulfur and other odors Sally couldn't identify. She dropped to all fours and crawled to the edge of the hole, spreading her weight out as much as possible, like she was crawling on a thin sheet of ice over deep water.

The edges of the hole were razor sharp, and Sally knew she was spread-eagled across a thin crust of rock. Her cat's-eyes adjusted to the light and she saw a chamber below her, roughly round, like she was looking into the interior of a room-sized basketball. Warm air wafted up, bathing her face with it and making her whiskers tickle. "Don't do it, Sally. Don't go down there. You'll never get back up here again. Don't be stupid."

She waited to see how she felt about the warning she'd spoken. The smart thing would have been to turn around and head back to the cave entrance to wait out the night. If she slept, she'd be rested by the morning. If not, well, it was still a dream, wasn't it?

Her sense of curiosity about the cave beneath her was almost overwhelming. It subsumed her rational thought. She *needed* to continue onward, not go back. This was her journey, and the next leg of it lay deeper inside the mountain. *Volcano*, she reminded herself in one last, half-hearted attempt to talk herself out of further descent. Volcanoes, full of burning hot lava, choking ash, poisonous fumes. Maybe she couldn't really die in a dream, but maybe she could.

The edge crumbled beneath her and she fell. Her reflexes kicked in and she twisted in midair just like a cat would, landing in a three-point stance upon the chamber floor several feet below her original perch. Her muscles quivered with the sudden, surprising impact, but nothing important cracked or broke. The floor was warm, but not uncomfortably so. The warm breeze was stronger in the chamber, swirling around in a capricious circle and only reluctantly rising to the tube above where it could find its way to the outside.

"Well, here I am." Sally stood and surveyed her surroundings. A corridor she hadn't seen before fell away from the chamber at a steep, curving slope downward. When the chamber had been full of lava once upon a time, it must have drained away the magma into a lower chamber. Prudence dictated she shouldn't pursue it any further, but she was already giving prudence the metaphorical finger with both hands.

Whatever answer she sought would be deeper into the mystery of the mountain. She entered the lower corridor and padded along the stifling tube, wishing she had a breather mask like the one she wore when running at high speeds. The rotten egg smell of sulfur was growing overpowering the further she went. It made her eyes stream, matting the fur around her face, and made her throat sting and swell, like she was suffering a virulent allergy attack. She grimaced at the thought of her fur, which she'd begun to think of as rather lovely, carrying the volcanic stink in it for days afterward.

Maybe she could find a place to take a bath. She was steadfast in her refusal to believe she would need to groom herself with her tongue. Dream or not, there were certain lines she wouldn't cross.

As the corridor curved deeper into the roots of the volcano, the air became so hot that she found herself panting like a dog. She longed for a simple cool breeze to break up the headache-inducing heat. A popsicle. Air conditioning. She passed by a small pool that under other circumstances might have been an inviting respite, but it was boiling, full of bubbles that stank of rotten meat. Even the floor was growing hot and Sally's curiosity might not be enough to overcome the sheer physical discomfort. She might be forced to turn back after all. And yet, she knew, she had to press onward. Maybe she'd find the so-called Ticking Lord. Maybe it would only be another clue to the puzzle of Reggie's Dream-world.

What she found was a lake of lava with a large black rock floating in it, bearing a white-hot salamander relaxing upon it.

Eleven

The Travelers' Questions Three is not based upon concepts of fairness.

Sally didn't know how she knew the creature was a salamander; some things seemed to be instinctive in the Dream-world, whereas others required learning. It basked on the large black rock like some great dragon. Its scales were a brilliant white and it glowed with an inner light visible even in the harsh orange light from the lava. Sally wrinkled her nose and felt one of her whiskers crisp into ash in the heat. The salamander turned its head to regard her with bejeweled eyes the color of amethyst. It flashed out a shocking pink tongue, tasting the air, and twitched its tail.

"Greetings, traveler. Welcome to my abode. I am Hiss, the Salamander of Wisdom." Sally didn't know what a lava-dwelling salamander was supposed to sound like, but Hiss had a throaty tenor, loaded with sibilance and a slight lisp that might have come from the long tongue constantly slapping around.

"I'm, uh, Sally. I'm just passing through."

The salamander's nostrils flared and its tail splashed a bit of lava into the air as it twitched. The lava struck a wall of the cave and stuck, its glow diminishing as it cooled. "I do not believe you will pass much further, unless you can tolerate this heat."

"I'm from Arizona. I don't mind the heat, but yeah, I see what you're saying."

"I have never been to Arizona. The name sounds as if it might be warm and dry. I might enjoy it, but I suspect it might prove too cold for my tastes. I'm rather particular about my climate, you see."

A cloud of insects twirled through the cave. They looked like dragonflies made of diamond. Hiss lashed out with its tongue and caught one, then crunched it into powder in its mighty jaws. The other insects swirled around just over the lava, dipping down occasionally to snag tiny pebbles that floated on the surface without melting.

Sally knew better than to ask how such a thing was possible. It was the Dream-world, of course. "I felt a compulsion to come down here. I was climbing the mountain and stopped in the cave above to rest."

Hiss licked its scaly lips with that pink tongue. "It is quite chilly that far outside, but I suppose you are better suited for it than I."

"Do you—"

Hiss splashed more lava with its tail and the splatter struck the shore near Sally, who jumped back to avoid the burning splash. "It sounds as if you are about to ask a question. I presume you wish to invoke the Travelers' Questions Three. You will, of course, confirm that."

Sally paused. It sounded important. She could almost hear the capital letters in the creature's words. She thought back through their conversation. Neither of them had asked a question. Maybe they were only allowed three questions, and then . . . something would happen? "I, uh, I don't know what that is."

"It is an ancient game, far older than Animal, Mineral, or Vegetable, or Twenty Questions, or even the Riddle Game. You are young, and I can see how you might be unfamiliar with the rules." Hiss gathered its legs beneath it. "Please stand aside. My heat may be . . . uncomfortable to you."

Sally pressed herself back against the wall of the cave. It felt like leaning on a radiator. Her fur insulated her skin from the heat somewhat, but when Hiss sprang across the lava lake to land on the shore, it was like an inferno approaching. Sally gasped at the creature's radiant heat and light.

"Now, then . . . the Travelers' Questions Three. The rules are very simple. We may converse as long as you like, but the game begins once one or the other of us asks a question. Whoever is asked must answer honestly. The answerer is bound to remain until the third question is asked. Once the third question is answered, the answerer is released and may depart. Simple, really. Note, though . . . the answers must be honest, but they may be veiled in riddles. I will not ask if you understand these rules, for I have no questions to ask you and do not wish to bind you here until I think of them. I fear you might burn up while waiting. Your tail is smoldering, by the way."

Sally squealed as the heat reached her backside. She shook it before it actually caught fire. "I'm sorry. You're really hot. Maybe I should just go."

"No. I apologize. It was most inconsiderate of me to approach you, as you are my guest." Hiss jumped back onto its floating rock once more. "Please accept my apology."

"Sure, no problem." Sally checked her tail and discovered to her dismay a patch of fur that crumbled into ash as she touched it, leaving behind pale skin tinged with the angry red of a burn. She wondered if it would grow back. Was that a thing in dreams? "Ow."

"Again, I apologize." Hiss snagged another crystalline insect with its tongue and crunched it into dust.

"Okay, I guess I'm invoking the, uh, the Travelers' Questions Three. How do—oh." She realized she'd nearly wasted a question on needing a clarification of the rules. Questions were such an integral part of all conversations. Even the simple, pointless ones that nobody expected to be answered still had that question mark at the end of them, and letting one of those pass her lips meant a wasted opportunity. Hiss had explained the rules to her, and the salamander was still hanging around on that floating rock in the lava. It wasn't bothered by the heat of the lava and it wouldn't have surprised her in the least to see it dive right into the molten rock with no more thought than an amphibian splashing into the ocean. She cleared her throat. "I'm prepared to begin if you are."

Hiss stretched out on its belly, resting its chin on its forelegs. "You may commence."

"Where can I find the Queen of Elephants?"

Hiss rolled onto its side and scratched at its belly with one rear leg. "The Queen of Elephants is imprisoned by the Ticking Lord in the Iron City."

"And, uh . . . Go on." Sally had been about to ask another clarifying question but remembered just in time to use a different sort of conversational prompt.

"The Iron City, as I recall, is many leagues north of here. Across the Black River, deep in the Burning Sands."

"But I don't know where those things are! I've never heard of any of them."

The salamander wasn't built for shrugging, but managed to convey exactly that motion by a general wiggling of its forelegs. "All you need to do is ask. Whoops, hold onto something solid."

Just as the salamander spoke, a distant rumble overshadowed the throaty hiss of the lava's circulation through the chamber and the ground shuddered. Sally didn't see anything sturdy enough to brace herself against that wouldn't immediately blister her skin, so she dropped into a low crouch, digging her claws into the pumice stone around the edge of the lava pit. The shaking continued for what felt like a few minutes. Small rocks fell from the roof of the chamber to disappear in the lava without so much as a bubble to mark their impact. For a few terrifying seconds, Sally thought the ceiling was about to collapse, but just when the quake seemed like it would escalate into wholesale destruction, it tapered off and stopped. Sand and small pebbles trickled from a few new cracks in the ceiling but no large pieces fell.

Sally got back to her feet, keeping herself low and ready to jump in whatever direction she needed to if something collapsed. Her hands were shaking like leaves in a gale. Her first instinct was to cry out, "What was that?" but the yammering, logical part of her mind screamed at her not to waste a question. She only had two left. She clamped her teeth down on her tongue until her panic had subsided enough to keep her from blurting out a question.

"You don't look harmed." Nevertheless, Hiss leaned forward, teetering at the very edge of its rock island.

"I'm okay." Sally clasped her trembling hands behind her back. If the ceiling collapsed, or her exit was cut off, how would she ever reach the summit? And what if the volcano erupted before she did? Then it occurred to her that something was still calling her upward. Whatever the next step of her journey to find the Elephant Queen was, it lay at the top of the nameless volcano. "Hey, Hiss, I have another question for you."

"I am ready."

"So you already know that I'm on a quest for the Elephant Queen. Something at the top of this mountain is calling to me. What's up there that's so important?"

Hiss yawned. "A difficult decision."

Sally paused, trying to figure out the best way to word her next sentence so it couldn't be construed as a question. "I don't understand what that means."

"It means exactly as I meant it to."

"You said you had to answer questions honestly. You said those are the rules."

"I did, they are, and I have."

Sally stamped her foot. "That's not an answer, though!"

"Of course it is."

"But . . . but that's not fair!"

"The Travelers' Questions Three is not based upon concepts of fairness."

Sally wrinkled her nose into a snarl. "I don't have to ask a third question. You can't leave until I do. Those are the rules."

"Yes, they are. I expect you'll get quite hungry after a while. I presume you don't eat these delicious crystal flies."

"This is a dream. I don't have to eat. I can wait."

"You don't know that."

The volcano rumbled again. Sally instinctively arched her back like a house cat trying to scare down a larger foe. A large slab cracked off a chamber wall and splatted down into the lava, sending smoking hot droplets in all directions.

"Perhaps you should ask your final question."

Sally wanted to argue, but she was terrified at the prospect of being buried alive. She asked the first thing that came to her mind, and the unexpected subject surprised her. "Why am I a lioness?"

"All people have a spirit animal. A totem, if you will. An animal that for whatever reason has deep, special meaning to them. Yours is clearly a great cat."

"But why a lion and not a horse? I mean—" Sally stopped, for as soon as she'd said *But why*, Hiss slipped off the rock island into the lava with a *bloop* sound.

She waited to see if the salamander would resurface, but it soon became apparent the creature would have nothing more to do with her. Whether it was only due to the conclusion of the game or because she'd somehow offended Hiss, she figured she would never know. A distant rumble far below her feet encouraged her not to tarry in the inferno a moment longer, and she turned her back to the lava pool and made her way back toward the surface.

The night air was cool and as refreshing as a lemonade slush in Arizona in high summer. It invigorated her after the sweltering interior of the grumbling volcano. Sally stood in the mouth of the cave and let the gentle breeze ruffle her lioness' fur. So the lioness was her spirit animal. She'd always thought of herself as more of a horse. After all, she was the third in her line to take on an equine name, after her mother's Pony Girl and her grandmother's Colt. She'd always wondered why her grandmother had taken *Colt*, when that was unequivocally a male horse. Her grandmother had laughed and said nobody would have taken her seriously if she'd called herself *Filly*.

What would Grandma Judy have said if she could have seen Sally, all decked out in fur with her tail twitching? Sally didn't know, but she did know the compulsion for her to climb had grown even greater once she knew something important awaited her at the summit. Hiss had said it was *a difficult decision*. She didn't know what that meant, but the sooner she reached the top, the sooner she could figure it out. She tilted her head back to look up the steep, rocky slope.

The stars were very bright as she dug her claws into the rock and began her climb once more.

TWELVE

I'm going to free you.

The closer Sally came to the summit of the peak, the more certain she grew that it was not a question *if* the volcano would erupt, but *when*. The ground shook with tremors on a disturbingly frequent basis, and even when the mountain wasn't threatening to shake Sally loose from its slopes, the rocks carried within them a low level humming vibration, like a motor running on the far side of a wall.

She struggled upward in the increasingly smoky air as a constant snowfall of hot gray ash drifted around her. She discovered that if she held her furry arm up to her face, she could breathe better, as if the fur was filtering the air. Nothing protected her feet, though, and from time to time she stepped on patches of ground that were hot enough to make her recoil until her toes were aching with every step.

A tremor shook the slope and a rock bigger than Sally crashed down the side of the mountain, passing only a few feet away. She hadn't seen it coming between the thick, ashy air and smoke that had finally obscured the valiant starlight. It bounded past her and sailed off into darkness, distant bangs and cracks the only indication of its journey downward. Another tremor, far more violent than the one that had dislodged the rock, shifted the entire slope downward several feet, sending Sally grasping at rocks to keep from an ignominious, and probably fatal, descent.

A fissure opened somewhere above her and steam smelling of gunpowder and ash shrieked into the sky. Sally nearly jumped out of her fur at the sudden whistle and her own plaintive yelp of surprise was lost in the power of the earth's voice. She changed her path to steer well clear of the new steam vent. The ground was hot beneath her feet, like pavement under the relentless blaze of a July afternoon. She wished she had a pair of boots instead of graceful cat's feet, but she couldn't make them materialize within the dream.

The volcano shuddered again and crimson light flared behind the edge of the slope. Lava bombs screamed away from an unseen split in the rock. Sally watched the display in mute terror. She was going to die. The volcano would split apart beneath her and she'd get to spend her last moments being burnt alive. If only she could wake up! She didn't remember ever dying in her own dreams before, and didn't want to discover what would happen if she died in someone else's. The smartest thing she could have done, she knew, would be to flee. She may not have been *Mustang Sally* fast in the Dream-world, but she was still plenty quick, and she would have bet she could have run to safety before the eruption came on full force.

But that compulsion to reach the summit still gnawed at her like an icy wind finding its way through a crack beneath the door. Would the top of the volcano be a crater, awash in fresh lava? Or would it be a cinder cone, covered with razor-sharp obsidian shards to cut her to shreds? She kept on climbing, coughing and choking at the fumes, eyes streaming from the smoke and heat, until all of a sudden she reached a flat spot as near enough to the top as she realized she was likely to get.

She found herself standing at the edge of a broken bowl in the mountain. Perhaps it had once been a lava cavern like the one where she'd found Hiss the salamander. It had eroded over time until one side of it was worn away. The process that had created it was far less important than the reason for its existence, and that was to contain a prisoner.

The prisoner was a bird-woman the same way Sally was a lion-woman. The woman's slender, feminine form was covered in mottled brown and white plumage, marred by a thick coating of gray ash as it drifted down from the clouds above like stinking hot snow. She had no arms, but her great broad wings were spread out and up, pierced with iron rings, and chained with rusting padlocks to a monolithic slab of granite behind her. Her feet were sharp black talons that curled and uncurled repeatedly against the hot rocks beneath them. She stared at Sally with unblinking eyes the color of the sun, hooded beneath a heavy brow ridge of feathers in a flat face with a sharp beak. She said nothing—nor could she have, for another iron ring had been drilled through her beak and a padlock held it shut. She could do nothing more than stare at Sally, entreaty deep within her eyes. Feather tufts atop her head marked her as an owl, and given the way she'd interacted with other beings within the Dream-world, Sally had no reason to believe she wouldn't also learn valuable information by conversing with the owl-woman.

Over the owl-woman's head hung two gleaming white keys, untouched by the falling ash, and Sally understood the nature of the difficult decision Hiss had mentioned. Three locks, two keys. Sally could release the lock holding the woman's beak shut, could ask her questions, could get a clue as to the next leg of her voyage. And then she could leave the owl-woman the way she'd found her, chained and unable to escape the forthcoming eruption. Or she could release the woman's wings, leaving her to fly away with Sally's questions unanswered. As if to remind her of the threat it represented, the volcano shook itself hard enough to throw Sally to the floor of the bowl. Sally looked up and the gray of the ash clouds had taken on a distinctive pinkish orange hue, and she knew the eruption might happen at any moment. She struggled back to her feet with the ground quaking beneath them. A distant roaring sound filled her ears and the heat threatened to crisp even more of her fur.

Hiss had warned her she would find a difficult decision atop the volcano, but in Sally's mind there was no contest at all. She couldn't stand by and watch someone die, or leave them behind knowing she'd abandoned them to certain death. That wasn't what heroes did, and dream or not, it wasn't what she would do.

She staggered across the bowl, more than once being hurled to the ground by capricious quaking. Steam vents opened around the edges of the bowl, whistling and screaming their freedom into the sky. Sally wished she could fold her ears flat against her head as she gritted her teeth against the noise.

The owl-woman watched her every move as she approached, eyes pleading for help. Sally reached up and pulled the first key down from where it hung on an iron hook. It was finely-carved ivory of much higher quality than the piece of tusk she'd hung around her neck. The flutes and barrels of the ivory key looked far too delicate for the rusted iron padlocks, but Sally knew she had to try. "I'm going to free you," she shouted over the rumbling of the volcano. "Here goes nothing."

She blew into the padlock's keyhole, hoping to clear out any accumulated ash and dust, and then slid the ivory key into it. Tumblers clicked into place as the lock rearranged its own insides around the key. Sally turned the key and the lock fell open without any fanfare or drama. The iron ring tumbled from its chain and slipped from her grasp. The ivory key shattered into splinters when the ring hit the floor of the lava bowl. Steam rose from around the pieces and they began to sink into the softening rock. Sally gasped as part of the bowl simply dropped into a roiling abyss of lava. She sprang for the granite monolith upon which the owl-woman had been imprisoned. Her claws found just enough purchase and she hauled herself up onto the top of it. She looked down and stared into the mouth of hell.

The owl-woman stayed silent, but she flexed her recently-freed wing, seemingly unharmed by its piercing. Heat and fumes rushed upward from the swirling lava beneath them both. As Sally reached for the second key the entire monolith tilted, tipping toward the pool. Sally screamed and splayed her arms and legs wide to keep her grip on the scalding rock. Blood began to stain the owl-woman's feathers as her pierced wing took more of her weight. If Sally didn't hurry to free her, it might not matter. She kept as tight a hold as possible on the top of the obelisk as it swayed over the lava pit below. A lightning quick lunge and then the second ivory key was clutched in her fingers. If she dropped it, all would be lost.

Sally's lungs burned from the fumes, and her eyes were streaming so much she couldn't see the keyhole in the lock and had to feel for it with her other hand, leaving her perched on the edge of the granite tower with a blast furnace below her. The heat evaporated her tears before they could soak into the fur on her cheeks.

The key found its way into the lock and Sally turned it. The iron padlock fell away, turning end over end like the One Ring falling into the fires of Mount Doom. The owl-woman spread her wings. The blasting thermals made her shoot up like a rocket into the swirling clouds of dust and ash. Sally didn't even have time to wave before the woman was out of her sight. Before Sally could think about how to get herself to safety, the whole granite monolith toppled, almost in slow motion, like a tree falling in the forest. As it tilted, Sally ran along its length, thinking she would leap for the edge of the bowl, but the entire lip of the bowl collapsed as lava had worn out the rock beneath it. The huge chunk of granite came to rest at about a forty-five-degree angle, with the lower end sinking slowly but steadily into the lava while the upper end was too far away from anything for her to reach. She was surrounded by magma with nowhere to go.

Amazing heat washed across Sally as the granite slipped ever so slowly into the crucible of lava. She backed up as far as she could, perched on the very tip that was still raised out of the magma. Fumes filled her lungs, making her head spin. She coughed and gasped, but the air was burning her from the inside out. It looked like she was about to find out what happened when she died in a dream for real. Steam rose from her cheeks where the tears from her streaming eyes evaporated into steam. Lancing pain shot through one of her feet as a vein of lighter material within the granite obelisk conducted heat from the molten rock. She lost her balance and toppled off the back corner where she'd perched.

She didn't even have time to wonder whether she'd sink or float in molten rock. A shadow came at her from above, golden talons flashing in the light. The owl woman cupped her wings, braking hard against the rising hot air, and dug her talons into Sally's shoulders, embedding them deep into muscle and, for all Sally knew, bone. She screamed at the tearing pain, and yet it was far different from the pain of immolation she'd expected.

The owl woman beat her wings furiously, struggling to gain altitude with Sally's weight dangling beneath her like helpless prey. Magma burbled and roiled only inches below Sally's feet, but she didn't dare move in case the owl woman lost her grip. The woman banked sharply just before crashing into the wall of the bowl and as she came around, her wings caught a thermal and they shot up and out of the bowl like they'd been fired from a catapult. Sally squealed at fresh pain as the owl woman's talons tightened around her shoulders, digging deeper into the muscles. They spun through the air, fighting capricious air currents, dodging sudden jets of scalding steam and plumes of choking ash. The volcano's groans and rumbles increased to a shriek as the pressure mounted. Lava bombs shot past them like screaming missiles.

Then, with a sound like the end of the world, the volcano split its top open and vomited out lava, sending it coursing down its sides like a burst boil. A shock wave flashed across the owl woman and her precious cargo, nearly sending the two of them spinning to their deaths on the smoking plain below. Sally felt her shoulder muscles tearing apart. The pain was the most intense she'd ever felt, and yet her mind wouldn't do her the courtesy of letting her faint. It hurt so much she couldn't even cry out, or scream, or do any of the things that people did to mitigate their pain. She clenched her teeth until they threatened to crack from the pressure and swung, helpless in the grasp of the owl woman's talons.

She could taste blood in her mouth and nose and wondered if she'd inhaled so much ash that it had shredded her lungs. All the owl woman's efforts might have been wasted if they both died from pulmonary hemorrhaging. Beneath them, a shock wave of high-speed ash raced down the volcano slopes, mowing down anything in its path as the mountain shook itself apart in fantastic and violent death throes. The pain in Sally's shoulders reached mind-numbing levels and she felt consciousness slipping away from her.

"No," she gasped as her eyes started rolling in her head. "No sleeping. It's a dream. No sleeping."

The stars appeared once more as the owl woman flew beyond the edge of the ash cloud and found her way into clear air. After so much stifling heat and smoke, the cool night air over the plains felt like a soothing balm and almost made Sally forget about the talons digging deep into her shoulder. The healing Moonlight rained down upon her, somehow feeding her strength to carry on despite her grievous injuries.

A broad, dark shadow rose up from the savannah, resolving itself into a tall escarpment stretching as far as she could see in either direction. Temperate forest covered the top of the high cliff and it was toward this that the owl woman flew. Sally nodded. They would be well beyond the reach of the volcano unless it reached gargantuan, world-shaking proportions. That might not be beyond the realm of possibility, given some of the things she'd encountered in the Dream-world, but she hoped it would remain no more than a distant notion.

The owl-woman reached the edge of the forest but her forward progress halted as her wings gave out. She dropped Sally into a mass of feather-soft heather and collapsed on the ground next to her. Blood rushed out of the ragged wounds in Sally's shoulders where the owl-woman's talons had dug in with such cruel force.

Sally glanced back toward the erupting volcano, an angry red wound on the face of the Earth, swollen with infection and fire, leaching death outward. She managed a weak smile. They'd done it. It was too far away to reach them.

And if it could, she was beyond caring. She laid herself down upon the heather and drifted into the unconsciousness of dreaming-within-dreams.

THIRTEEN

Not again. Not on her watch.

A clinking noise brought Sally out of her slumber. She sat up with a jolt, and the pain that shot through her body was better than an air horn for bringing her to full alertness. She hissed like a cat at the unexpected burning. Her wounds had been dressed, packed with mud and bandaged with large green leaves bound in place with woven vines. She tried to move her arms and discovered an entirely new level of agony. The way her shoulders had been torn, it was a wonder she could move her arms at all. She didn't relish the idea of fighting, much less moving, but knew she'd have to brave it if she was to continue in her quest.

The clinking noise repeated. Sally turned her head to look and discovered even that movement wasn't immune from pain. The owl woman was bashing her head against a large rock at the edge of the escarpment. No, it wasn't her head, Sally realized, but she was smashing the lock holding her beak shut. It clinked when it hit the rock. The owl woman pulled her head back and shook it as if to clear anything she'd jarred loose inside her skull with the impact and repeated it again.

Something about the owl woman's shape and coloration seemed oddly familiar as she perched awkwardly upon the ground and tried to break the lock once more. Some owls had two feather tufts that stood up like horns, but the owl woman's tuft was more like a mohawk, shocking crimson feathers rising in a crest more like a cockatoo's than an owl's.

And then, with a gasp, Sally realized the owl woman was Minerva. She could see her friend's posture as she hunched over to get a better angle against the rock. The lock clinked against it once more but didn't fall away. Sally opened her breath to ask Minerva how she could help, but the question choked itself off at the source. She was suddenly mindful of the Traveler's Questions Three. Was that applicable in this situation? She didn't want her friend to be bound by the rules of the game, and then have to depart when it was completed. Better she shouldn't ask any questions at all. Besides, Sally thought wryly, it wasn't as if her friend could answer any of them with her beak bolted shut.

She took a soft step toward Minerva, her claws making the faintest of scratches against a rock, but the owl woman whirled as if Sally had blown a bugle to announce her presence. Sally swallowed against a dry mouth and a throat still stinging from the steam and volcanic gases. The owl woman's bright, unblinking eyes bored into her like searchlights, even in the gray pre-dawn light. Sally cleared her throat. "I, uh I presume you are Minerva, and I am not asking any questions to confirm it. I do not wish to begin the Travelers' Questions Three with you. Do—"

Minerva whirled around and smashed her beak against the rock once again. Sally gasped. She'd nearly asked *do you understand?* Would it have counted as the beginning of a new game? She didn't want to risk the possibility.

"I understand. Please warn me again if you anticipate I will slip." Sally sighed. "I'm not really good at this. I ask a lot of questions. Especially here, in this dream place." She looked around at the new, unfamiliar surroundings. "Because I really don't understand anything."

Seen in the slowly brightening dawn, the escarpment upon which they'd landed was every bit as grim and foreboding as the volcano they'd left behind. It was a great black cliff, perhaps formed millions of years ago by a great crack in the dream-continent, like half the continent thrusting itself high above the other half. The jagged edges seemed fragile, like they might collapse into the valley below at the slightest provocation. The valley itself was sheathed in gray and white clouds, making it feel like the cliff edge was the edge of the entire world. Perhaps in a way, it was. A distant rumble reminded Sally there were things beyond, and she spotted the volcano rising above the clouds like a distant, angry pimple. Its red glow lit the clouds around it as it rained soot and ash down across the valley.

Her shoulders twinged in pain and she regarded the dressings upon them in wonder. It was a silly thing, but she couldn't understand how Minerva had treated her wounds without arms. Had she used her feet? Sally was aching, desperate to ask a question, but she feared locking herself into an unwanted challenge.

No.

This was the Dream-world, yes, and there were rules, but Sally didn't have to play by the rules of the game. She could elect not to participate. Nobody was forcing her to abide by them. Just like in waking life, she could turn the tables. When she'd been down in the volcanic cave, speaking with Hiss, they had both agreed to play Travelers' Questions Three. Sally hadn't thought there was any other option at the time. She knew now, she could simply refuse to engage. If Minerva likewise refused to engage in the game, neither of them was bound by its rules.

She turned to Minerva. "I will not play Travelers' Questions Three with you. I will not be bound by its rules, and neither will you." She took a deep breath, knowing she was risking a lot by flaunting those very rules. "Do you agree?"

Minerva's nod was clear and precise.

"Good. Let's get this thing out of your beak."

The sun rose, turning the thick clouds of the valley below the escarpment into a blazing field of white, like

Colorado sun shining upon a snowfield. Behind them, the foreboding darkness of the jungle transformed into a less-threatening collage of a thousand different shades of green. Sally closed her eyes and heard the songs and cries of uncounted birds and insects, and the rich scents made her head spin.

None of it was helping the two young women remove the lock through Minerva's beak, though. The stubborn circle of iron resisted their attempts to break either the lock box or the band itself. Levering it open would be impossible without shattering Minerva's beak. That left picking it open as the only other viable alternative. Sally had never picked a lock in her life and didn't know the least bit about the theory of how to do it beyond what she'd seen on TV. Even if she knew anything about it, the jungle didn't seem to be a likely place they would find something they could use to fashion implements fine and strong enough to do the deed.

Stymied at every turn, Sally at last had to admit defeat. "Let's move on. Maybe we can find something further along in the journey."

Minerva nodded. Even though her feathered and beaked face was far more difficult to read than one of human appearance, Sally could see the exhaustion wearing on her friend.

They entered the jungle.

Traveling amid the thick undergrowth and closely-packed tree trunks was more of an exercise in solving a three-dimensional maze than actually making any kind of linear progress. Sometimes they would have to crawl beneath massive fallen branches, their faces pressed into the mud. Other times they would clamber over them, testing fur, feathers, and skin against razor-sharp thorns. More than once they found themselves at an impasse and were forced to retrace their steps until they could find a fork in their path. Sally lost all sense of direction after the first few minutes. Indeed, if it wasn't for the pervasiveness of gravity, she wouldn't even be sure which way was up.

Fortunately, Minerva's sense of direction was unfailing, and Sally turned over the responsibility of choosing paths to her friend. Given Minerva's lack of arms, anything involving crawling was especially difficult for her, and after a while her brilliant plumage, like Sally's fur, was sodden with mud and more than a few bloody scratches.

Even with Minerva selecting their route, it was still fraught with numerous dangers and discomforts. Dangling vines were sometimes awash with fire ants, or entwined with poisonous snakes, or even dripped with caustic fluid that itched and burned like salt in an open wound. It was giving Sally the strange sensation of waking nightmares while she was already asleep in someone else's Dream-world. She kept flashing back to one of her first missions with Just Cause, where she traveled to Guatemala with some of her teammates and not all of them returned. They hadn't lost their lives *to* the jungle so much as they had to those who were prowling within it. Sally would hear the sounds of creatures, nearby yet unseen, and she would have to keep herself from clutching at Minerva in a panic.

Just when Sally didn't think she could do it any longer, Minerva pushed past some giant leafy fronds and the two young women staggered out onto an animal path. It was barely wide enough for the two of them to walk side-by-side, littered with uncounted piles of dung and the skittering creatures that lived among it, and speckled by the occasional beams of sunlight that filtered down through the overhead canopy.

Sally took a deep breath and tried to calm the panicked hammering of her heart. "This is good," she said as her brain tried to wrap itself around the millions of scents rampant in the air. "A path always leads *somewhere*, right?"

Minerva nodded. The poor young woman could crack her beak open just enough for Sally to pour water from a curled leaf into it, but getting any sort of food into it had proved impossible. Ants would fit into the crack, but Sally couldn't grip them well enough to shove in without crushing them to pulp, which she discovered she could only smear on the surface. If they couldn't get the lock off Minerva's beak soon, it wouldn't matter any longer.

Surely, she couldn't starve to death in a dream.

Sally kept telling herself that.

They followed the path. The canopy rose high above them like the flying buttresses of some great organic cathedral. The air was thick with humidity, at times making it feel to Sally more like she was swimming rather than walking. Brightly-colored birds dove between the tree branches, snagging juicy insects or the tiny iridescent lizards that scurried up and down the boles like squirrels. Noisy animals of some kind squalled and shrieked at each other in the high branches, making Sally think of monkeys. Once she glanced up a nearby tree trunk and met the sulfurous gaze of a speckled great cat of some kind. It snarled at her and she jumped in surprise, but the creature only climbed higher, its razor-sharp claws making short work of the smooth bark.

Some amount of time passed as the two young women trudged through the jungle, following the path toward what Sally hoped was salvation. The passage of time being what it was within the Dream-world, Sally couldn't tell if they'd been wandering for five minutes, five hours, or five days. She had no frame of reference except for the growing hunger pangs making her belly clench and her throat sting. She kept thinking how she was in the jungle and she was a hunter by her very nature; there should have been food of all kinds just waiting for her to take it down, but the Dream-world was being notably stingy with sustenance.

And then they froze when they heard it. Laughter, just at the far range of Sally's exceptional hearing. The feathers along Minerva's crest rose erect at the sudden, unpleasant jocularity. It wasn't joyous laughter; it was cruel amusement at someone else's discomfort.

"No." Sally growled in the pit of her throat, her hackles rising like a jackal on the hunt. She caught the scent of blood in the turgid jungle air, mixed with a heady musk. It was a deeper tang than the sharp ammoniac odor of the cat-men who'd slain the elephant a lifetime ago in the Dream-world. Not again. Not on her watch.

She ran.

Vines slapped at her as she pelted through the jungle, reaching down with their deceptive snares, eager to trip her up in her headlong flight. Fallen boughs crossing the path threatened to trip her, but she wouldn't be denied her passage. Her powerful legs carried her over every obstacle while her feline grace kept her from running into anything dangerous or unyielding. She outdistanced Minerva in seconds. The owl-woman didn't have enough room on the cramped animal path to really stretch her wings, and the canopy wouldn't have let her gain much useful altitude anyway.

A sharp crack rent the air, followed by a weak cry of pain and more harsh laughter. She'd heard that sound many times in movies. Someone was being whipped.

The jungle grew brighter ahead, and she burst into a clearing to confront a scene out of an exploitation film.

A black-furred panther-man had been lashed face-first against a pole outside of a mud-and-grass hut. His fur was stained with blood that was his own and bodily wastes that were not. Other men with piggish heads and protruding fangs cavorted around him with gleeful taunts. Their filthy manes were more akin to dreadlocks than fur, coated with mud and slime, and they stank of open sewers. One of them was amusing the others by urinating across the back of the panther-man's legs while another was pulling back his whip to deliver another blow. With horror, Sally realized that the panther-man's tail had been torn away and hung around the whipper's neck like a crude feather boa.

Not caring about losing the element of surprise, Sally roared a challenge like a lioness, startling the boar-men into frozen indecision. She zeroed in on the whip-bearer as her primary target and charged at him. The stench of the filth caked in his fur would have turned her stomach inside out, had she eaten anything. He raised the whip in uncertainty, as if its bloody braids would dissuade her. She poured on the speed, far slower than she'd ever attacked in real life, but faster than anything in the Dream-world. She sprang at him, leading with naked claws and following with fangs. The shock of impact carried through her entire body as she torpedoed into him like a furry missile. They tumbled head over heels and when Sally came up, remnants of the boar-man's throat dripped from her claws.

His feeble death rattle galvanized the others, and they snorted and squealed at her, trying to gin up the courage to attack her. They outnumbered her, and indeed even the smallest of them probably had twenty or thirty pounds of muscle mass on her, yet they balked at openly charging. Cowardice, it seemed, ran in groups.

Sally grabbed the boar-man's whip and cracked it at one of the other boar-men. Its tip laid open a bloody gash across his chest and he shrieked, fleeing into the jungle at the edge of the clearing.

One took a half-hearted step towards her, his yellowed tusks flashing in the surprising sunlight of the clearing. Sally pointed at him, inverted her hand, and motioned him to come-hither, brandishing her whip with undisguised menace. He fled after his brother.

Then a pair of strong arms grabbed Sally from behind and she found herself trapped in the reeking grasp of a boar-man. "You stupid nigger bitch," he whispered in her ear. "You shoulda got off at another stop. Now you got to pay with that ass." A filthy hand cupped one of her breasts, stroking it suggestively before pinching with cruel force. Sally cried out at the sudden pain and surprise. She tried to fight back but the boar-man's strength was inhuman, and all he did was laugh. A solid blow struck the back of her head. "You uppity cunt. I was gonna show you a good time, but now I'm gonna beat another hole in your head and when I'm done, maybe I'll fuck that one t—"

A sudden shadow raced across the clearing, sweeping the boar-man off his feet and tearing his grip loose from Sally. She whirled, her skin still crawling from where his hands had touched it, and saw him dangling from Minerva's talons, struggling in vain to free himself from her iron grasp. She beat her wings with furious effort, climbing and circling around the clearing until she suddenly dropped the boar-man. His arms and legs flailed as he fell, but he never reached the ground, instead coming down upon a wooden pole that might have been used to support a clothesline. The end of it punched upward through his chest and he slid a couple of feet down it before the friction of his constricted ribs and organs brought him to a halt. His frantic movements halted as death swept over him, leaving behind a stinking, leaking husk that had stained the pole above it black with blood and shit.

Sally sank to the ground, shivering in uncontrollable terror. The way he'd spoken, how he'd come at her from behind . . . she was certain it was maybe the last coherent memory Reggie Washington had of the night she was attacked all those years ago, filtered through the Dream-world.

If it had happened to Sally, she might have retreated into a Dream-world of her own making as well.

FOURTEEN

Everything in dreams has a meaning.

By the time they got him cut loose from the pole he'd been tied to, the panther-man had lapsed into unconsciousness. Sally was no doctor, and besides, who knew how injuries worked in the Dream-world, anyway? Maybe he was out from blood loss after the forcible removal of his tail and his lash wounds, or maybe it was shock, or perhaps even exhaustion. Minerva probably could have told her if her beak hadn't still been locked shut. Minerva's wings were mainly useless as arms, so it fell to Sally to cut the panther-man down and carry him to the nearby stream flowing through the clearing. At its deepest, it rose to her waist, and the cool water was nearly as refreshing as a strong cup of coffee after a restorative nap. She bathed the black-furred man in the water until all the filth of the boar-men had been rinsed away and the water once again burbled clear away from him.

With Minerva keeping a watchful eye out for the return of the cowardly torturers, Sally brought the unconscious man back into the hut where he would at least be out of view of anyone watching from the cover of the surrounding jungle. Minerva fluttered up to perch on the roof, rotating her head around in the unnerving way owls could do so she could keep an eye on the entire clearing.

The hut was a simple mud-and-grass dome daubed over a framework of wooden poles lashed together. A hole was cut in the center of the roof for smoke to escape from the fire pit directly beneath it. At one point, the panther-man's few possessions must have hung from the hut's walls and roof, but the boar-men had trampled and befouled many of them. Sally found a small folding cot that had been overturned and kicked against the side of the hut. It was the sort of thing that might have once occupied a cheap hotel. She spread it out and carefully laid the unconscious panther-man upon it, careful to prop him up on his side so he wouldn't lay upon the stump of his tail. Blood still oozed from the wound and Sally knew the first order of business would be to bandage the injury.

Although the boar-men had done a lot of damage to the hut's interior, Sally did find a ragged blanket. She tore it into strips and tied them over the stump of tail. She hoped he wouldn't develop an infection from them. Her nose told her they hadn't been particularly clean even before the boar-men had gotten at them. She'd have to chance it.

Once she'd staunched the flow of blood, she turned her attention to the rest of the hut. She threw the worst of the spoiled items out past the hut's entrance. She'd deal with them later. In the meantime, she needed to see what assets she had available.

After a thorough search of the hut, she learned she had much more to work with than she'd originally thought. A couple of gourds and skin sacks hung undisturbed from the hut's framework. One gourd held only water, but the other contained a treasure in salt. One sack held numerous pouches of carefully-separated dried herbs, their pungency enough to make Sally's stomach rumble in hunger despite the befouled mud on the hut floor. Another held strips of dried meat of some kind, and Sally let herself eat a few as she searched. She had to keep her strength up in case the boar-men returned before she had an opportunity to rest.

The last thing she found gave her the most hope of all. It was incongruous object for a world seeming to follow African themes: a large, weatherbeaten steamer trunk that might have looked brand-new in the early Nineteenth century. Its brass fittings and corner guards were tarnished and blackened with age, while the leathery coating of the sides had cracked and split to reveal termite trails in the wood beneath. And yet, Sally felt immediately that it belonged in the hut with the same kind of certainty as if the trunk had always been there and the hut grew around it. She fiddled with the unfamiliar locking mechanism before discovering that by flexing one part sideways, the latch would pop free. She raised the lid, eager to see what secrets lay beneath.

Tools!

Sure, they were rusty, and some were even broken. Nevertheless, Sally pulled out a pair of pliers and grinned at them. Minerva's imprisoned beak would soon be released. Once more, Sally would converse with her friend, who was by far the wisest person she knew. She started to leave the hut with the pliers clutched in one paw, but then thought better of it. She glanced back at the unconscious panther-man and decided he would rest better if he wasn't being constantly disturbed by Sally running in and out of the hut. She returned to the trunk and hefted it. It was heavy, but not so much so that she couldn't carry it for a few yards. She brought it outside into the sunlight and set it upon the hard-packed dirt in a cloud of rust particles.

"Minerva, come down here. I've got tools to get that lock off your beak." Sally raised the pliers for emphasis. They fell apart in her hand. "Shit. Okay, there are others."

With a fluttering of feathers, Minerva glided down from her perch atop the hut. She looked down at the selection of ancient tools Sally showed her and shook her head.

"No, I won't accept that. There has to be something in here that will work." Sally rummaged through the trunk. "Look, here's a . . . a file. We can use that, right?"

But the second she touched it to the iron lock, it crumbled away into shavings. "Or this screwdriver?" The screwdriver snapped in two like a candy cane. "No. There's got to be something we can do. Why would these tools even be here in the Dream-world if we weren't meant to use them? They've got to have meaning, right? Everything in dreams has a meaning. They can't just be . . . useless."

Minerva's wings popped up in a gesture Sally took to be a shrug.

Sally stamped an angry foot and spun around, fists clenched at her sides in useless fury. She wanted to hit something, to tear at it with her claws, to rip it apart with her fangs and bathe in its blood. Her eye fell upon the remains of the dead boar-man and she took a step toward the corpse before realizing the enormity of her intent and tried to shake some sense back into herself. As she did so, she felt the makeshift pendant she'd fashioned from the gift of the dead elephant's tusk bounce between her breasts. She raised it to examine, as if it might hold secrets to share.

It would guide her, the elephant had said. Well, it wasn't doing much guiding now, was it? It sat centered in her field of vision, a polished bone-white arrow pointing right at . . . the boar-man's tusks, Sally realized. She'd used ivory keys to release Minerva from her chains at the volcano. Maybe she needed another key of ivory. She let her pendant fall back against her chest and bent down to claim the boar-man's tusks for her own. She raised the grisly trophy and considered how to best shape it to suit her needs. "Minerva, come help me with this."

Minerva joined her and the two of them examined the lock holding the owl-woman's back shut. At last, Minerva picked one of the rusty tools from the steamer trunk and scratched out a pattern on the tusk with her talons, a slow, laborious process. Sally forced herself to sit still and not disturb her friend. At last, Minerva surrendered the tusk back to Sally and indicated where she should remove material.

Sally began filing away ivory, making a snowfall of tiny white particles in her lap while Minerva alternately stood watch or ducked inside the hut to check on the panther-man. The sun crawled across the sky and the jungle sang and screamed as Sally worked. Once, Minerva launched herself aloft with furious flapping to chase something back from the edge of the clearing. Sally leaped to her feet, the tusk forgotten, expecting to have to fight once more. Nothing materialized from the leafy green wall at the clearing's edge, and whatever Minerva had seen must have fled back into the underlayer.

Sally picked up her tool once again and got to work. After a while, she called Minerva down to test the key. It slid partway into the lock but no further. She smiled at the progress she'd made and returned to it. After another period of carving, she tested it again and the key went all the way into the lock but wouldn't turn the tumblers. "What did I do wrong?"

Minerva held the key up in one foot to examine it for imperfections. She even went so far as to sniff it. At last, she returned it to Sally and pointed out a small but crucial piece for Sally to remove. She pried it out and slid it into the lock. "Here goes nothing."

With a single, anticlimactic click, the lock popped open and fell free from Minerva's beak.

Minerva shrieked with joy, opening her beak wide. She half-ran, half-flew over to the stream to drink. She had to hold a wingtip over the hole in her beak but managed to get water down her throat. Thus satiated, at least for the moment, she turned back to Sally. "Thank you. I feel much better."

Sally wrinkled her nose in a smile. "I'm just glad I don't have to figure this all out on my own anymore. Or do all the talking. Do you know anything about what we're supposed to do?"

"No more than you do."

An idea occurred to Sally, and it seemed so natural she couldn't believe she hasn't considered it before. "That guy in the hut. The panther-man. Do you think that's March?"

"Yes." Minerva didn't hesitate in her answer. "It's the only thing that makes sense. Otherwise, why would he be here unless it was to give you something?"

"Well, we did get your beak freed up. Maybe that's why he's here."

"I suspect he has more of a role to play than that." Minerva blinked, nictitating membranes flashing across her yellow eyes. "I am very sleepy, and hungry. But mostly sleepy."

"Rest, my friend." Sally patted her friend's feathered shoulder. "I'll keep watch."

Minerva flapped up to the roof of the hut, fluffed it her feathers, and shut her eyes against the afternoon sun.

Sally went inside to check on their patient and grinned when she saw he was awake. "How do you feel?"

"I've been b-b-better." The panther-man, clearly March, rolled into his side and grimaced as he bumped the stump of his tail.

"I'm glad you're here." Sally crouched down beside him. "I'm just sorry we didn't find you sooner. Before . . . you know."

He twisted around to look at where his tail had once been. "It's all right." He managed a toothy smile, fangs gleaming in the near darkness of the hut. "I was waiting for you."

"What's your role in Reggie's dream?"

"I'm a g-guide. I know the way through the . . . the jungle. To reach the Burning Sands."

Sally's heart jumped. She'd nearly forgotten her quest with her mission to free Minerva's beak. Now she had the next step of her journey laid out before her, ready to take. "Are you strong enough to travel? The sooner we can leave . . ."

March shook his head. "I don't think so. Maybe tomorrow. It's nighttime now."

As he spoke, the last rays of sunlight vanished beyond the edge of the jungle perimeter, bathing the clearing in brightening starlight. His breathing became deep and slow in the blackness inside the hut. Sally could barely see the outline of his black fur in the shadow. She wasn't the least bit sleepy. After all, she was still technically asleep in someone else's dream.

She stepped out into the night and caught her breath at the unexpected beauty of the jungle. Luminescent fungi and moss decorated the perimeter trees, and glowing insects flitted to and fro on their nighttime business. Colors ran from pink to yellow to blue, giving everything a mystical feel.

And that's when she heard, from beyond the edge of the clearing, a low voice call her by name.

"Sally . . ." The voice repeated again, and Sally felt the fur on the back of her neck stand on end. What new mystery was this?

It had to be Harlan, of course. It was the only thing that made sense. She'd met everyone else who was on the Moon with her in the Dream-world. The voice didn't sound like his, though. It was a friendly, husky voice not at all like Harlan's precise, clipped tones.

Sally took a few steps in the direction of the voice and stopped, sniffing the night air, listening for the sound of a heart beating amid the leaves. "Who's there? Is that you, Harlan?"

Her only reply was the jungle symphony.

"I warn you, if this is some sort of trick . . ." Sally stopped, for she'd caught a scent of hot blood, fur, and power. She brought all her feline senses to bear, seeking the source. "I can smell you," she said at last.

A shadow rose amid the other shadows. Broad shoulders, a thick mane, eyes that gleamed in the starlight. The King of the Jungle had arrived. "*Xiao mu shi*," he said.

Sally blinked. "I'm sorry?"

"No apology is required." The man stepped out from beneath the tree where he'd crouched. Although the clearing was only lit by luminescent plants and stars, Sally could tell his fur was tawny like hers instead of black. He shook out his magnificent mane and wrinkled his muzzle into a smile.

"Who are you? Get back, I'm warning you." Sally flexed her fingers, feeling the claws push their way out. "This place is under my protection."

"I'm not here to cause harm. I came to speak to you. I am Shi Xin."

"She's in?"

"Close enough, *xiao mu shi*."

"What's that?"

"A name, nothing more."

"What's it mean? Everything here means something."

"It is meant for you to discover, not to be told. That would be cheating."

"Cheating who? Myself?"

"Yes."

Sally felt like stamping her foot in frustration. "I don't understand."

The lion-man stepped away from the shadows, letting starlight sparkle in his mane. "You are being played for a fool, Sally."

"How do you know my name?" She paused. "Never mind. Of course you do. It's a dream. What do you mean, played for a fool?"

"Your mission. Your quest. It is a ruse. A distraction."

"How do you mean?"

"You must abandon your quest to find the Elephant Queen. It could mean your life."

Tendrils of suspicion crawled up Sally's spine. "What do you mean? Are you threatening me? Trust me, that's a very bad idea. It could go . . . poorly for you."

"Not a threat. I'm trying to protect you." The lion-man turned to face her. His own face was buried in the shadow of his mane, but his eyes gleamed in the darkness. "You've been told an inaccuracy. A falsehood."

"A lie?"

"If you wish. You believe you must rescue the Elephant Queen, that she is being held prisoner against her will."

"And what's your point of view?"

"She is being cared for by the Ticking Lord. He keeps her alive in much the same way as the medical machines keep her body alive."

"She's on life support in the Dream-world? How does that work? Isn't this all her dream and we're just guests in it? What you're claiming doesn't make any sense, stranger. Sorry, not buying it." Sally cleared her throat and ran her tongue across her teeth as if checking them for sharpness. "I think you'd better clear out of here now before something . . . happens."

The stranger took a step back and Sally could smell the indecision rippling through his muscles. "Let me make it plainer for you. If she dies in this dream, she dies in real life, and anyone whose mind is ensconced within hers at the time of her death will likewise perish."

"If she dies, I die too?"

"Yes. Can't you see I'm trying to save you? To protect you?"

"Why would you even care? You're just a figment of Reggie's imagination. Or of mine. You're not real."

The lion-man lashed out with blinding speed, faster than Sally could react. His claws flashed right across her nose, not deep enough to break the skin but hard enough to leave her face tingling. She jumped back, spreading her own claws wide, prepared to fight for her life once more, but the lion-man didn't move again. "Did that feel real?"

Taken aback, Sally rubbed her nose and checked it for blood. Not a single spot marred the fur on her fingers. "Yes."

"Consider it an object lesson. Things that happen to you here, in the dream, can have effects in the real world. Consider how powerful a tool your brain is, *xiao mu shi.* Given enough information, it can be convinced anything is real. Including your death in a dream."

Sally snorted, wrinkling her nose and noting how it still stung from the brush of his claws. "I still don't see why you care. You came here to talk me out of my mission, and that makes you my opponent."

"I . . . couldn't bear it to see you perish. I know I've been dead in the real world for many years, but I still exist here, within this Dream-world. It is . . . my home."

"It's the home of a ghost. You died before I was even born. You're him, aren't you? Lionheart."

He bowed. "Naturally. I'm so proud of the hero you've become, *xiao mu shi*, and I'm so sorry I haven't been able to be involved with your upbringing at all."

A knot twisted in Sally's guts like she'd eaten one too many bean burritos. "What do you know about my upbringing? You died at the same time as my f-father." It was like peeling a scab away from an unhealed wound, the feeling of admitting to herself that she was helping the man who'd killed both her father and Lionheart. They, along with many other heroes, had died at the hands of the Destroyer, of Harlan Washington. What kind of monster had Sally become, to make entreaty with such evil?

"*Xiao mu shi.*" Lionheart's voice dropped to a low growl, barely enough to carry over the whisper of the night breeze through the nearby jungle canopy. "You must not go to the Iron City. Without the Ticking Lord's constant monitoring, the Dreamer's spirit will twist away into nothingness. All that she has been, all she might ever be, will vanish. Turn around. Go back. Find your way back to the light and leave this darkness behind forever. Please, Sally. You must."

Sally felt herself to be on the verge of tears. A tremendous swirling maelstrom of conflicting emotions was threatening to burst forth. It was as if she were simultaneously on the verge of losing something invaluable or winning something amazing. She almost blurted out the question dancing on the edge of her lips but then she realized she still had a card to play. "I think you're l-lying to me. You already said I'm on a journey. That makes me a Traveler, and I'm invoking the Travelers' Questions Three. You are bound to answer me honestly."

Lionheart nodded, making his mane flutter like dandelion fluff in a breeze. "I understand and accept this challenge. Ask away, Traveler." He watched her from beneath his heavy brows, his eyes pools of liquid obsidian but for a single speckle of reflected starlight in each one.

"Were you sent by the Ticking Lord to interfere with my progress?" Sally watched Lionheart carefully, waiting to see if he would try to dodge the question. He would have to answer honestly, but that didn't mean he couldn't veil his answer in a riddle.

"It wouldn't be inaccurate to say that. There could be any number of reasons why I'm here. Following orders might only be a very small portion of that reason."

Sally sniffed. Because he'd agreed to play the game, he was bound by the rules, and therefore he couldn't be dishonest in his answers. There was nothing preventing him from speaking in riddles or half-truths, so long as he didn't outright lie. His answer at the very least meant he'd agreed to come to Sally on the Ticking Lord's orders, even if he had his own, separate motivations for doing so.

"How long is the journey to the Iron City?"

Lionheart smiled. "As long as it takes to get there. If you stop moving, it will take you forever."

Sally had to clamp her sharp teeth down on her tongue to keep from lashing out with a follow-up question, which was exactly what Lionheart had intended her to do. She would have wasted her third and final question and he would have been free to depart. The sound of his breath halted as he held it, waiting for her to make that crucial mistake.

She wouldn't give him the satisfaction. She already knew what her third and final question would be, and she'd picked it because he would have to answer honestly and then he would leave, so she wouldn't have to deal with him in the aftermath of his answer, whichever direction it might take. She would have held her own breath if she didn't need it to ask the question.

"Lionheart . . . are you my . . . my f-father?"

His smile saddened. He reached out a hand toward her, claws withdrawn into his thick, furry fingers. "Only the living can truly answer that question, *xiao mu shi*."

Sally reached for his hand and only brushed her fingers against his before he vanished like smoke in the breeze.

FIFTEEN

We spend so much time fighting, as superheroes.

Sally didn't know how long she stood outside the hut and pondered Lionheart's final words to her, but by the time she forced herself to stop thinking about them, the sky had grown light in the east and the song of the jungle was switching from nighttime creatures to daytime.

She knew once she finished her mission in the Dream-world, she'd have to take a trip back home, to Arizona, to speak with her mother. She'd never considered the possibility that her mother's husband Bobby, who had been a low-powered superhero and member of Just Cause named Audio, hadn't also been Sally's father. Now she wasn't sure, and wouldn't be until she spoke to her mother. If Lionheart was truly her father instead of Bobby, that meant her mother had been unfaithful at some point, which was a real blow to Sally's feelings. On the other hand, Lionheart had, from all she'd heard about him, been a stellar example of a superhero and Just Cause hero, and Sally could have done worse than to carry on his line.

She gasped as she realized that Lionheart being her father would mean Yunbao was her sister. Or at least, her half-sister. Growing up, Sally had always wanted to have a sibling—preferably a sister, because boys were icky—but her mother had said she had no time or energy to look after more than one parapowered child at a time. Indeed, she'd barely even dated again since Bobby—and Lionheart —had been killed by Destroyer at Tornado's funeral. It had always been Sally, her mom, and her grandmother. Three generations of superheroes, speedsters all.

The sun peeked over the edge of the canopy, flooding the clearing with golden light, and Sally knew she'd waited long enough. She whistled through her teeth and Minerva raised her head from beneath her wing to look down at her from her perch atop the hut. "Good morning."

"Good morning yourself. Are you going to sleep all day? We've got a journey to take."

Minerva fluffed out her feathers. "No, of course not. I've been waiting for you to decide it was time to leave."

"Why me?"

"Because this is your journey. I'm just here to accompany you."

"You're the sidekick?"

"So it would seem."

"And here you're not even wearing pixie boots."

Minerva clacked her beak in amusement. "I'll do my best to find some."

"Did you listen in overnight?"

"Listen to what? I was asleep."

"You didn't hear me speaking to Lionheart?"

"No, but this is a dream. Perhaps I wasn't meant to hear it."

Sally shrugged. "Maybe not. I'm still trying to figure out what the rules are for the Dream-world."

"There may not be any rules. Or they may be fluid."

"You're not really helping, Minerva."

Minerva matched Sally's shrug with a flick of her wingtips. "I'm still trying to figure out exactly what my role here entails myself."

"Speaking of tails, we should check in on our patient." Sally twitched her own tail and wondered if it might not in fact be a legacy from Lionheart.

They went into the hut to find the panther-man awake and crouched beside his fire pit, working to start a fresh blaze. He looked up as the two women entered his home and grinned at them, his teeth shocking white against the black of his fur. "Welcome to my home. I'm sorry I haven't g-g-gotten breakfast ready yet."

Sally hunched down beside March. "How's your tail?"

He grimaced. "What tail?"

"Does it still hurt? Here, let me check the dressing on it."

"No, that's okay." March moved out of reach of Sally's hands. "It's fi-fine. I don't even notice it now."

Sally wondered why he still stuttered in the Dreamworld created by his mother when she'd never heard him speak. Or perhaps she had, deep down, even while in her coma. It was comforting to her in a way; it added a note of familiarity to an otherwise alien setting. "You said you know the way to the Burning Sands. Can you help me?"

March nodded. "Yes, although it's many miles from here."

"Then we'd better travel light." Sally looked around at the supplies, recalling what she'd seen when she'd cleaned up the mess left by the boar-men. Nothing more than a gourd of water and a gourd of dried meat for each of us. That will have to be enough to get us through the distance. We can refill our water along the way if we need to."

"Wait, you want t-t-to leave right now?"

"Sooner we leave, sooner we reach the Iron City and save the Elephant Queen. That's got to be your mom, March. I don't know why she's got the whole elephant thing going on but that's the way it seems to be here in the dream."

"I don't know . . ."

Sally reached out and clasped his hand. He tensed like he wanted to pull away from the unexpected contact but he stayed in place, muscles quivering. "The Ticking Lord is afraid of me. Of *us*. He sent a . . . a minion to try to stop me from going. That means he's worried about us succeeding. As far as I'm concerned, that means we should give him a real reason to be afraid."

"Are you sure you want to do this?" Minerva preened her wings as if she'd always had them. "The challenges are bound to be more difficult the closer you get to your goal."

"Of course they are. I already figured this out. I'm Mario, and the Elephant Queen is Princess Peach. She just better not be in another castle when I get there."

Minerva canted her head sideways and stared unblinking at Sally, but March snickered at the reference.

"You know, at first I came here because of the favor I owed Destroyer, that is, your uncle, March. Now it's different. It's personal. I want to succeed. I want you to hear your mom tell you she loves you. I want her to see your face and smile. I want to save her." Sally swallowed against a sudden, unexpected lump in her throat. "We spend so much time fighting, as superheroes. We fight against villains. We fight against nature. Fighting, always fighting. But being a hero doesn't always have to mean fighting. It should mean saving too."

"That's a n-nice thought." March's hand twitched like he wanted to reach out toward her but was afraid to.

"Do you know how far it is through the jungle to the Burning Sands, March?" Minerva asked.

"N-no. It's not a straight line. Many miles."

"I won't be able to travel alongside you. The trees are too densely-packed for me to fly, and I will slow you down on foot. I'll fly over the top of the canopy and meet you at the edge of the jungle after you emerge."

"No!" Sally leaped to her feet. "We shouldn't split up now. I need you, Minerva."

"I'm not abandoning you or your quest, Sally. It's just that I can see I will be a liability during this particular stretch of your journey." Minerva straightened up from her roosting position to stare straight on into Sally's eyes. "You only think you need me. Think of this as . . ." She canted her head to one side as if by doing so, she would see Sally in a completely different perspective. "Throwing you into the deep end of the pool."

"You know I hate swimming." Sally grumbled as she gathered up some undamaged gourds and made impromptu slings for them from some loose cloth the boar-men had trampled but otherwise left unsoiled. She looked down at her handiwork. "Hey, these are pretty good. When did I learn how to do this?"

"It's a d-dream." March took one of the slings and hung it over one shoulder and across his chest. It fit snugly against his midnight-colored fur, breaking up the darkness with a splash of red and gold. "You can do anything."

"But it's not my dream. It's your mom's." Sally slipped her own sling over her shoulder. It rode comfortably against her torso without rubbing, although she didn't think that would be the case once they started running.

"Your p-presence is coloring it. So's mine. And Min . . . Min . . ."

"Minerva's, yes. I get that." Sally winced. "Sorry. I didn't think. I bet you hate when people finish your sentences for you."

March shrugged. "Sometimes it's better that way."

"You ever text or Facebook or anything? Lots of people communicate that way these days."

"Who would I text? I don't kn . . . know anyone."

"You could text me. I wouldn't mind. I mean, uh . . . It's all right." Sally bit the inside of her lip with her sharp fangs, wondering what sort of message she was sending. March's social skills were terribly stunted, and it was no wonder with his upbringing. Sally was glad to see he could interact with others at all.

March didn't reply. Instead, he tucked two gourds into his shoulder sling, one capped with a cork to hold in water, the other with a wide mouth and a piece of cloth tied over it to keep insects away from the dried meat within. The awkward silence between them made Sally wish she was somewhere else. She hoped he wasn't misinterpreting her words, but didn't know how to ask him directly how he'd taken them without embarrassing both of them, so she stayed quiet.

Minerva was the first to step out of the hut into the bright morning sunshine flooding the clearing. She spread her wings wide to stretch them as the two cat-people emerged, blinking, from the dusk inside the hut.

"I think I'm more nocturnal." Sally squinted at Minerva, shading her eyes.

"I know I am." March wrinkled his face into a snarl. "I'm already hot."

Minerva clacked her beak in amusement. "I'm sure the jungle will provide shade. Which direction are the Burning Sands, March?"

He scratched at his chin for a moment and then pointed to the north.

Minerva nodded. "I'll meet you at the far edge of the jungle. I'll wait as long as necessary."

"But what if we take a really long time?" asked Sally.

"Then I will wait a really long time." Minerva sprang into the sky, her powerful wings carrying her aloft in silence. She circled the clearing once and then disappeared beyond the edge of the canopy with naught but the remnant of a breeze to flick at the fur on Sally's face.

"I guess that's that." Sally turned to March. "Any reason we need to stick around here any longer?"

March shook his head.

"Lead on, mister. Pick your pace. I'll keep up." Sally smiled at him.

March raised his head as if sniffing at the air. Sally matched the action to see if she could detect anything amiss coming from the jungle, but all she caught was the overwhelming aroma of rich vegetation and rot. March jumped up and down a couple of times, like a football player trying to keep warm on the sidelines, and then trotted off toward the clearing's edge. Sally followed and the green darkness swallowed them like a verdant whale.

The two cat-people ran through the jungle, vaulting over fallen trees awash with moss and insects. Hanging vines threatened to ensnare them, dripping with stinging, poisonous sap. Sally lost all sense of direction within a minute or two as March picked his path between the titanic black trunks, sprinkled with mushrooms of every color. Occasionally, they would happen across a moment of unexpected beauty. Once it was a pair of mating dragonflies whose bodies sparkled like diamonds. Another time it was a brilliant crimson and gold flower emerging from a thicket of dark green that reminded Sally of her costume. Yet another time they found a monolith of granite as old as the world, thrusting from the rich loam of the jungle floor, covered with a thousand colors and varieties of lichen and moss.

They paused for a break when they'd been running for a while and Sally sipped at her water, rationing it to keep from slowing her down with cramps. Although her strength had always been in the sudden sprints, the bursts of super-speed that let her defeat most opponents in a moment, she'd done her fair share of distance running as well. "You know what this reminds me of?" She popped a piece of jerky into her mouth and sucked on it to soften it. "This one time I ran all the way from Guatemala to Arizona. There was a lot of jungle that time too."

"Why did you d-d-do that?" March leaned back against a bole as big around as a house.

"I was . . ." She paused. Did March need to know the truth? Had Harlan ever told him about Destroyer's history with Mustang Sally and the rest of Just Cause? Yes, she decided. He deserved that much. "At first, I was just running away. From your uncle. He was down in Guatemala, doing some really terrible things to people in the area. Killing hundreds of them. When we discovered what he was doing, we went down there to stop it."

She stopped as a lump thickened in her throat. She closed her eyes for a moment and could see the shoulder guns on the Destroyer battlesuit belching fire, tearing apart her friends. Glimmer's dying words, sent to her telepathically, still rang in her mind: *Sally . . .*

run! And run she had. Just Cause had sent her and three other heroes to investigate Harlan's actions in Guatemala. When she fled, Glimmer was dead, and Crackerjack and Doublecharge were prisoners. Sally had only been eighteen, barely a hero, and had only gone on the mission at all because she spoke Spanish and her powers were exceptional.

One time, months later, she'd worked out on a map how far she'd run: roughly eighteen hundred miles. It had taken her six hours. She'd nearly run the boots right off her feet, and if not for her rapid healing abilities, she might have permanently crippled herself in her panic to reach help. She turned up on her mother's doorstep in the early morning hours, and her mother, a former member of Just Cause, had called out the cavalry. Several super-teams from around the U.S. had stepped in to help rescue Crackerjack and Doublecharge, and to stop Destroyer's plans permanently. Even so, more of Sally's friends had died. Their names graced statues in the Just Cause Memorial Garden in Manhattan: *Trix. Esther. Forcestar.* In the end, all their deaths, along with so many others, could be placed squarely upon Harlan Washington's shoulders.

She told March.

He was silent for a long time after she finished speaking. He wouldn't meet Sally's gaze. "Maybe . . . th-that's not who he is anymore."

Sally tucked her water bottle back into her sling and stood, ready to run again. "It's who he was then."

SIXTEEN

I'll make you a bet.

The two runners settled into a regular rhythm. They trotted through the jungle for stretches of time as indeterminate as the passage of the sun overhead. Sally knew time was passing by the waning amount of water in her gourd. Neither she nor March were keen on risking whatever passed for intestinal parasites in the Dream-world, so they avoided the pools of standing water that stank of rotten eggs and had green films covering their surfaces.

Whenever they stopped for a break, sipping water and chewing some of the hard, dry jerky, Sally would catch March staring at her. He hid it well, keeping his eyes hooded underneath his dark brows and staying in the shadows as much as he could, but nevertheless, Sally could feel his gaze upon her. She'd been the object of others' infatuation long enough that she'd developed a sort of sixth-sense about it. That sense seemed to have been amplified in her current feline body. Her hackles rose at the touch of his eyes, which was far more noticeable and nerve-wracking when the fur across the back of her neck was long and luxurious. At first, she wondered why he was staring at her, but then she could have slapped herself for being so blind to it.

The poor boy was clearly crushing upon her with all the subtlety of a fourteen-year-old freshman in high school. She could hardly believe he wasn't shuffling his feet and staring at the ground when talking to her. He'd grown up in social isolation. He'd probably never had a girlfriend. For that matter, he was probably still as inexperienced as Sally had been when she first came to Just Cause. She remembered how tongue-tied and anxious she'd been around Jason, the tall, handsome, muscular superhero known as Mastiff, and how tender he'd been the first time they were together. It was no wonder she'd married him.

She wasn't worried about March. He was no threat to her. Indeed, Sally doubted he was much of a threat to anyone, parahuman abilities notwithstanding. In person, he'd come across as, well, more of a pussycat than a panther. She wondered why the Dream-world had cast him in the latter role. Minerva as an owl, now, that made sense. Her wisdom was one of the foremost aspects of her personality, and even without her abilities, it made her a formidable opponent. Sally as lioness, well, maybe that was the dream's way of confirming she was Lionheart's daughter. But the Dream-world was a construct of Reggie's mind, not March's, which meant Reggie's subconscious had been the deciding factor when casting the characters. Maybe Reggie was somehow trying to affect the outcome of her own dream, pushing Sally and March toward each other. That implied Reggie had some level of consciousness, which meant in turn Sally was on the right path to try and rescue that consciousness, to bring it back out and help Reggie's mind to awaken.

In the meantime, she resolved, she'd keep an eye on March just in case. She watched him during breaks from behind lowered lids. She kept herself in shadows as much as possible and used her exceptional feline vision to examine the play of his muscles beneath his pelt of thick black fur. Her eyes traced down the sinuous curve of his spine, ending in a bandage of rough-spun cloth where his severed tail had been bandaged.

She shook herself. What was she doing? She'd been staring at him as much as he had at her, with her mind wandering in directions that were both inappropriate and unwelcome. Why was she doing that?

It had to be the influence of the Dream-world. She couldn't allow herself to fall under its sway. Even though it was only a dream, she didn't want to risk letting any of March's feelings take root. And likewise, she needed to keep on top of her own feelings and recognize they were not likely her own. "Hey, how's your tail?" It was the first words either of them had spoken since they departed the clearing, many hours earlier.

March's green eyes widened at the sudden, unexpected interest in his well-being. "It hurts, but I c-can manage."

"Doesn't seem to have affected your stride or balance at all. I've been watching." Sally felt like tearing out her own tongue. She'd basically admitted she'd been watching his ass. Of course she hadn't, she told herself. She'd been looking out for a companion's well-being. The quality of his ass had nothing to do with it, regardless of it being a very nice ass.

Dammit!

Sally was glad she had fur covering her face to keep her blush from showing. "So, uh, how far to the edge of the jungle?"

"Not far now."

"Then let's run."

They ran, toe claws digging into the rich soil of the jungle path. As they traveled, the canopy began to lighten, showing more bright spots of sunlight leaking through in isolated puddles of gold. The ground itself became softer and wetter, until their forward progress slowed as it became less about running and more about wading. The water stank from algae and slime, but it still seemed cleaner and more wholesome than the pools they'd encountered on their travels. It reminded Sally of the Everglades she and Jason had visited on a long-weekend vacation to Florida a couple years back.

And then, they reached the edge of the jungle. It was like approaching a wall of brilliance with the last trees as dark shadows against it. As they emerged, blinking, into the sunlight, they saw a broad, slow-flowing river with sticky mud flats lining both banks. Beyond the far bank rose hills of blinding white sand against an azure sky. The breeze carried away swirls of iridescent dust from the dune crests. The river itself was full of beings. Given the way the Dream-world had seen fit to put predators in Sally's way, she wouldn't have been surprised to discover a bunch of crocodilians, but instead, the river denizens appeared to have far more in common with hippopotamuses.

They were still humanoid in the peculiar way the Dream-world transformed creatures. They looked like gray-skinned sumo wrestlers, with stubby legs that seemed far too small to hold up their barrel-shaped bodies. Their heads were pure hippo, with jaws that spread wide in threatening yawns, flashing their tusks at one another. Occasionally one would roar and charge toward another, and that worthy would either flee or stand and fight. Most fights were over in moments as the loser fell into the river, bleeding out from fatal puncture wounds inflicted by the vicious bites of the victors.

An exceptionally large hippo-man splashed out of the shadows until he was standing in ankle-deep mud on the near bank. He looked Sally and March up and down with his thick, stumpy hands on his hips before he spread his jaws wide and roared at them. "No. No way. Nope. Nuh-uh."

Sally stepped forward, wincing at the stink of the hippo-man's breath. "What do you mean, *no*? We haven't even done anything yet."

The hippo-man stomped a foot, splashing mud at the two cat-people. "I am Kiboko of the River People, and all you see here is mine. Every rock. Every droplet of water. Every cow. Every calf. Mine. All mine."

"That's all right. We don't want any of it. We're just passing through." Sally put on her most polite smile.

"Passing through? You want to cross the river. *My* river. And you have to walk across *my* banks to do it." Kiboko spread his short arms as wide as he could.

"We didn't say we were crossing the river." Sally had a sinking suspicion things were going to go badly no matter what she said. Maybe she could invoke the Travelers' Questions Three. Get him all tangled up in logic. Leave him thinking up an impossible answer while she and March fled into the Burning Sands. "I invoke—"

"You think you're going to invoke that silly game with me? Well I refuse to play it. This is my land. My rules. And my rule is that you have to pay a toll if you want to cross."

"What toll?"

Kiboko snapped his mouth shut for a moment, making a thunderous clapping sound. "I think ten years each should do nicely."

"Ten . . . years? For what?"

"Whatever I choose. Ten years servitude, and then your toll is paid."

Sally snorted. She could tell Kiboko wasn't going to be impressed by manners. He was boisterous, brash, and full of self-importance. She'd met a hundred politicians like him. "Well maybe we'll just head up the river, then. Eventually we'll leave your territory and then you have no sway over us."

Kiboko squeezed his eyes into threatening slits. "You can try. If you leave, I'll kill you. Nobody disrespects me that way. *Nobody!*" He splattered mud in all directions. "Nobody!" His bellowing made several of the more skittish hippo-men back away from him.

Sally could practically see the veins in his head throbbing. One little scratch, she thought, and his blood would spray out like a fire hydrant. She sighed and popped her claws. It was going to be another fight. It seemed like the Dream-world solved all its problems through the use of violent conflicts. A wry grin worked its way across her mouth as she realized the similarities to real life. And then an idea arose, and she held it up to the light of consideration. "Tell you what, Kiboko. You don't want to play a game. Maybe you don't have the intellect for it. But that's okay. I'll make you a bet. Plain and simple."

"What bet?"

"I bet I can beat you in a fight. Straight up, no rules. Play as dirty as you want, with one exception."

"Exception?"

"Neither of us gets help. One on one. Me versus you, winner takes all."

"All what?" Kiboko's bluster shrank as he struggled to wrap his brain around the concepts to which Sally was introducing him.

Sally puffed up her chest. On one hand, she was deathly serious with Kiboko, but on the other, she recognized how ludicrous the situation was, and she was making it worse by showing off for March's benefit. *Look how heroic I am as I'm fighting to save your mom.* "I win, you let us continue our journey unharmed."

"And when I win instead?" Kiboko thumped his chest. "What then, pussy-willow?"

Sally growled in the back of her throat. She had formed a plan and intended to stick to it, but if Kiboko started calling her degrading names, she might forget herself and just kill him instead.

She was, unfortunately, getting used to slaying as a way of life in the Dream-world.

"If you win, I will be your slave for life, but my friend will be free to travel onward unharmed."

"W-wait, what? N-no, Sally!" March stepped up beside her, grabbed her arm, spun her to look at him. His eyes were cartoony wide. "You cuh . . . cuh . . . " Being upset was making his stutter worse, and that in turn embarrassed him and upset him even further, making it a vicious cycle where he had a great many things to say but couldn't speak them.

Sally removed his hand from her arm, gently, and squeezed it with as much reassurance as she could muster. "This way at least one of us gets to move on to save your mom."

"B-b-but . . ."

Sally took his other hand and stood facing him, gazing into his eyes. "It should be you, March. She's your mom. She doesn't know me, but you're her flesh and blood. Deep down, even in a coma, she'll know her own son, and I believe you can awaken her." She glanced over her shoulder at Kiboko, who stood fuming in the mud. "But I've been watching that guy since he came out of the water. Don't worry. I can take him." She said it with far more confidence than she felt, but that was what March needed to hear.

"Be. Cuh . . . careful." March took a deep breath as he tried to settle himself down.

Without understanding why she did so, Sally stepped in close to him and bussed his cheek. His arms came around her in an awkward embrace, as if it were something he didn't know how to do. She moved back quickly before he had a chance to cling. "I will. Watch this."

"Let's go!" Kiboko looked hopping mad, flapping his stumpy arms like wings.

Sally pointed at him. "Do you accept my terms or not, Kiboko?"

"Yes, fine, whatever."

"They're binding terms. You can't renege."

"I won't." Koboko paused, and then roared a challenge at her. "Let's go! I'm tired of waiting!"

Sally grinned a mouthful of razor-sharp fangs at the hippo-man. "Ready or not, here I come."

One of the truisms Sally had come to learn over many years in the superhero business was that given her slight stature and build, most opponents were going to be physically stronger than her. And when parahuman abilities came into the mix, many of them were *much* stronger, to the point where one bad move on her part would result in her being the Formerly Fastest Girl in the World Who Is Now Dead. Her husband Jason was one of those super-strong types, who secretly referred to unpowered humans as *crunchies*, who could toss around cars like toys and punch holes in concrete walls. He had always been very careful around Sally, even when they tussled like pups at play. Kiboko would have no such compunctions about injuring or killing her, but Sally was counting on that premise. She'd spent years learning how to analyze opponents and their fighting styles. Perhaps she wasn't as fast as she was used to being in the real world, but she was still much faster than the slow, awkward hippo-man, and she was going to use that to her advantage.

Unfortunately, Kiboko had other advantages, and Sally could tell he knew how to use them as she approached him. The mud grew deeper and stickier the closer she got to him. It clutched at her feet with all the greed of a hungry infant, and if she'd been wearing boots, she'd have lost them in seconds. It would do much to negate her speed and quick direction changes, whereas Kiboko was simply strong enough to muscle his way through the mud without it being much of a hindrance. However, he was naturally slow, and as long as Sally could keep him from grabbing at her, she felt like she could pull off the win. With his enormous head and tusks like blunted daggers, if he managed to clamp his jaws over her, she'd likely be crushed into pulp.

Maybe she could reduce that threat, she thought, and her foot flashed across his jaw, connecting solidly with one of his lower tusks and snapping it loose in a spray of blood. He bellowed in surprise and pain.

"That's one." Sally grinned as she circled around him, wary, careful to plant her feet on the occasional hillocks of vegetation amid the muck, where she could keep her balance and had some traction. Kiboko charged at her with all the subtlety of a derailing locomotive, roaring and flailing his stumpy, useless arms. Sally sprang to one side, raking his flank with her claws as he passed. She landed and her feet promptly slid out from beneath her, plopping her down ass first with the stinking mud all the way to her waist.

Kiboko spun around and lunged at her, intending to drive her deeper in the mud where he could trample or suffocate her. Sally struggled to stay clear. The mud embedded between every stitch of her fur, making her feel twice as heavy. Kiboko's heavy foot crashed down, just glancing off Sally's ankle before she yanked it away. Despite his bulk, he was faster than he looked.

In combat practice, Sally had learned to use opponents' strength against them. Her friend and teammate Yunbao had grown up in a martial arts school in Hong Kong and had started teaching Sally a style called *baguazhang*. It focused on flexibility, and circles, and a half dozen things Sally could barely remember as the hippo-man pressed his furious assault.

Other hippo-men and women stared in open-mouthed shock as the two combatants fought their way down toward the river. None of them moved to help either Sally or Kiboko, but they shuffled back and forth to see better.

Bedraggled, with water and mud streaming off her sodden fur, Sally found a sand bar and relished in the sudden improvement in her traction. She'd stayed out of Kiboko's range largely from luck. With her toes getting purchase in hard-packed wet sand, it was going to be an entirely new fight.

And then Kiboko kicked a glob of mud right across her face and blinded her. Sally staggered back, trying to wipe the sticky muck away from her eyes, and tripped over something hard and unyielding. She landed on her back and gasped as the wind flew out of her lungs. Kiboko laughed and stomped toward her. She scratched at her own face, trying to clear her vision and scramble away from the hippo-man at the same time. A heavy kick caught her in the side and she cried out as one of her ribs broke. The force of the blow rolled her over and she landed face down in a puddle of water.

Kiboko's foot came down on her head, not stomping, but pressing her inexorably deeper into the water, forcing it into her nose and mouth. She scrabbled at the sand but couldn't get any purchase to free herself. Kiboko leaned his weight on her and he was as heavy as the entire world. Sally felt she was seconds from blacking out if she didn't do something. But what could she do? She was used to having her accelerated perceptions handy to plan out her moves at super-speed, but in the Dream-world she was only a little bit faster than others.

But that might be fast enough, she realized.

There was only one part of Kiboko's body she could reach in her present condition: his foot. She couldn't take a deep breath because she was suffocating in the sandy water, so she had to trust there was enough oxygen in her bloodstream to let her complete her action. She lunged up and behind her, using the innate flexibility of her catlike body, dug her claws deep into the back of Kiboko's leg, and tore apart his Achilles tendon.

Hot blood poured down across her back as he recoiled from her sudden, vicious strike. His bellows sounded like they came from the far end of a long tunnel as Sally pushed her weary self out of the mud. The first breath of air was the sweetest she'd ever tasted, and if she'd had time, she would have savored it over and over. Sides heaving as she struggled to get herself back to an even keel, she wiped her face and saw what had tripped her in the first place. It was a piece of driftwood, a broken tree, naked of bark, bleached bone-white by the sun. She lashed out at it with one foot and kicked free a jagged piece as long as her forearm. She bent to pick it up and then regarded her opponent.

Kiboko was hopping mad—literally, as he couldn't put any weight on his damage foot. Froth flew from the corners of his mouth as he screamed obscenities at her. "You bitch, you fucking cunt, I'll make you pay for that!"

Sally swung the chunk of wood like she was backhanding a tennis ball, and one of Kiboko's tusks snapped off to fly all the way to the river. "Say that again."

"Dumbfuck whore!"

Crack. Another of Kiboko's tusks fell victim to Sally's piece of wood. "What are you going to do to me?"

"You bitch! You slut! I'm gonna kill you! Kill you! K—"

Sally lunged forward with the piece of wood and jammed it upright deep into Kiboko's mouth. One splintered end buried itself in his soft palate while the other impaled into his tongue. He screamed at her, hot breath making her fur flutter, but that was all he could do. He couldn't shut his mouth and snap the wood and his arms were too short to reach up and pull it loose. He gagged at the wood and more froth ran from his mouth but he couldn't do anything else except whine at her. He took a half-hearted step toward her, lost his balance, and fell to the sand.

Sally looked at the other hippo-men, ready for another challenge, but they were all backing away from her wide-eyed, creating a clear avenue for her to reach the river. She wondered if any of them would help Kiboko. Given the hard gleam in most of their eyes, she guessed not. He hadn't made any allies in his jockeying for alpha male status in the pod. Perhaps they'd let him die. Even if someone took pity on him eventually, he had lost every bit of standing he had when he got beaten by someone half his size.

Her head hurt where he'd stood his weight upon it, and the broken rib was demanding attention every time she took a breath, but in the end, she knew she'd beaten Kiboko, and that meant she'd won the wager. Her foot bumped against something and she saw it was the hippo-man's tusk that she'd knocked loose. Grunting from the pain of her broken rib, she squatted down and retrieved it. She'd *earned* it, dammit, and she wasn't going to leave without her trophy. She reached a hand out toward March, who looked as shell-shocked as many of the hippo-men. "Let's go."

Hand in hand, they waded into the river.

SEVENTEEN

She wants to see you with her own eyes, not in a dream.

The Burning Sands lived up to their name.

Sally wished she had her boots, or some regular tennis shoes, or even some beach clogs as she and March crested one dune after another of sand bleached the color of bone. Growing up in Arizona, she'd gotten used to walking on hot surfaces, but the sand was another creature entirely. It swished and slid with every step, threatening to slip out from beneath her feet, send her tumbling down the side of a dune, and then bury her in its unforgiving depths. As it heated the sands to intolerable temperatures, the sun also beat down upon their heads until both March and Sally were panting like dogs. Her thick cat-fur only made the heat worse, and if someone had handed her a razor, Sally would have cheerfully peeled away her pelt until the razor was too blunt to cut.

As uncomfortable as Sally was, she knew March had to be suffering even worse with his inky fur. He marched on in stoic silence, and she took inspiration in it and managed to keep herself going despite her broken rib and burning feet.

When they reached the summit of the next dune, Sally paused, shaded her eyes, and squinted into the horizon. In all directions, she could see nothing but sand and more sand. The jungle behind them had melted into the frozen waves of white, and the only hint the river left was a shimmering mirage floating well above the surface of the sand. Nowhere did she see the shadowy blight she imagined the Iron City to be. She didn't even see Minerva cruising over the dunes. Her friend's failure to appear was unnerving. How long had they been in the dream, anyway? Had Minerva awakened prematurely? Or was she truly lost and unable to find them, despite March's fur making him look like a lump of charcoal in a snowfield?

"How long do you think we've been walking?" Sally thought she saw a dark speck on the horizon, but it vanished when she blinked. "It feels like it's been days since the sun set."

"Maybe it has." March panted like a dog. "I just want some water. I'm so th-thirsty."

"Me too. Maybe we'll find an oasis."

That was the last thing either of them said for another lengthy stretch of walking. They fell into the peculiar rhythm of traveling across the sand. Climb slowly to the top of a dune, treading as lightly as possible. Pause at the top for a momentary rest. Check the horizon for any sign of Minerva, of the Iron City, of water. Slip down the face of the dune into the valley between them. Pause again at the bottom for another rest. Repeat. Repeat.

"Damn it, Reggie, quit trying to kill us!" Sally lashed out at the air with a fist as she reached the top of another dune. The merciless sun beat upon her with an almost tangible force. "We're trying to save you."

"Maybe she d-doesn't want to be saved." March swayed on his feet. The heat had gotten to him hours ago. It rose off him in waves. He fell to his knees and picked up a handful of the scorching white sand to watch it fall through his black fingers. "M-maybe she doesn't care."

Sally knelt beside him. "Of course she cares, March. She wants to see you with her own eyes, not in a dream. I can't imagine any mother not wanting the chance to hold her son at least once."

March bowed his head and said nothing.

Sally licked her lips with a tongue that felt like a piece of pumice. "Look, it's hot, and we're thirsty, and we're both exhausted. Let's rest. Like, really rest."

"Where? There's no sh-shade."

Once again, Sally scanned the horizon for Minerva. Or the Iron City. Or anything that could cast a bit of shadow in which they could huddle and wait for nightfall. And then it came to her. "The sand. It's white. It reflects sunlight. It'll be cool underneath." To illustrate her point, she took March's hand in hers and plunged it into the sand. He started to pull away from her but stopped as he realized the temperature beneath the sand was several degrees cooler. "You're right."

Sally was so tired it took her awhile to realize she was still holding March's hand in hers. The tiny pricks of his claws played a strangely soothing counterpoint to his skin and fur beneath hers. She imagined what it would look like. Black and white wrapped in each other. Yin and yang. She shook herself. "Come on. The sand will be easier to burrow into at the bottom of a dune." She didn't know that to be a fact, but it sounded good, and would give her a rational reason not to keep holding March's hand. She knew she needed to stop leading him on. Because that's what she was doing, wasn't it? She wasn't developing any sort of feelings for the earnest young stutterer she'd just met. That was unrealistic.

Of course, so was traveling through the dreams of a comatose woman.

The two cat-people slipped down the side of the dune into the loose sand at the base, letting the grains they'd dislodged on their descent surround and flow over them until only their faces were still uncovered. It was still hot, and the sun was like a thousand-watt spotlight shining directly upon them, but beneath the sand, the heat was merely tolerable instead of incinerating. "We'll wait for nightfall, and then we'll travel. We'll find water then, too." Sally found that she'd taken a position beneath the sand where her fingers rested upon March's forearm.

"S-so thirsty . . ." March's voice was faint and his eyes, barely visible beneath a roof of alabaster sand, shut against the timelessness of the desert.

Sally squeezed his forearm and she, too, shut her eyes to conserve her waning energy for nighttime travels. She didn't dream, exactly, while resting inside someone else's Dream-world, but she found her introspective thoughts bubbling to the surface and taking hold of her. First she had her companion to consider. She could understand his attraction to her. He had been isolated for years, and honestly, she'd filled out a bit in her twenties and looked better than she had as a gawky teenager. What boy wouldn't feel a little twinge of appreciation when he looked at her? That was only realistic, right?

But then why was she finding it so difficult to shut it down in the Dream-world? In the real world, when she was awake, all she would have to say was "I'm married," and that should be the end of it. In the Dream-world, there was no ring around her finger, and maybe March saw her as fair game. Seduce her in the dream and perhaps she'd weaken in reality. Yes, that had to be it.

She shouldn't have been attracted to him either.

But she was.

Damn it, why was she even allowing herself to entertain such ridiculous fantasies? He was the nephew of a *supervillain*. That supervillain had killed her father!

The real question, burning in her mind in letters spread across the landscape in fifty-foot flames, was *who was her father*? Her entire life, she'd only ever thought of one man, her mom's husband, Bobby "Audio" Thompson as her father. Her mother had told her many stories about him and how loving and caring and forgiving he could be.

That last one was bothering Sally something fierce. Why would her mom be so careful to mention he was *forgiving*?

What had she done to require his forgiveness?

She'd cheated on him. Of course she had. It was the only transgression she could imagine for which her mother would need to be forgiven. Sally had once thought Jason had cheated on her, and if it had turned out to be true instead of a misunderstanding, it would have been the end of their relationship.

Did that mean she was in fact Lionheart's daughter? Had their cheating led to a pregnancy? She didn't look like a cat or a lion in the real world. Did she really have anything that suggested part of her genes had come from the half-man, half-lion? No, of course not. Then she thought about her hair. Her mom's hair wasn't naturally blonde—she'd always dyed it. It wasn't very thick, either. Her father—or at least, her mom's husband Bobby—had brown hair as well. Sally's thick blonde mane might have been Lionheart's legacy. Or maybe it was just the vagaries of genetics.

So many questions, Sally thought, and no way to find out the truth short of confronting her mother. She didn't have the slightest idea how to even broach that kind of subject. *Hi Mom, how are you? By the way, did Lionheart get you pregnant with me?*

Yeah, no. She couldn't do that. The embarrassment alone might kill both of them before they ever got around to an answer.

This was still Reggie's Dream-world, though, and Sally couldn't explain how a woman who'd been in a coma for more than twenty years was suggesting the question in Sally's lineage. Of course, Reggie had lived with her older sister Irlene and Irlene's husband Javier, who were the Just Cause members Imp and Javelin. Like Sally, she'd grown up around superheroes. The difference was Sally hadn't watched her brother destroy half of Harlem first. Reggie might have been in a position to see something going on between Lionheart and Sally's mom. Maybe she'd taken something she'd seen and run with it all the way into her dreams . . .

. . . All of which would be academic if Sally couldn't get her out of the coma.

She shut her eyes against the glare of sunlight against the bleached grains of the Burning Sands and tried to put the brakes on the whirlwind of her thoughts.

When she next opened her eyes, the sun had faded away, leaving behind a sky like she hadn't seen since running through Wyoming in the middle of the night. She saw a billion stars scattered across the Universe, like looking back through time. The band of the Milky Way was clearly visible over the horizon. The white sands had transformed into a bluish gray under the brilliance of the full Moon low on the horizon. Somewhere up there, she thought, she was asleep and hooked up to machines through March's and Minerva's focus, allowing her to exist inside Reggie's dreams. The quantum unreality of feeling like she was in two places at once was enough to make the sci-fi nerd in her geek out just a little. She raised a hand out of the sand and looked at the furry digits with their claws. "I really am Schrödinger's Cat."

"What's that?" March rose out of the sand like a shadow. He shook himself and a cloud of white dust spread away from him.

Sally shook herself as well. "I'm the cat in the box, but you don't know if I'm alive or dead. I'm existing in a quantum state, both alive and dead at the same time. Except now I'm in two places at the same time. I'm here, in the Dream-world, and I'm up there on the Moon." She pointed at the shining silver disc in the sky. "And so are you. We're in a quantum state right now."

"If you s-say so."

"Just run with it." Sally smiled. The rest beneath the sand had done her well. She felt re-energized enough to take a quick running pace for a while. "Are you up for a jog?"

"Yes." March reached up to brush a bit of sand off Sally's nose. The Moon reflected in his eyes, making them look large and bright. Sally had to tear her gaze away from them for fear of getting lost. Damn it, she wasn't supposed to be doing that! "Whuh . . . which way?"

March's question derailed her thoughts. She had no idea how big the Burning Sands were, or where in them they might find the Iron City. They could wander lost in the desert until they dropped dead of dehydration or exhaustion without ever even seeing a speck of black against the white landscape. She'd kind of counted upon Minerva being with them, which might give them an edge in the form of her parahuman awareness of sensory details, not to mention her general wisdom. Minerva's way of examining problems had proven to be far more useful a trait than any of her abilities, and Sally hadn't realized how much she'd come to rely on the wisdom and observations from her friend until she didn't have them handy.

"I don't know." She hated admitting the truth, because she wanted March to think better of her. "You don't have any ideas?"

"No."

"I wish Minerva was here. We could really use someone with wings and excellent vision." She looked up at the stars, like grains of the Burning Sands cast across a bolt of black velvet. "Back in the old days, people used to navigate by the stars. I always thought that was a really neat idea, but I never did figure out how they did it. I'm hopeless without my GPS." Her side twinged and she felt around where her rib had been broken. It was tender but it seemed like the break had solidified. At least it seemed her quick parahuman healing still existed in the Dream-world. But then a gleam in the sands caught her eye and she forgot about where she'd been injured.

She knelt in the sand and hunched down in spite of the pain in her side. The glow seemed to be coming from beneath the sand. Unlike the bluish gray of the sands under the Moonlight, it was a red glow. She started to scrape away sand, working with slow, careful precision so as not to disturb whatever was providing the crimson light. Soon she'd brushed enough sand aside to see what was emitting the gleam. It was Kiboko's tusk that she'd knocked out in their fight and claimed as her prize for winning. Without a pocket to keep it in, she'd carried it in her hand on their first day's journey across the Burning Sands. She must have lost track of it when they buried themselves to escape the sun's heat.

Why was it glowing?

She lifted it out of the sand and saw the light blazing from the broken end of the tusk, like the dried blood itself was shining. As she turned it over in her hands, the light faded to dark. "Huh. I guess that's that." She thought about tossing it away, to let it be swallowed up by the Burning Sands forever, but no, she'd *earned* it; she was going to keep it. She lowered her hand and the light blazed forth from the tusk again.

March figured it out first. "It only l-lights up when it points . . . points . . ." He grimaced and stomped on the sands in frustration over his speech impediment. He pointed in on direction, his dark fur blotting out the stars beyond.

Sally held her breath and slowly turned the broken tusk around. Sure enough, when it faced a certain direction, its glow brightened. A bit of experimentation showed them the tusk worked like a Geiger counter, giving off its strongest light when it was pointed in exactly the correct direction. "That has to be it, our clue."

"How do y-you know?"

"I don't, but it's the only thing giving us any sort of guidance at all, and I'm willing to bet that here in the Dream-world, it's guiding us to *somewhere* we need to be, whether or not that place is the Iron City or something else."

"Are you betting your life on that? We might not . . . not survive an . . . an . . ." March spun around, his fists clenched. Sally could see the tension in his shoulders. His arms were quivering and she wouldn't have been surprised if he hauled off and hit himself in the face.

She put a hand on his shoulder. The muscles stood out underneath her fingertips like steel cables. She pulled gently to turn him back around to face her. He had his head bowed far enough forward that no starlight reflected in his eyes at all. "I hate it. I ca . . . ca . . . ca—"

Surprising herself as much as she did him, Sally took his head in her hands and pressed her lips against his.

Kissing him with their cats' muzzles was odd but not unpleasantly so. His fur was soft against her face, and his whiskers intertwined with hers in an intimate sort of way. His hands fluttered helpless at his sides as he didn't know what to do with them. At last they found a resting spot at the small of her back. She pulled her hands from his face and wrapped them around his neck, pulling him in closer. She felt her body responding in the way that normally led to shenanigans with Jason.

Jason!

She jumped back as if she'd scalded herself.

"I'm sorry!" March turned away, embarrassed.

Shame threatened to overwhelm Sally. "Don't be sorry, March. That was all me. I was . . . I was trying to help you relax. It always works in the movies when someone stutters." She realized she was mumbling, every bit as embarrassed as he was. She'd felt his excitement as they kissed, and her own had risen to match it. It wouldn't have taken any effort at all for them to take the next step and turn their desert-wandering dream into a sex dream. The truly scary part for Sally was she wouldn't have minded it. It was a *dream*, and that didn't really count, did it? Still, the thought of Jason had driven any thoughts of imaginary infidelity away for the time being. "I'm the one who should be sorry." She took a deep breath, trying to calm her rushing heartbeat. "Maybe we should just hit the road." She raised the broken tusk. "Follow our beacon."

They ran across the dunes, neither speaking to the other out of some sense of embarrassed propriety. At least, that was Sally's reason for staying quiet. It was easier to keep focused on putting one foot in front of the other, following the guiding light in her hand, than talking to her companion. Any conversation would be stilted, awkward, as they danced around what had happened before.

Time passed.

Sally's thirst and exhaustion climbed in equal measure until all she could think about was how tired and thirsty she was. If presented with a comfortable patch of grass beside a pond of clear water, the agony of decision over which to experience first might be fatal. Where at first the two cat-people had kept up a steady pace, eating up mile after mile of blue-gray sands beneath the stars, now their steps were ragged and irregular, more of a stagger than anything.

The Moon, which hadn't moved during the entirety of their evening travels, simply faded from existence. The nighttime sky brightened to a brilliant turquoise as the sun appeared directly overhead. It blazed its fury down upon them from above while blinding them with its reflection on the pearly sands once more. The beacon of their broken tusk hadn't the brightness to overcome the burning sun. Once more, they had lost their way, and didn't seem to be any closer to their goal.

Sally's legs gave way and she collapsed at the top of a dune. Nothing but miles upon miles of pristine white sands as far as she could see in any direction. No Minerva. No water. No Iron City. "No . . ." she whispered through swollen lips. "We can't fail."

March flopped down beside her. "We tried. Maybe it wasn't meant to b-be."

If she had the strength to sit upright, Sally would have

hung her head in defeat. "March, when we wake up . . . What happened last night . . . that was just part of a dream, all right? That's not a thing in the real world."

"I know."

For a long time, no words were spoken between the two as they sprawled on the sands beneath the merciless sun, waiting to die.

EIGHTEEN

I won't quit.

Sally's eyes flew open, but the light stabbed her eyes like needles. She gasped for breath, but no matter how hard she tried, she couldn't inhale, couldn't scream. A burning lump clogged the back of her throat, like vomit she couldn't spit out. Trembling with mounting panic, she forced her eyes to focus. Blurry objects took on sympathetic vibrations. Something nearby shattered.

A sharp pain hit her thigh and every muscle in her body tensed up while her heart tried to explode. Air rushed into her lungs and she coughed, gagging on whatever had stuck in her throat. She kept swallowing, but the burning wouldn't go away. The world returned around her like she was emerging from a long, dark tunnel.

She saw the world as a frozen tableau, a scene of frantic and imminent destruction. March lay on a nearby bed, staring at her in mute, unmoving shock. Minerva was halfway off her own bed, blurred in the act of motion like a paused video. The scene culminated in a wide-eyed Harlan standing beside Sally. One of his hands reached out toward her forehead as if he were an ancient priest trying to draw the evil spirits forth, while the other held a syringe in her leg with the plunger depressed.

She realized at last that she was back in the real world. She'd been rudely withdrawn from Reggie's Dream-world with neither invitation nor warning. Her perceptions were accelerated, as they often were when she was utilizing her super-speed, but never so fast that the world around her ground to a halt. Her eyes wandered toward the screen beside her, which Harlan had said would monitor her vital signs. Every line was flat—not at the bottom, which would indicate her death, but jammed at the top. According to the machine, her heart rate was 999. She was quivering as whatever drug Harlan had injected her with raced through her system. Objects were flying off the table at the side of her bed, including a container of water which was in the process of exploding into a thousand shards.

The burning in her throat became overwhelming. She gagged and choked and her stomach heaved. She vomited out a thick slurry of shiny, silver-streaked mucus. It splattered onto the floor beside her and froze, losing the power of its acceleration once it was no longer connected to her body.

She immediately felt better, as one often did after a powerful purge. She lay back on the bed, shaking as chills raced through her. Lungful after sweet lungful of air flowed through her body, giving her racing heart a chance to slow down. At last, she managed to control her perceptions and slow them back to the same speed as the rest of the universe. The pitcher beside her finished breaking and the pieces flew in all directions, making Harlan recoil. Minerva and March were both shouting in surprise and concern.

"I'm okay." Sally's chattering teeth belied her words, but she really did feel improved. It was like coming down off a tremendous runner's high, except . . .

She coughed and spat another silvery glob onto the floor.

"Guh. I'm sorry." She held up her hands and they shook and fluttered like leaves in a gale. "What happened?"

Harlan spread his nano-membrane between his hands and held it, looking at Sally through it as if it were an x-ray scanner. "It would appear your body has rejected the nanites I gave you earlier. I believe you suffered a severe allergic reaction." He brought his hands together, allowing the membrane to disappear back into his skin once more. "I had to give you a shot of epinephrine or you would have suffocated."

"Why now? The stuff has been in me for days." Sally tucked her hands beneath her armpits trying to warm them and stop them from shaking.

"I don't know. I'm not a doctor. Something changed. Maybe it has to do with your powers. Somehow, your body identified the nanites as a dangerous foreign substance and your immune system attacked them."

"She has a fever," said Minerva. "A bad one. I don't need my powers working at full strength to know that. You need to get her cooled off right away."

"There's a shower in m-my room. It's closest." March swung his legs off the bed. His face was drawn tight and his eyes were shadowed from exhaustion.

Minerva wobbled on her bed. "I don't think I can fly. I don't feel well. I need electrolytes and carbohydrates."

"March, get her something. And you'd best get something for yourself. You look about as terrible as she does." Harlan picked up Sally as if she were a baby. "I'll take care of Sally." He carried her easily in the lunar gravity out of the medical suite and down the hall.

Sally burped and spat out another gooey chunk of silver. "I'm sorry."

"I'll take care of it." Harlan stared straight ahead, woodenly, as if lowering his eyes to look at Sally might betray his fortress of equanimity.

The room door slid aside at his approach and he took her right into the bathroom and set her in the shower without removing her shift. An adjustment of the knob sent water sluicing down upon her in slow motion, soaking her thin garment with cool droplets. Her shivers became frantic, then passed to full-on vibration until the shower walls sang with sympathetic harmonies and the falling water took on a waveform appearance.

Harlan stepped back, as much to avoid Sally's quaking as anything else. "Stay there. I'll get you some medication."

Sally couldn't even have stood up. Her muscles tensed and relaxed thousands of times per minute. She couldn't remember ever feeling so terrible, which was significant considering all the insane trials she'd put her body through during her years with Just Cause. The real world was suddenly unbearable, the way it must be for a newborn fresh from the womb. Each droplet of cooling water was an icy needle poking into her skin. The light and the air were deadly assassins seeking to blind and suffocate. How could Minerva stand such hypersensitivity in her everyday life? Sally would have gladly died just to turn it all off.

Harlan returned a short eternity later with a plastic bottle of clear fluid and a syringe. Sally puked up one more globule of silver and it flowed down the drain. "This is electrolyte, and this is for your fever."

Sally tried to stop her hands from shaking enough to take the bottle and then held still while Harlan injected his concoction into her dripping arm. Her metabolism processed the medication in seconds and a moment later she stopped shuddering from the fever. She collapsed against the back of the shower. "C-c-cold . . ." Her teeth chattered as heat poured from her body.

Harlan reached in and turned up the temperature a couple of degrees. "You should feel better soon. I need to figure out what went wrong."

March burst into the bathroom. "How's she—oh!"

Sally realized his embarrassment at the same moment. Even though she was wearing the cotton shift in the shower, it had soaked and clung to her like a wet t-shirt. It was practically transparent, meaning he could see pretty much everything. With her skinny runner's body and ragged hair, she was willing to bet she looked more like a washed out meth head than a superhero.

But somehow, even though March was staring, she didn't mind his gaze so much.

Harlan turned back to look at his nephew. "She will be fine." His soft tone barely carried over the sound of the shower, but it contained enough implicit threat to make Sally shiver for an entirely different reason.

March fled.

Harlan turned back to Sally. "I see that you're improving. I'll bring you some clothes." He, too, left the bathroom.

Left alone at last, Sally felt she could let down her guard and allowed herself to cry. She'd failed, and that was hard for a perfectionist like her to take. Somehow, the Dream-world had bested her, in spite of help from March and Minerva. She hadn't completed the quest, hadn't rescued the princess from the tower.

But video games had save points, had 1-UPs for extra lives. Maybe this interruption was a save point for her. Maybe she could reload the game and try the next level again. There had to be a path to the Elephant Queen. She was too close to give up now.

"No," she said aloud. "I won't quit."

She drank the electrolyte Harlan had brought her. It tasted like salty-sweet lemon candy. It made her thirsty afterward, but she could almost feel it permeating her tissues, adding much-needed hydration and nutrients back to her body. Her appetite raged and her stomach growled. She could have matched Jason slice for slice in a pizza-eating contest.

Jason.

Thinking of him was like a punch in the face. It made her dizzy yet brought the entire world into sharp clarity. A wave of guilt assailed her as she remembered all the thoughts she'd had about March, how her body had responded to him in the Dream-world, how it had here in the Preserve. She wanted him. Lusted for him. But she had to stop, somehow. Physical separation would be best, but she needed March's help until she finished her mission to save Reggie.

She got out of the shower and pulled off the dripping cotton shift. Once she'd wrapped a towel around herself, she peeked her head out of the bathroom. She was in March's quarters for sure, because the room smelled like him even though the surroundings were otherwise sterile with no personal touches at all. Even the bed was made. A clean shift, briefs, and a folded jumpsuit sat at one corner of the bed, and some soft slippers on the floor beneath. She dried off her hair then dropped the towel beside the bed.

She glanced toward the door, making sure it was shut and she was alone in the room. Then she bent down and inhaled from his pillow. The scent was stronger, and it warmed her the way brilliant sunshine could on a cold morning. Her body responded in kind and she jumped back as if she'd just received an electric shock. Guilt wracked her and she dressed in hurried shame. The sooner she got out of March's room, away from him, the better.

She needed to call Jason, to hear his voice.

Unfortunately, she knew that was next to impossible. Even if Harlan had added cell phone repeater towers on the Moon—something she highly doubted, given his interest in total isolation—she knew it was almost a second and a half delay for communication signals between the Earth and the Moon. That would not only make conversation difficult and awkward, it might be enough to raise suspicions. Whatever else Sally might think about Harlan, she could respect his desire to stay away from the planet. As long as he was up here, focused on his projects, looking inwardly instead of outwardly, he might not think about living up to his *nom de guerre* of Destroyer back home. He might never destroy again.

She trotted out into the hall, the light gravity making her bouncier than she felt. She went back to the lounge and found Minerva and March there already, in the process of microwaving entrees. March turned to look at her and smiled and she nearly tripped over her own feet because of it. Only her parahuman reflexes allowed her to keep from face-planting. She staggered, caught herself, and pirouetted gracefully to safety in the lunar gravity.

"Are you all right?" asked March, aghast.

"She's fine." Minerva pushed a pair of pot pies toward Sally. "I expect you'd like these."

Sally smiled at her. "Yes, very much. But not just yet. Where's Harlan?"

"In the sleep lab. He's trying to figure out what went wrong before."

"How does it look?" Sally knew it didn't matter if Minerva knew nothing about the technology Harlan had built. She knew people, and if Harlan was having a real problem, he couldn't hide it from her no matter how hard he tried.

Minerva shook her head. "Not good."

"Shit." Sally turned and left the lounge.

When she found Harlan, he was leaning on a desk, an untouched cup of coffee cooling beside him, staring at a computer screen as he ran simulation after simulation. "Harlan?"

He didn't look away from his work to acknowledge her. Instead, he started another simulation. "After you've rested, I'll have March fly you and your friend back home."

"What? Why?"

"There's nothing more you can do here."

"No, I—"

He jumped to his feet and pounded a fist on the desk. "You failed!" At last, he turned his head to look at her, and Sally saw pure misery in his eyes. His voice dropped to a whisper. "And I failed."

Sally took a step toward him. He needed human contact—an embrace, a reassuring pat on the back. Something. But she knew the man would never accept such a thing. For just a moment, though, she was ready to throw away all her history with the man before her and offer him that embrace he needed. "We didn't fail. We were close. Do you understand? March and I, we made it to the Burning Sands. The Iron City is there. We just need to get to it. It's the last leg of the journey. We can do it. We can rescue the Elephant Queen. We just need to go back for a little bit longer."

Harlan shook his head and sank back into his seat. "What you're saying makes no sense to me, and even if it did, I won't risk you going back into the Dream-world without any protection. I can't keep you safe. I'm not even sure I can keep you alive."

Sally was about to ask him what did he care if she lived or died, but like a flashlight in the darkness, she suddenly understood that he did care. Maybe it wasn't the same kind of caring that she had for Jason, or for her friends and teammates, but he felt . . . responsible for her. When they'd met, years ago in Philadelphia, and she exchanged a favor in return for his technology to save the world, he'd said something to her. He'd said he was practically a father to her, a role model in the sense that he'd guided her life and choices through his actions as Destroyer. Somehow, Sally understood, he was worried about her like a parent worries about a child.

Destroyer cared about her.

It was almost enough to make her faint. She cleared her throat. "I want to stay. I want to see this through to the end. I believe you're doing the right thing here, and I . . . I'm proud of you for it. I want to be a part of that for you. I want you to see your sister again. Really see her. Speak with her. Tell her stories. Listen to her laugh. I want March to have his mom tell him she loves him. I can't do that from Earth. And I can't do it without you." She crossed the lab to stand beside him. She couldn't believe what she was about to say, but it was true. "I . . . I trust you."

He looked up at her. "You shouldn't. Not after everything I've done."

"No, I shouldn't. But today, I'm trusting you. I'll go back into the Dream-world. I'll do it without your nanites. I'll have Minerva and March to help me. I'll go find your sister and I'll bring her back to you. And if anything happens to me, I believe you'll save me. Like you did today." She hesitated a moment, then put her hand on his shoulder. She could almost feel his skin crawling beneath her fingers, but she kept her touch light, so he wouldn't feel too discomforted by it.

And then he reached up and took her hand—not in anger or fear, but in companionship. "All right."

NINETEEN

I don't have to answer that.

March raised his head from the sand. "Someone's coming."

Sally raised her own head. She didn't remember the journey into the Dream-world. Maybe she'd slept through it. Or maybe it was getting easier.

The approaching apparition wasn't Minerva as Sally had hoped. It was an honest-to-goodness sledge shaped like a teacup, floating across the sand on wide polished runners and pulled by fourteen deer, although they were no deer like Sally had ever seen before. They were all the size of a medium dog, with delicate legs and fangs hanging down from either side of their mouths. They arrived in a cloud of musk strong enough to make Sally's head spin. The sledge driver hauled back on the reins, shouting "Whoa!" at his team. They came to a halt and waited, stamping the sand, impatient at the delay in their headlong rush.

If the tusked deer were strange, they looked almost mundane in comparison to the sledge driver. Although Sally had come to expect humanoid animals in the Dream-world, it was still a shock to see a baboon sucking on a corncob pipe with a wide-brimmed straw hat perched at a jaunty angle on his head. He perched on a seat at the very front of the teacup sledge, while bundles and parcels were haphazardly stacked inside, with a cargo net tied down tight over everything to hold it in place.

The baboon took his time tying off his reins while he reached up with a prehensile foot to pull the corncob pipe from between his lips. He blew out a lungful of blue smoke and watched it drift away with satisfaction plastered across his dog-like muzzle. At last, he turned to regard Sally and March. "Ho, travelers. Yesyes."

"Uh, hello." Sally's lips were cracked and would probably have bled had her body not been jealously guarding every last bit of moisture.

The baboon stood up on the very edge of his seat. His long, kinked tail helped him balance as he swept his hat from his head and bowed deeply to Sally and March. "I am Papio, a simple merchant and trader in rare goods, yesyes. Who would you strangers be?"

"I'm Sally, and this is March." Sally's mouth was so dry she could barely summon enough spit to swallow and rehydrate her voice box. "We're looking for the Iron City. Do you know where it is?"

Papio put his hat back on, covering the tufted fur atop his head. "The Iron City. Yesyes. It is my destination, for I have a great cargo of rare tusks to spend there. Narwhal and walrus. Both very rare, very valuable in this part of the world, yesyes." His tiny eyes narrowed and he puffed on his pipe for a moment. "Perhaps you would like to acquire one, young lady. A narwhal tusk would set off your fur magnificently. Sir, perhaps you would like to purchase one for your lady-love, yesyes?"

"She's not . . . not . . . not . . ." March fell silent.

Sally tried to clear the persistent dryness from her throat but only succeeded in making herself even more hoarse. "Do you have any water?"

Papio puffed his pipe again, regarding the two cat-people with cool, simian detachment. "Why not? I have enough to share. Never let it be said that Papio would not help out someone in need. Yesyes." He reached beneath his perch and withdrew a battered canteen. A flip of his wrist and it spun through the air into Sally's hands.

She opened it right away and passed it to March.

He shook his head. "You first."

She wanted to argue. She was the superhero. She was supposed to sacrifice her comfort and safety to protect others. But she was so terribly thirsty. The water inside the canteen was flat, lukewarm, and somehow the most delicious thing she'd ever tasted. She made herself sip it, savoring every mouthful, only swallowing it when she couldn't stand it any longer. It was the longest drink she'd ever taken in her life, and somehow through the magic of the Dream-world, the container stayed roughly half-full. She handed the canteen to March. "Drink slowly. Too fast and it'll come right back up."

He nodded and raised the canteen to his lips.

Sally turned back to the baboon trader. "Thank you, Papio. That was a gracious gift."

Papio nodded. "Keep the canteen. I have more. Yesyes. And now I must depart."

"Wait!" cried Sally, the water giving her voice strength at last. "You said you're going to the Iron City. Will you take us there?"

Papio snorted through his long, dog-like snout. "Nono. My sledge is already full, and my team is straining at the weight as it is. You will have to find your own way there."

"We'll die if we d-don't go with him." March's voice was barely a whisper, but Sally heard him clear as day.

"Good luck, travelers." Papio gathered up his reins and whistled past his pipe at the fanged deer. They stopped their nosing around in the sand and leaped to attention, ready to be commanded.

"Wait!" Sally shouted again. "I invoke the Travelers' Questions Three!"

Papio nearly inhaled his entire corncob pipe at Sally's outburst. His face broke into an angry snarl, spread further apart in an aggressive yawn, and concluded with furious eyelid flapping.

All of it was to no avail, for he was bound by the rules of the ancient game once Sally had issued the challenge. His tantrum came to a sudden end and he narrowed his eyes at Sally. "I counter-invoke."

Sally gasped. "You can't do that!" She whirled and turned to March. "He can't do that . . . can—" She clamped her mouth shut as she realized she had nearly given away a question by asking it of March.

She would have to be more careful. She cleared her throat and thought carefully about her next statement. "We must take turns with our questions. Since I invoked first, I must be granted the right of the final question, so you must ask first."

Papio puffed his pipe. "Yesyes." He rolled the pipe around in his lips and then asked, "Why do you wish to go to the Iron City?"

"I must rescue a . . . friend, who has been imprisoned there by the Ticking Lord." Sally held her breath, waiting to see if her answer had been suitable enough. When Papio nodded, she'd already thought of her first. "Why are you lying to us about not being able to take us there?"

Papio rocked on his perch. "Oh, I didn't want you to ask me that, nono. I'm a merchant. I don't do anything if there isn't a percentage in it. If I don't show a profit, I starve, yesyes. You don't look like you've got anything worth anything to me."

Sally raised her prize, the hippo-man's broken tusk, to show it to Papio. "Look at this."

Papio tried to put on the affectation of being supremely bored, but Sally could see the avarice in his beady little eyes. "What is it?" His face fell as he realized he'd burned one of his questions on an inconsequential answer.

"It's a hippopotamus tusk." Sally smiled. "It was my prize for defeating him at the riverside. It's also a beacon that lights the way toward the Iron City. Is it an acceptable fee to you in return for a ride to the Iron City?"

A mighty struggle played out on Papio's face, but greed won out over fear. "Yesyes. Gimme." He held out his hand and Sally passed him the tusk. He sniffed it, sighted down its lines, and cupped his hands around the end to see the crimson glow. He giggled and cavorted around the sledge, toying with his new prize as Sally and March made themselves as comfortable as possible amid the baboon's parcels. At last his dancing subsided and he returned to his perch at the front of the sledge, dangling his lumpy ass over the edge.

"I think perhaps I will wait to ask my final question. Yesyes. If I am careful, I'll have a servant in you for a very long time, especially if you ask your final question first. I think you'll agree that is the best possible outcome in this case, yesyes." He whistled at the fanged deer. They quit nosing around the sand and tugged at the sledge, struggling to gain traction against the additional weight of the two cat-people. In the end, they succeeded in overcoming inertia and shortly, the sledge flew across the Burning Sands once more, kicking up a wave of ivory grains in its wake.

"You're not any better off if I don't ask my final question. You can't leave either." Sally sat back against a bundle of narwhal tusks, careful not to let any pierce her skin.

"I don't have to leave. I know where I'm going, yesyes."

Time passed as the sledge raced around dune after dune, traversing the valleys. Sally watched their guide as he controlled his team of deer, grumbling to himself, but the combination of heat, exhaustion, and dehydration was taking its toll. Her head lolled and more than once she jerked herself awake. Beside her, March had given in and passed out, his mouth open just enough to show his shockingly pink tongue amid his black fur. Sally noticed his hand was clutched in hers and smiled at the way things happened in the Dream-world without any conscious effort.

A sudden, heavy impact shook the rear of the sledge, dislodging a screaming Papio from his perch.

Sally experienced the unusual sensation of her fur standing on end much like a cat's. Papio rolled off the sledge and shrieked, "What is that thing?"

Sally turned to see a crimson crest arising from a dark feathered head and piercing yellow eyes. "It's Minerva, and you just used your last question, Papio."

Papio's eyes widened. "Oh! Oh damn!" He stomped all around the sledge, screaming incoherently, kicking sand, punching the air.

While she waited for the baboon's temper tantrum to subside, Sally trotted around the back of the sledge to embrace Minerva. "I missed you so much," she whispered in the owl-woman's ear hole. "Where were you?"

"Looking for you. It's a large desert." Minerva clacked her beak. "What's his problem?"

"He wasted a question on your arrival and now he's got nothing on me."

Minerva flapped her wings and hopped up to the very top of the sledge to perch like a gargoyle at the edge of a skyscraper.

Papio rounded on Sally and pointed the stump of his corncob pipe at her. He must have broken it or bitten through in his fury. "You cheated! I don't know how, but you cheated me!"

"I did nothing of the sort." Sally folded her arms. "You asked the question of your own accord. You have no hold on me any longer."

The baboon stomped in exasperation. "Ask your last question, yesyes. Ask it so I may leave."

"No. You agreed to take us to the Iron City. You accepted trade for it. You're obligated to follow through."

Papio's eyes narrowed. "Or what?"

"I don't have to answer that. I've already answered your three questions." Just the same, Sally wondered what exactly kept people from breaking the rules of the Travelers' Questions Three. It wasn't like there was a police authority going around arresting people who didn't follow the rules. Just the same, she'd felt no desire to cheat or lie when she'd played the game. Maybe it was the Dream-world itself that enforced the rules. She wondered what would happen to someone who attempted to circumvent those rules.

Papio clenched his fists. "It's not fair! None of this is fair, nono!"

"Life isn't fair, not even in the Dream-world." Sally boarded the sledge. "Now I believe you still owe me a journey to the Iron City. Let's hurry, please. I'd like to get there soon."

TWENTY

Wait for something to happen.

The sledge flew across the sands, carrying a cargo of tusks, two cat-people, and one angry baboon. Minerva flew overhead, escorting it, circling around to check for pursuit, for threats, or for any sign of their destination.

Every once in a while, Papio would glance back over his shoulder at Sally and March, his long snout wrinkled into a snarl. "Ask your final question."

The third time he did so, Sally snarled back at him, baring her sharp teeth at him. His grimace disappeared as he shut his mouth with a clack.

He didn't turn back a fourth time, although he did keep up a steady stream of barely-heard invectives, muttered under his breath.

The tireless deer continued their journey across the sands, cloven hooves flying in a rapid, muted tattoo like a snare drummer playing with foam mallets. Sally laid back against the cargo, snuggling against March, and watched Papio as he drove. Something about the baboon's method was disturbing her, but she couldn't quite figure out what it was. It wasn't anything overt that raised her suspicions. All he did was perch on his seat, the reins clutched in his long fingers. His pipe had broken during his tantrum so he could only hold a wad of tobacco in one distended cheek. Brown spittle stained the fur at the corner of his mouth as he spat over the side from time to time. The hippo tusk Sally had traded for a ride sat in a pouch behind his seat, nearly forgotten, and then she figured out what was bothering her.

The unchanging landscape had shown nothing but white-upon-white sand dunes for many hours, and yet Papio was guiding the sledge with all the confidence of someone who could follow a route with his eyes shut. Sally hadn't seen any kind of landmarks or path or any indication of the way to the Iron City. Her only hope would have been to use the hippo tusk to find it. Papio hadn't even bothered to look at it.

Either he knew where he was going, or he was lying to Sally about taking her there.

If he was lying, he had done so in full violation of the rules of the Travelers' Questions Three. She replayed the question she'd asked in her mind, as well as his answer, to see if she could remember anything that could be interpreted differently from her intent. No, she was quite sure she'd asked if the broken tusk was an acceptable trade for a ride to the Iron City and Papio had said yes. If he wasn't actually taking them there, he'd broken the rules and Sally figured there must be some kind of consequences.

Conversely, if he'd been truthful as the rules required, they were heading for the Iron City, which meant he knew how to get there when there were no obvious indicators. He was following some kind of path or beacon only he could see, and that made Sally very nervous.

Minerva dropped from the sky to perch on the edge of the sledge. Her talons dug in to keep her upright while the swaying sledge cruised down the side of a dune. "I just spotted the Iron City. It's not far."

Sally cleared the dust from her throat. "Papio, I'm not asking these questions of you, so you don't get to answer them."

Papio's grumbling rose in frequency and volume for a moment before subsiding to the ongoing dull roar.

"Are you sure that's what you see?" Sally asked. "It's real? Not a mirage?"

"Yes, I'm sure. It has the look of industry and metal and rust about it. It's not a mirage, and this sledge has been heading toward it since I first spotted it about an hour ago."

Sally was convinced. If Minerva said something was real, that was a better endorsement than if Sally had seen it with her own eyes. She squeezed March's hand. His eyes opened and he smiled at her. "Are we there yet?"

"Almost," said Sally. "Hey, Papio, I'm ready to ask you my final question."

Papio glanced back over his shoulder. "Good."

"Are you leading us into a trap?"

The surprised baboon spat out the remains of his corncob pipe into the flowing sand beneath the sledge's runners as he yanked on the reins, bringing the team to a halt. "Yes. I can't believe you would waste your final question on such a simple, yes-no question. You are without a doubt the stupidest person I have met in the world, yesyes. Now get off my sledge."

Sally didn't move. "No. You made a deal with me. You take me to the Iron City."

"That wasn't a deal. You tricked me."

"You took the tusk in payment. Are you saying you'd refund it to me?"

Papio reached behind his seat and lifted the hippo tusk, weighing it in his hand as if considering whether or not it held enough value for him to keep it.

While he took stock of his options, Sally turned to March. "I want you to go with Minerva."

"What? Wh-why?"

"Papio just confirmed he's leading us into a trap. I don't want you falling into it."

"But you're g-going to fa . . . fa . . ."

"With my eyes open, yes."

"Extra eyes are better." March opened his wide and Sally felt like she could dive into the cool green pools within them, which was an even better reason for them to separate. She was finding it more and more difficult to reconcile the feelings the Dream-world seemed to be encouraging with her feelings for Jason. It was growing more difficult for her to determine which were her own feelings and which were being implemented by whatever consciousness was guiding the Dream-world. Splitting up would be for the best.

"Yes, but in this case I want you with Minerva."

"Why?"

"Because we may have to rescue her." Minerva clacked her beak.

Sally pointed at Minerva, who had been as alert as ever. "Yes, exactly. We already know this is a trap. If I'm the only one who falls into it, I can count on the two of you to get me out of it."

March didn't look convinced, but he stepped off the sledge. "I g-guess."

Sally reached out and squeezed his hand. "I'm counting on you, March."

He managed a faint smile beneath his furry muzzle. "Okay. I trust you."

"Minerva, find someplace safe for you and March and wait."

"Wait for what?"

Sally shrugged. "Wait for something to happen."

Minerva nodded, the crimson feathers of her crest bobbing up and down.

"I'll see you guys soon enough." Sally turned to Papio. "All right, let's go spring this trap of yours."

"It is not my trap, nono." Nevertheless, Papio tightened his reins and clucked the fanged deer into motion once more. Sally looked back once and was amazed at how quickly they'd pulled away from her friends. Both were barely more than dark smudges against the gleaming white of the Burning Sands.

She turned her attention forward, eager to catch her first glimpse of the Iron City.

Before she ever saw any of the construction, a dark smudge appeared over the horizon, growing thicker and darker as the sledge drew closer. It reminded her of the pollution that hovered over New York City on miserable summer days without so much as a whisper of breeze. She caught a hint of soot and smoke in the air, like the perpetual Diesel fog hanging around a truck stop. Over the hiss of the sledge's runners on the sand and gentle thudding of the fanged deer hooves, she became aware of the gradual rhythms of machinery.

Then the sledge rounded a dune and the Iron City appeared before them like a ghostly apparition of rivets and rust.

The city was like something out of an acid-tripping steampunk fan's mind. Soaring walls of rusting iron arose from the sand as if they'd been there before the desert. Bolts the size of Sally's legs connected wall sections. Patch plates were held in place with rivets, and stood out as clean, dark spots amid the delicate patina of rust and pits that covered the older sections. As she looked up toward the summit of the walls, she saw they were capped not with parapets like some ancient stone castle, but by slowly-turning gears that must have been as big as houses. Beyond the walls, she could see smokestacks spewing flame and black smoke. A spiderweb of gantries spread between the stacks, supporting hundreds or thousands of wires sparkling with raw electricity. At what must have been the city center, a great tower reached into the sky, marring the azure expanse with its smog-enshrouded framework. Pipes wove in and out of its walls. Vents shot smoke or steam into the sky. Gears and shafts spun as machinery below the ground worked at some nefarious purpose. The subsonic vibrations made Sally's fur stand on end as the sledge came to a halt before a pair of gates as tall as the walls themselves.

Sally stared up at the top of the walls, having to lean back to do so. The construction was obviously designed to make people feel inferior when confronted by such grand scale, and it was working. Never had her mission seemed as hopeless as it did when she stood before the gates of the Iron City, wondering how she could possibly rescue the Elephant Queen from within those titanic walls. "I feel like I'm about to enter Mordor."

Papio bounded from his perch. "I've fulfilled my part of the bargain, yesyes. No more help from me." He pointed at Sally and shook his other fist in triumph.

"Whatever you say, Papio. I'm just waiting for you to spring your trap."

Sally turned to the gates and called, "Are you in there, Mister High-and-Mighty Ticking Lord? I'm here. Come and get me." She didn't know what kind of response she was expecting, but all she got was stony, metallic silence from the giant gates. After waiting for something—*anything*—to happen, she stamped one of her feet in frustration and turned back to look at Papio. "You're terrible at springing traps."

Papio paid her no attention. He had grabbed a bundle of his wares and scampered across the sand to a spot to one side of the colossal gates. As Sally watched, he slid open a hidden panel and pulled a lever. That released another panel from which emerged a wheel. After opening a second hidden panel, Papio entered a code onto an old-fashioned typewriter keypad within it. A loud *kachunk* came from behind the wall. Papio returned to the wheel and cranked it. It made a ratcheting sound that ended in a clank. Papio released the wheel and raised his bundle up over his head to display it to an armature that emerged from within the wall. The armature sparkled with numerous camera lenses in the sunlight. "Many wares, yesyes. Great value."

At first Sally thought the equivalent to ringing the gates' doorbell was unnecessarily complex, but then she realized without Minerva's help, she might have never figured out the combination. Even so, someone must have been behind all those cameras, and that person would still have the ultimate decision-making power.

The cameras turned away from Papio to regard her with their cold, glassy eyes. She'd expected something like that, but it was still sudden and made her jump. Any thoughts of brave words fled, leaving her tongue-tied. She felt like C-3PO outside of Jabba the Hutt's palace in *Return of the Jedi*, only not as eloquent.

The armature bearing the cameras withdrew back into the walls of the Iron City once more. Sally turned to Papio. "What does that mean? Are they going to let us in?"

Papio bounced back onto his sledge. "Yesyes. But from here you walk. No more riding Papio's sleigh, nono."

"Suit yourself."

The clanking sounds of machinery ramping up increased around the gates, echoing up and down the walls until Sally had to clap her hands over her ears. The sand shuddered around her feet like popcorn in hot oil as massive gears began to turn. The stench of industrial lubricants and coal fires blew out from vents around the gates, making Sally's stomach turn flip flops. With a grinding squeal, the gates shuddered, shaking loose a cloud of accumulated sand and dust.

The gates were deep, showing how thick the Iron City's walls were. Sally guessed they were a good thirty or forty feet thick and she wondered whether they were intended to keep people out or to keep them in. Instead of a solid floor, the gates had opened over an oil-streaked grate, punched with round holes. Heat and greasy moisture rose through those holes as Sally followed Papio's sledge through the opening in the walls. It felt like the inside of a fast food restaurant's kitchen with all the atomized oil and grease floating through the steaming air. After suffering so much dehydration in the Burning Sands, the application of moisture was a strange but welcome change in the air.

The space beyond the gate opened up into a bizarre steampunk and junkyard-chic world like the fevered imaginings of a hallucinating engineer. The road beyond the gate was paved not with asphalt or cobblestones, but with row after row of rusting license plates bolted to some surface underneath. Where another city might have a line of decorative trees on either side of the thoroughfare, the Iron City had strange sculptures made from the twisted wreckage of crushed automobiles. Their broken headlights shone with dim, flickering light like accusations against those who had wronged them. As she passed by one, Sally heard a starter grinding slowly, repeatedly, as it tried to engage an engine no longer capable of turning over. It gave her what her grandmother called the screaming heebie-jeebies.

A moment later, when another sculpture honked its horn at her, she just about jumped right out of her fur. The angry tone echoed up and down the block, picked up by other sculptures until she felt like she was in the middle of a New York traffic jam.

Sally and Papio weren't the only beings on the streets, either. The Iron City bustled with mechanical activity. Small carts and scooters whizzed to and fro, purely mechanical creations clanking and hissing as they went about their business. Overhead, other devices traversed the numerous electrical cables and steam pipes crisscrossing the sky, brachiating like mechanical monkeys. It was all an orchestrated ballet of gritty, homemade machinery.

At the center of the city, the great tower oversaw all. Now that she was inside the walls, Sally could see the huge clock face on the tower's side. It was unlike anything she'd ever seen, with six different hands traveling at different speeds and rotations, with more markings around the edge than she could count, or even recognize. The subsonic vibration she'd felt outside the walls was more pronounced inside, and within the vibration she felt a rhythm. "The Ticking Lord," she whispered.

A crane lunged downward and clamped itself around Papio's sledge, raising it up and away in the blink of an eye, leaving Papio's fanged deer to choke and strangle in their harnesses. They thrashed and kicked away the last moments of their lives. Sally only had time to gasp a single breath of shock before a dozen nasty-looking guns popped out from hatches in the ground to surround her in a ring of blackened lethality.

Sally raised her hands. Now, at least, she was getting somewhere.

TWENTY-ONE

Not another king in the entire world can say that.

Only moments after her surrender, machines rushed in to surround Sally. They burped black smoke into the sky while dribbling noxious chemicals from their underbellies. Each machine had four gimbal-mounted legs with a wheel at the end. Spinning gyroscopes hung in cages beneath them, keeping them upright as they lurched across the roads. Each bore a variety of weapons ranging from simple blades and crossbows to what Sally figured were railguns, humming with barely-contained electromagnetism. They had head-turrets with mismatched cameras to focus upon her. She could almost feel the malevolent force behind those camera eyes watching her every move. The rolling robots, if that's what they were, aimed their weapons at Sally with clear intent and began herding her down the street.

She went willingly. Sooner or later she knew she would have to confront the Ticking Lord, and then she could really get to work on rescuing the Elephant Queen. But first, she'd have to survive her journey across the Iron City. She kept her paces slow and measured, and kept her hands in plain sight of the machines. She'd come so far, and she didn't want her journey cut short at the last second by a skittish robot cutting her apart with ultrasonic electromagnetically-fired projectiles.

Overhead, the brachiating machines skittered and beeped as they swung limb-over-limb along their pipes and cables on whatever mysterious business kept them moving. Occasionally one would slip and crash to the license plate-tiled ground, often as not breaking apart into several pieces upon impact. Smaller machines, perhaps the equivalent of rodents, would creep out from piles of rubbish to pick at the remains, sometimes stealing pieces and dragging them back into their dark lairs.

As she was escorted through the Iron City, Sally began to develop a sense of the place's purpose. It was an organism of sorts, in the same way that any city could rightfully be called alive. This Dream-world city seemed to have the sole purpose of keeping time, and all aspects of the city's structures were devoted toward keeping the giant cogs and springs turning with the appropriate speed. When parts of the city-machine broke down, other parts immediately locked into place, rerouting what Sally was calling the flow of time. Perhaps the Iron City kept time for the entire Dream-world. If it stopped, maybe the Dream-world would vanish. If it did so, would Sally vanish with it? Would she be lost forever, a soul seeking a path home, perpetually denied? The idea gave her the shivers, and for the first time ever, she wished maybe she hadn't been quite such a science fiction buff.

A furry figure dropped from an overhead gantry, startling Sally enough to make her surrounding robotic guards skittish. Their weapons flailed around wildly for a moment as they assessed the newcomer's arrival. When everyone and everything realized it was only Papio the baboon, the guards righted themselves to aim at Sally once again.

"Got you," crowed Papio. "We got you. Oh my, yesyes. You will suffer greatly at the hands of the Ticking Lord, that is for certain, and I will be rewarded for sure. Yesyes."

"What are you doing here?" Sally asked. "I thought you were selling all your collected tusks."

Papio chittered a laugh. "You are a fool. Nobody cares about tusks. Not in this place. All that matters in here is machinery, yesyes. The Ticking Lord rules over all, and I am sure to be rewarded."

"Yeah, I just bet you get what's coming to you." Sally turned her attention away from the gleeful baboon to stare up at the great tower as the party approached it.

It was an even mix of careful architectural planning, naked girders and gantries spread out in intelligent ways, with crossbeams where they ought to be and everything held in place by multiple layers of rivets and welds. And then there was the junk. There wasn't a better way to describe it. Parts of the tower looked as if some giant had taken handfuls of wrecked cars from a salvage yard, crushed them into blocks, and stacked them like Lego bricks. As they drew closer, Sally realized the crushed cars were still alive in some twisted mechanical way. Headlamps flickered on and off in an unreadable machine-language code. Electric antennas would push out from the debris like the feelers of an insect, then withdraw. Occasionally a sad, muffled horn would blow a somber note. Once, a glove box popped open, discharging a handful of greasy, stained papers that blew away on the hot breeze that came from numerous exhaust vents.

Above it all, the great tower ticked like a clock. Each slow, thunderous clack was preceded by an orchestra of ratcheting gears and tightening springs until the cacophony made Sally wince and plug her ears. After the clock ticked, steam vented all around the tower, blasting sulfurous humidity up into the sky while gritty oil and lubricants dribbled down the tower sides to form a hydrocarbon sludge along its base.

A swaying platform held by four grease-sweating steel cables dropped from the thick fog above. Slippery green slime coated the platform, with tendrils dangling from the irregular holes rusted through the ancient metal. One of the three-wheeled machines nudged Sally until she stepped onto the platform. It creaked with the addition of her weight, and groaned when Papio bounced onto it, making it swing back and forth with his momentum. He giggled as Sally had to grab onto the greasy cables for support when the platform lurched into the air again. It rose past gears and gantries, past steam-belching pipes and exhaust vents, through stinking chemical rain spilling fat droplets of sulfur-yellow goo. At last, it came to rest against a narrow plank thrusting out from the side of the tower.

Papio stepped onto the plank and sauntered toward the irregular opening in the tower wall, enshrouded in shadow, reeking of decay and rust.

Sally hesitated, and one of the cables supporting the platform snapped. Unbalanced, it nearly pitched her over the side. She sprang for the plank just as another cable snapped to drop the platform like a trap door. Sally found herself dangling from the very edge of the plank, her feet swinging out over nothingness. She dug her claws into the plank's surface, struggling to keep from falling to her doom. The plank creaked and splintered under her claws and she knew she was losing her battle with gravity.

"Come on . . . you wanted . . . me here." If the Ticking Lord wanted to talk to her, he was going to have to give her a helping hand. He wouldn't bring her all this way simply to watch her fall to her death, would he?

The plank lurched as machinery started pulling it back into the side of the tower. Sally quit struggling to pull herself up and concentrated on keeping herself from falling instead. Once the plank got close enough, the tower wall itself would give her the traction she needed. Sure enough, when her toes touched the wall, she managed to use it to climb back onto the plank just as it retracted all the way into the side of the tower.

A wall of metal slid shut behind her, locking her inside the stinking fortress of the Ticking Lord. It took her eyes a few moments to adjust to the rusting darkness within. She focused on her other senses to get a feel for her surroundings. The air stank of sulfur and rot, rust and oil. It was hot and humid and left a metallic chemical taste permeating her mouth, like sucking on a penny. Machinery droned in the walls, beneath her feet, over her head. The massive ticking sound repeated at slow, regular intervals. Each time it did, the walls and floor would shake and tiny flakes of rust would fall from overhead like snow.

The scent of an animal brushed her nose and she knew Papio was nearby. "Thanks for nothing."

Papio chuckled, a furry shadow against a reddish glow down the corridor. "I get my reward anyway, yesyes."

Sally didn't reply. Her eyes had grown accustomed enough to the dim corridor she felt she could advance once more. The floor sloped downward, leading toward a room aglow with the flickering light of torches or candle flames. More of the acrid green slime coated the floor and Sally had to move carefully so she didn't take a tumble. The floor of the corridor seemed to be suspended within a tunnel, and she didn't know what kind of awfulness flowed beneath her and didn't want to find out.

At last, she and Papio emerged into what she could only call a throne room. It was broad and hemispherical, with gears turning in the walls and crankshafts dripping oil into troughs. The stink of propane filled the air as gas jets burned from nozzles to provide light. The air was smoky enough to make Sally's eyes water, but even so she was appalled at the apparition in the room's center. At first she thought it was some kind of giant pulsating slug with pipes ramming into it from the floor, but then she made out the puffy human arms operating levers, switches, and dials on control panels that hung from the ceiling or sprouted from the floor.

"My Lord, I have brought her as you asked, yesyes. I await my reward."

With a gesture, the control panels swung out of the way to reveal the Ticking Lord in all his biomechanical glory. No seamless melding of machine and man, he was everything that could have gone wrong. A cranking pump pushed black fluid through a tube into his body while another withdrew it into a centrifuge of some kind. His skin wasn't any color at all. Gray, brown, black, red—all fought to be seen in between the machines and devices protruding from his flesh. The stink of offal, decay, and never-washed flesh made Sally's guts twist and if she'd had anything in her stomach, she'd have vomited.

The Ticking Lord had Harlan Washington's face.

Sally shouldn't have been surprised, but it was still a shock to see a strangely youthful Destroyer staring back at her from yellow-encrusted eyes as a machine held his head upright. His lower jaw hung loose, like it was detached, and a tube entered his face beneath his jaw. A speaker beside him crackled to life.

"A reward . . ." Dust drifted from the speaker grille as a hoarse voice emerged from it.

"Yesyes, a reward! I tricked the lioness, I did, all by myself. Brought her here as your prize. And a choice pile of tusks to boot, yesyes. Reward me, my Lord, for I've done your bidding."

"Your reward, baboon."

An armature detached itself from the ceiling of the throne room to lower a leathery box lined with rivets. Papio's eyes gleamed with greed and he cavorted in place as the armature came to a halt before him. He grinned at Sally, showing off his fangs. "You see?" He turned back to the box, undid the latch, and opened it.

An explosion blew his head off.

Papio's furry body tumbled over backward, his shredded straw hat falling upon the throne room floor like chaff escaping from a harvester. His body came to a halt and one hand opened to spill out the remains of his corncob pipe.

It had been such a swift, brutal attack that Sally was at first inclined to feel sorry for the baboon, until she remembered he was selling her out for a handful of baubles. He was a figment of the dream anyway, so she turned away from his body as it drained the last of its blood into holes in the throne room floor.

"I do not . . . part with my wealth . . . easily." The Ticking Lord's rheumy eyes focused upon Sally.

Sally waved a hand at the rusting walls. "You call this wealth? This is a junkyard."

"That is what you see." The Ticking Lord's voice grew stronger, as if practice was improving his output. "Everything here, in this city, is mine. From this great tower down to the smallest machine, it belongs to me. I built it all. Not another king in the entire world can say that. This is not just my city. It is *me*." As if to demonstrate his absolute power, a swarm of tiny crawling devices emerged from the base of the throne. Each of them twisted and rolled like a mechanical sidewinder as they converged upon Papio's body. Like a group of leafcutter ants, they worked in concert to raise the dead baboon off the floor and carried the corpse to a floor vent. When it slid aside, they pushed Papio into the shaft below it.

When the operation was completed, Sally turned back to the Ticking Lord. "I was going to ask why you are in this dream, Harlan, but I don't think it's really you. I think you're just another aspect of this messed-up Dream-world. The goal of my entire journey has been to come here and rescue the Elephant Queen, and I see now that you must be her captor. You will release her to me now." Sally tried to put every ounce of whatever Jedi Mind Tricks she might possess in the Dream-world into her entreaty. All she needed was for Harlan—the Ticking Lord—to say yes, and then it would all be over. Reggie's mind would be freed. She would wake up from her coma. She could embrace, and be embraced by her son for the first time ever.

That was how it was *supposed* to work, but maybe nobody had explained that part to the Ticking Lord, who burst into laughter. His sides heaved, requiring leathery bellows to flex themselves to provide additional air, while greater quantities of fluids raced in and out of the pipes and hoses protruding from his flesh.

Sally felt her face grow hot beneath her fur.

Thick, yellow mucus leaked from the Ticking Lord's eyes and a tiny nozzle emerged from the side of the throne to spray them clean. The mucus rolled halfway down his face and stopped at a protruding pipe, where it began to dry into a dull crust.

"You are nothing, lioness. Nothing at all. I am the Ticking Lord and nothing happens in my kingdom without my say-so. You would have the temerity to issue me orders like I'm some simpering teenager? In my own throne room? Here is my decree. I consign you to my dungeon, where you will be fitted and implanted with machinery to become a soldier in the service of the Iron City."

Machines dropped from the ceiling like spiders descending upon lines of silk. They surrounded Sally and wrapped cables and chains around her arms. She struggled but more and more mechanical tentacles wrapped around her until she was nearly entombed. "I'll never fight for you, Washington. Never!"

Harlan Washington's terrifying last words echoed in her ears as the machines dragged her through a vent in the floor and into a shaft that dropped into a deep, dark hole. "I don't believe you."

Twenty-Two

Please, you have to wake up.

A machine wrapped a leathery bag over Sally's head, making it impossible for her to see and nearly impossible to breathe. She struggled against the myriad chains and cables wrapping her up but to no avail. They banged her off solid surfaces as twisted around and around until she had no idea which way was up. Her head glanced off something, only barely deflected by the bag, and she squealed as stars flashed in front of her eyes. She knew it was only a dream, but in the waking world, she had a bad history of concussions, and had been warned that if she didn't start taking better care of her noggin, she could kiss her career as a superhero goodbye. Jason had even gone so far as to make a tactful suggestion about updating her costume to include a helmet. Sally told him she couldn't run right in a helmet. She depended upon the feel and sound of the air around her when moving at super-speed as much as she did any other senses, and a helmet would degrade that sensory input.

Eventually, the banging became replaced by dragging, and Sally figured she was close to her final destination, wherever that might be. Without any pronouncement or preparation, the cables and chains whipped away from her, ripping out patches of her fur where it had twisted around them. The stark pain brought tears to her eyes and for a while, she hurt too much even to open them to look at her surroundings.

The sounds of departing machines dissipated, leaving Sally alone in the near silence. Besides her blood rushing in her ears, the only sound was a grating, nearly subsonic hum that set her teeth on edge. Somewhere else in the tower, if that's where she was, the ticking sound was barely audible. A rich, chemical odor assailed her face and she realized she was lying on a corroded metal grate slimy with a slick substance like old mineral oil.

She would have jumped up to get away from it, but she couldn't tell how high the ceiling above her was, so she got into a crouching position before slowly rising, her hands reaching out to feel the air around her. At last, her cat's eyes adjusted to the darkness and gray blobs resolved into shapes.

She was in what she could only describe as a jail cell. It seemed to be almost like every cell she'd ever seen in a movie. The room was roughly six feet by nine feet, with grease-sweating walls on three sides and bars on the fourth. A window high up on one wall showed the faintest glimmer of Moonlight, suggesting Sally would get a few minutes of sunlight daily in her incarceration.

Sunlight was nice, but she didn't plan to stay long enough to have that be all she had to look forward to on a daily basis.

The rest of the cell was empty. She didn't have a cot or a toilet, although she supposed she wouldn't need one in the Dream-world. Apparently she was supposed to curl up on the floor when she was ready to sleep. She wondered if her jailer would provide food and water to her, but again, she supposed she didn't really need it. The chemical moisture running down the walls seemed to come from the corner where walls met ceiling and drained into the grate that made up the floor. Although the metal of walls and floor was pitted and corroded, it didn't seem to be weak anywhere Sally tested it. The high window on the wall would have been difficult enough for her to reach with a dry wall beneath it, but the oily slime made the idea of climbing up to it an impossibility.

A door was built into the wall of bars, and she padded over to investigate it. The hinges were on the outside and well-protected from tampering with plates above, beneath, and beside. Sally had just moved to start examining the lock itself when she caught a whiff of something organic, something alive.

She jumped back from the bars, her fur standing on end and claws pushing free from her fingertips. A growl tried to force its way past her teeth but she held it back, knowing silence would be more useful a tool than intimidation. She opened her senses to her surroundings, trying to locate what she'd smelled.

Her ears picked it out first: a gentle, slow inhalation. With the following exhalation, she soon caught another hint of sour sleep breath. Someone was down in the dungeon with her. She wondered if it would be yet another hurdle in her challenge or if she had at last discovered the Elephant Queen. The breathing didn't sound as if it came from something particularly massive, so it was probably another test of some kind.

Pale, dusty light began to filter into the prison through the small window high on Sally's cell wall. She gave her eyes time to adjust and watched as the bars of her cell became visible, then the corridor beyond the cell, and finally another cell across from hers. What she first thought was a pile of rags thrown haphazardly into the corner of the far cell resolved into a small girl, huddled beneath a ratty blanket, asleep. The girl had something clutched tightly against her and the more Sally stared at it in the gray light, the more she was convinced it was a filthy stuffed elephant.

Could it be her, the Elephant Queen?

At first, Sally was furious at the Ticking Lord. What kind of monster would imprison a child in such conditions? But then she remembered it was all a dream. Maybe it would have made more sense for Sally to be angry with the tortured mind that had created such conditions within the Dream-world, but that would solve nothing. She made herself relax, pulled her claws back in, and moved forward until her face was pressed against the bars. "Hey, are you okay?"

The girl didn't move.

"Hey, wake up. Please, you have to wake up."

Sally's entreaty garnered no response. She stepped back from the bars, considering her options. She was going to operate on the assumption the young girl was indeed the Elephant Queen. Her mission all along had been to rescue the Elephant Queen from her imprisonment by the Ticking Lord, and this seemed to fit the bill precisely. Without any more specific direction, and not knowing whether or not the girl was in fact the Elephant Queen, Sally decided to proceed like she was. Nobody should have to stay locked up in conditions like the Ticking Lord's dungeon, whether a queen or just an innocent little girl.

She returned her attention to the lock of her cell. It had an oddly-shaped keyhole, and that made Sally think of something. She found the very first piece of tusk she'd acquired on her journey, from the elephant she'd failed to save. It still hung on its cord around her neck despite all the rough handling by the Ticking Lord's machines. She pulled it off and examined the ivory. She'd already used keys of ivory before when she freed Minerva from the volcano. Her claws and teeth were sharp and strong enough to carve up the ivory. All she needed was time.

The small rectangle of sunlight moved across the floor as the hours passed. Sally's world was reduced to the *skritch skritch* of her claws and teeth against the ivory tusk fragment. She was thirsty, hungry, and her hands shook from exhaustion. At last the light faded and the sky beyond the tiny window grew dark once more. She'd passed her first day as a prisoner of the

Ticking Lord. Not once had she been interrupted. No machine brought her food or water. Nobody even checked to see if she was still imprisoned. It was as if the world had forgotten about her.

Sally suspected that was a similar sentiment to the feelings deep in Reggie's mind. She, too, had been forgotten by the rest of the world. Sally glanced up from her work toward the young girl who hadn't moved once the entire day. The last vestiges of light vanished, leaving the cell block bathed in darkness once more. The only sound Sally heard was the gentle breath of her fellow prisoner. It was a soothing rhythm, relaxing enough for Sally to set the tusk she was carving in her lap and lean against the cell wall to wait for dawn. She wouldn't sleep; not while a prisoner in the Ticking Lord's tower. She had a sneaking suspicion if she did, she might not wake up again any time soon. Or ever. Instead, she did something that ran against every natural instinct she had as a speedster.

She waited.

Meditation was foreign to her, as she was used to figuring things out on the fly, using her parahuman abilities to process information much faster than a typical person. But now it seemed she had nothing but time, and the lioness form she'd taken in the Dream-world didn't think any faster than normal. She did have a lot to consider. Lionheart might very well be her father, and that meant she'd lived her entire life believing false information. That in turn meant her mother hadn't been quite as faithful as Sally would have liked to believe. Clearly she had a lot to discuss with her mother, whether or not the Dream-world version of Lionheart had been telling the truth. Now that she had time to really consider it Sally realized her mother had glossed over a lot of details about her years in Just Cause. Much of what she'd told Sally was echoed in official reports of the time. Sally hadn't even known Tornado had died from AIDS until John Stone had told her years later.

And then on top of it all, she had her feelings for March to consider. She was trying very hard to convince herself they weren't real, but a byproduct of her existence within Reggie's Dream-world as facilitated by March himself. If anything, those feelings might be a psychic echo of March's feelings for her. She had a lot easier time believing March had developed a crush upon her and that was causing ripples through the Dream-world. She'd have to put a stop to it once they all woke up. Cut it off at the source. Go back home to Jason.

Sally realized she could make out shapes in the darkness once more and glanced up toward the window. The sky beyond was a lighter gray than the surrounding shadows of the wall. Somehow she'd spent all night thinking. Or maybe the nights in this part of the Dream-world were much shorter. And yet, when she looked down at the tusk in her hands, she saw it was shaped like a key. She must have been working at it for a great many hours but she didn't remember spending any time on it at all. Her hands ached and she knew she'd been working hard. Maybe there was something to meditation after all. It might be worth looking into once she woke up.

She snorted softly in amusement. She was the leader of the world's premier team of superheroes. She was lucky if she had enough time to finish her morning cup of coffee before lunch most days. The only way she was going to pull off meditation would be to do it at super-speed, which kind of defeated the purpose.

The key in her hands represented as much of a question as anything she'd encountered so far in the Dream-world. Every choice she'd made had serious consequences, and everything seemed to revolve around the tusks. The last time she'd used ivory keys, they'd broken in the locks when she used them. Would this one do the same thing? She only had the one key, and she'd have to open two locks, hers and the young girl's. She thought about trying to wake the girl and tossing her the key, but even if she could wake her, which Sally doubted, all she might accomplish was to release the child into a hostile environment without anyone to protect her. That wouldn't count as a rescue in anyone's book, and it certainly wouldn't to Sally.

No, she had to free herself first. If the key broke upon opening the lock, Sally would have to figure out some different way to release the young girl. Whatever it took, she'd make it happen, or die trying, she thought with grim finality. She thrust her hand between the bars, twisting her wrist around to fit the key into the lock. Would it break when she turned it? Or would it even turn at all? She had shaped it based partly upon her wiggling a claw into the hole but mostly by instinct.

She jiggled the key a bit to see if it would slide all the way into the lock and after a bit of finagling, she heard it strike the back plate and she knew if nothing else, it fit. The next question was whether or not she had clawed it into a useful shape. She started turning it and inside the lock, she heard tumblers sliding around. The key handle cracked but it didn't break as she brought it all the way around. The latch clicked and the cell door swung open without any fanfare.

For a moment, Sally couldn't believe she'd actually managed to free herself, but then she clamped down upon that unproductive line of thought. She needed to stay focused, stay positive, and get the Elephant Queen out of the Ticking Lord's clutches.

She withdrew her key from the lock and padded across the corridor to the opposite cell door. Turning the key was much harder in the other lock, and just as the tumblers clicked, the handle broke off the key, leaving the rest jammed into the lock.

Sally didn't care. She'd accomplished that phased of her mission. She opened the door and went into the cell to hunker down beside the sleeping girl.

In the faint light, she could only see the most general details. The girl was far younger than Sally had thought. She might have been five or a very small six years old. Her hair was caught up into little rubber-banded puffballs and her face was buried against the filthy stuffed elephant. Sally gently pulled away the blanket and hissed to herself at the child's obvious malnutrition. She looked a lot like the kids in those late-night commercials begging people for a few dollars for clean water and food.

"Hey . . ." Sally scratched at the girl's back gently through the thin t-shirt she wore. "Hey, sweetie, are you okay?"

The girl rolled over, looking up at Sally with big, dark eyes. "I was s'eepin'."

"Do you want to get out of here?"

The girl sniffled a bit. "I want my momma."

Sally swallowed a lump in her throat. If this was Reggie, as she suspected, then her mother had been dead for more than thirty years. "Do you want to go home?"

The girl hugged her elephant tight. "Uh-huh."

Sally held out her hand. "Then come with me, kiddo. Let's take you home."

Twenty-Three

What is real?

"What's your name?" Sally asked the young girl.

The girl said nothing, only stared at Sally's fur with her dark eyes wide.

"It's okay, I promise. I'm not going to hurt you. I'm here to take you home."

"Momma said I ain't s'posed to talk to strangers."

Sally knelt before the girl. "My name's Sally, and I know I look kind of funny, but that's only here. The rest of the time I look just like a regular person."

"You look kinda like the cat that lived behind the trash cans in the alley, only he got hit by a car." The girl hugged her stuffed elephant.

Sally shivered. The innocent statement felt a little too on point for her liking. So many crushed cars had been built into the walls of the Ticking Lord's tower that it wouldn't have surprised her in the least were she to get hit by one. "Was that alley near where you lived?"

"Uh-huh."

"Would you like to go back there?"

"Uh-huh. I wanna see my momma."

Sally held out her hand as gently as she could. The girl seemed skittish, which Sally figured was wholly expected given her imprisonment. "I'll help you find her if you like."

The girl shrank back from Sally's offered hand, her arms still wrapped around her stuffed elephant.

"I like your elephant. What's his name?"

The girl looked down as if regarding her stuffed companion for the first time. "Babar."

"Like in the books?" At last, Sally had something she could relate to. She remembered those children's books fondly. Her oldest friend Juice had read them to her the way a father would read them to his daughter. "I loved those books. Is your Babar a king too?"

"No, he's just an elephant." The girl paused. "My name is Regina, Miss Sally Kitty. It's nice to meetchoo." She curtsied with all the grace of an ambassador meeting royalty.

Sally bowed back to Reggie. She knew she'd found the Elephant Queen at last. Now she needed to figure out how to complete her mission by rescuing her. The first hurdle had been the cell door. The next step was obvious as well. "Do you know how to get out of here?"

Reggie shook her head. "I was s'eepin."

"How long were you—never mind, Reggie. It's not important. What is important is that we get you to safety." Sally held out her hand again and this time, Reggie took it. The small girl's hand was cool in Sally's paw. It was rare for her to feel like a giant when all her teammates and most of the rest of the world towered over her, but Reggie barely reached up to her waist. "Come on, kiddo. Let's go this way." With only two directions to choose from, Sally figured they already had a fifty percent chance of getting the way out on the first try.

Unfortunately, after rounding the first corner in the corridor, they found a dead end with a yawning hole in the ceiling above them. Sally had a vague memory of falling while she was wrapped up in the cables and chains of the mechanical guardians. They must have cast her down to the dungeon through that hole. She supposed if they had to climb, they might find their way back up to the throne room where she could confront the Ticking Lord once more. She wasn't eager to face him again—at least, not on his own turf where he held all the power. Perhaps on neutral ground, she might have a chance against him and his machines. Within the tower, though? Not a chance.

"This is no good. Let's go the other way." Sally smiled down at Reggie who smiled back.

"Why ain't you the horse lady? I 'member the horse lady. You sound like she did, but you look like a kitty."

Sally gasped. Somehow in her dream state, the girl had connected Sally to her mother as Pony Girl. She almost knelt down beside the girl to ask whether or not Lionheart was her real father, but no, it was still a dream and she couldn't trust anything she learned while within it. "The, uh, the horse lady was—*is* my mom."

"Okay."

Sally wondered how much of the Dream-world was a construct of Reggie's, and how much influence she, Minerva, and March were having upon it. She led Reggie down the corridor to an apparent dead end consisting of crushed cars. "Oh come on," Sally grumbled. "There's got to be a way out. There's always a way out. Maybe we can find a garbage chute or ventilation shaft or something." She sighed. "There's always one in the movies." She began examining the corridor walls and ceiling.

Reggie pointed at the wall. "They's a door, Miss Kitty."

Sally turned around to look once more. There in the middle of the wall, amid the crushed automobile wreckage, was a sliding van door still on its tracks. She was certain it hadn't been there before when she first looked. "Did you put that there?"

Reggie shrugged. "I don't know."

The handle was stiff, but Sally got a good grip on it and pulled upward on it until it unlatched. The door slid along its tracks, letting in a blast of hot, smoky air and light brilliant enough to blind Sally. She winced and rubbed her eyes, trying to drive away the chartreuse and maroon spots floating in her vision. She hadn't expected a door to lead outside so soon. Dungeons were supposed to be deep underground, but this one was more like a fairytale, where the prisoners lived in a high tower. As Sally's vision cleared, she saw they were in an isolated tower at the opposite side of the Iron City. The Ticking Lord's tower rose from the depths of rust, wreathed in a sooty veil of smog, shaking the entire world with each tick of its giant clock. Their own tower was a tall, spindly affair, a precariously balanced stack of girders and pipes bound together by chains, cables, and naked welds. No chemicals or lubricants ran down the side of their tower, making Sally think it was really just an inert tower and not part of the intricate machinery of the city itself. She could see the Burning Sands beyond the city walls, so far below them. All she had to do was get Reggie down from the tower, escape the city, and hide in the desert until the Ticking Lord gave up looking for them both, and then . . . what?

"What am I supposed to do now?" Sally asked without expecting any kind of answer. "Do we just make it to the desert and then you wake up? Do I have to bring you somewhere? How do I wake you up in the real world?"

"What is real?" Reggie's voice was still a child's but her words carried the weight of an old woman. "It's as real in here as it is out there. An' in here, ain't nobody gonna hurt me."

"Reggie . . . Your brother is out there."

"He a monster. He done kilt a whole lot of people."

A lump rose in Sally's throat. How was she supposed to defend Harlan when the list of people he'd killed included several of her friends and both of the men who might be her father? "Yes, he has. But he sent me here to find you. To rescue you. He cares about you."

Reggie shook her head. "He don' care 'bout nobody but himself."

"That's not true. He brought you here. I mean here in the real world. It's a safe place where nobody can ever hurt you again. Everything he's done—all the bad things, I mean—he did so he could better help you. He even raised your son."

"I ain't got no son. I'm a little girl, Miss Kitty."

Sally sat on the rough metal floor beside Reggie so she could converse with the girl more easily. "You do have a son. His name is March and he cares about you too. He loves you very much. Without him, I wouldn't be here now."

Reggie said nothing but hugged her elephant tighter.

"More than anything, he wants to hear you say you love him."

"I can't do that. I don' even know who he is."

"You'll never get the chance if you don't wake up. Come on, Reggie. This is your Dream-world. Help me to help you. How do I get you out of here? Nobody told me the rules once I got this far."

"I don' know, Miss Kitty." Reggie drew her knees up to her chest, looking every bit the lost waif she was. "I been here a long time."

With a sudden feathery breeze, Minerva appeared in the doorway Sally had opened in the tower's wall. Her beak was open and she was panting like a dog in the stuffy heat. "There you are. I've been circling forever, trying to spot you."

Sally leaped up to embrace her friend. "You have no idea how happy I am to see you."

Minerva looked down at Reggie, who was staring up at the new arrival with wide-eyed apprehension. "Is this the Elephant Queen?"

Sally nodded. "This is her."

Minerva bowed low, sweeping one wing up and back while brushing the other against the floor. "Your Majesty. I got here as quickly as I could."

Reggie shrank back against Sally's legs and popped a thumb into her mouth.

"She's a little shy." Sally brushed her fingers across the girl's hair, gentle and tender, the way her own mother used to comfort her after a nightmare.

"I understand." Minerva clacked her beak. "I'm a friend of your friend, here. I'm here to help."

Reggie stared up at the owl-woman, still clutching her elephant tight.

Sally knelt down beside her. "Reggie, don't be afraid. She's my friend. She's here to help you too. She has wings, so she can fly you to a safe place far away from this tower, far away from the Ticking Lord."

Minerva lowered her voice. "I can't carry both of you. Not together."

"Take her. Right now. I mean it, Minerva. Get her out of here. Don't come back for me until she's safe."

"What if she wakes up while you're still trapped here?" Minerva touched Sally's arm with a wingtip. "I'm not certain you won't be trapped here forever. Even I don't really understand how all this works."

Sally nodded. When Minerva admitted she was in the dark, it meant there really wasn't any apparent solution to the problem. "We'll figure it out. We always do, right? But they could find out that we're not in our cells any moment, and then we're screwed."

"All right." Minerva bent down to look Reggie in the eyes. "Do you want to go flying with me?"

Reggie said nothing.

"Like Dumbo," said Sally. "You ever see Dumbo? The little flying elephant?"

"Uh-huh."

"You could be like him. The flying Elephant Queen." Sally squeezed Reggie's shoulder. "Are you scared?"

"Uh-huh."

"Don't be. This is a good thing. Babar needs clean, fresh water. Clean, fresh air. He can't get any of that here. Neither can you. Minerva will take you to a place where you will have both."

"Okay. Like Dumbo." Reggie stared into Minerva's eyes. "I ain't 'fraid of you now."

"Lift her up, onto my shoulders." Minerva turned her back to Sally. "I don't want to carry her in my talons." She looked back as Sally obliged. "I'll come back for you, I promise."

"Not until Reggie's safe. I mean it, Minerva."

"I know you do." Minerva walked to the edge of the hole and paused. "Any message you want me to give March?"

Sally's heart sank into her toes. She'd been suspecting things might go badly for her after Minerva left with Reggie, and now with Minerva's question, the owl-woman clearly thought the same thing. "Tell him . . . tell him I'll see him soon. Either in real life, or in his dreams."

"Will do. Hold on, Your Majesty." Minerva leaped from the doorway and spread her wings.

Reggie's squeal faded into the distance as Minerva tore across the Iron City, using the momentum of her initial fall to gain speed. She whipped around an isolated tower near the wall and dove beneath the grasping limb of a crane. In only a few seconds, the dark speck of her against the brilliance of the desert vanished as a wave of fresh outgassing from the ground vents sent plumes of sooty steam skyward.

"Well, I guess that's it. She's free. I can wake up now." Sally said it with all the unwavering faith she could muster. She'd completed her mission. She'd rescued the Elephant Queen from the Ticking Lord and any moment, the real Reggie would awaken from her coma and Sally would find herself on a gurney in Harlan Washington's Moonbase.

Any moment . . .

A sound behind her made her spin around, fearing the worst. She'd pictured one of the Ticking Lord's mechanical guards approaching with its weapons raised and pincers eagerly grasping. Instead, what came at her was a multi-tentacled behemoth out of a steampunk nightmare. Its body was a hissing metal barrel, churning with fuel and fire and sloshing with every movement. A dozen tentacles of cleverly-engineered interlocking plates and gears lashed at floor and walls, pulling at the bars of the recently-vacated cells as it flung itself toward Sally.

Any ideas Sally might have had at fighting vanished as the multi-limbed horror raced toward her. Her teeth and claws weren't going to make a dent in those tentacles. Flight seemed to be her best option, but without wings, she was going to have to climb for it. She raced to the hole in the wall. It was a long way down to the ground. One glance over her shoulder and she knew she had no choice. She jumped out, twisting as she fell, and caught the very lip of the doorway with her feet scrabbling for purchase against the tower's rough construction. She found a ledge a few feet down and swung down onto it just as the monster pushed through the hole in the tower wall. It clacked and hissed as it rearranged its limbs to thrust its way into open air.

Now that she was outside the tower, Sally could see it was made from stacked automobile wreckage. There were plenty of foot- and hand-holds, although so much rust decorated everything Sally didn't know what to trust. Unfortunately, the pursuing beast had no such concerns. Even though it was heavier than her, it could distribute its weight across a dozen limbs so that even if pieces of cars fell away to crash to the ground far below, it was in no danger of falling. It clanked after Sally, chasing her like a spider pursuing its next meal. She slipped and slid down wreck after wreck.

She accidentally grabbed onto a side mirror instead of car door and it snapped. Only by the grace of her cat-like reflexes was she able to grab the door frame with her other hand before plummeting to her death. She dangled over a yawning abyss for a moment, terrified to continue onward, afraid for her safety against the apparition behind and above her. A tentacle flailed at her and she yelped in fear and fell. Her toes slipped on the smooth body panel of a truck but her fingers caught hold of its Diesel exhaust stack. It creaked and bent but held. Her tumble had given her enough of a lead to take a moment to figure out her next move.

Down, of course.

If she could reach the ground in one piece, she thought she might have a chance. On the side of the tower, it was only a question of what would kill her first, the clanking mechanical demon chasing her or a slip and fall to her death.

As if she didn't have enough to worry about, crane derricks rose from the buildings below, pushing upward on great billows of steam with grasping claws hanging from the ends of their gantries. One of them, awkward in whatever means of control kept it moving, tore loose a piece of the tower. It slipped from the claw's grasp to crash down the side of the tower, banging as it fell as if insistent to stay connected to its foundation.

The spider-machine crawled down after her, bracing its tentacles against the rising crane gantries and lashing out with an occasional limb to try to snag her. She had lost all the ground she'd gained by falling earlier, and wasn't eager to reproduce the feat once again. She needed a change of tactics, and she turned away from the tower and sprang toward one of the crane gantries.

As the machine lunged after her, a crane swung around with its pincers open wide, attempting to grab her out of midair. The two collided in a tremendous crash of metal, burst hydraulics, and cloud of acrid steam. The spider-machine's shattered body tumbled down to the ground far below, leaving only one limb hopelessly entangled in the errant crane's cable. It swung to and fro as if whatever connection it had to its control had been severed.

Sally found descending the crane gantry to be much easier than crawling down the tower. The gantry had numerous handholds. Some were slick with mechanical perspiration, but even when she slipped from those, another was immediately below it. The crane around her quivered and shook. She hoped she was giving it fits about how to deal with the equivalent of an insect crawling down its spine.

She hoped she was making it itch.

A crash above her shivered the entire gantry and several steel girders rained down around her, narrowly missing her. Another crane, the only other within range, had sacrificed itself by beating its crossbeam against her crane's framework. Her crane creaked and groaned, its structural integrity ruined by the heavy impact. Rivets popped loose and ricocheted around Sally like bullets. One caught her up high, taking a chunk out of one of her ears. Crimson blood streamed through her white-and-black fur.

The shock made her miss a step and her foot slipped off an oily crossbeam. She misjudged when she tried to catch herself as she fell and snagged her wrist in a spot where two beams came together. In real life, such an incident might have torn her entire hand away, or at least dislocated her shoulder. In the Dream-world, it hurt as much as either of those things might have, but without any permanent damage beyond entrapping her in the gantry. She cried out at the pain and indignity of being caught so easily. She hung at such an angle where she couldn't get any leverage to pull herself up her own arm to free herself.

Something buzzed past her head like a giant mosquito. She glanced around, struggling to breathe as her own body weight pulled against her lungs. A creation reminiscent of a mechanical wasp the size of a softball hovered nearby. It even had a stinger, a hypodermic needle filled with who-knows-what, angled toward her as it approached. She swung at it and knocked it out of the sky as if she were King Kong taking on the airplanes.

Two more of the robot wasps rose from a building near the crane base. Then two more. In a moment, an entire fleet of the droning creatures floated near her just out of her reach. "You can stick me with those, but I swear I will take more than one of you with me if you do." She gasped for air but it felt like her arm was being slowly torn away from her shoulder.

Nevertheless, the first wasp that dove toward her got smashed into the gantry. The second buzzed in impotent fury as Sally lashed out and grabbed it just below its hypodermic stinger. Its mechanical wings beat the air in a frantic attempt to escape but instead she hurled it into a third.

The fourth one came at her fast, aiming for her face. She got her hand up in front of it just in time. The hypodermic needle punched right through her palm, emerged from the back of her hand, and deposited its chemical load down her arm instead of into her bloodstream. It hurt more than anything she'd ever experienced and yet it was one more second she'd remained alive and fighting instead of giving in to the inevitable; one more second Minerva had to get Reggie further away. "Come on . . . best you got?"

Something sharp poked her in the back, and another in the side. A third got her right in the back of her thigh.

She wanted to say something heroic, like an action movie hero, but instead the darkness took her.

TWENTY-FOUR

It's an old game, older than you or me.

Sally first became aware of bright white light filtering through her closed eyelids. She cracked them open but the brilliance blinded her and made tears stream down her cheeks. She realized she was lying on a surface on her back. The muzziness in her head made her think she was back on the Moon once again, slowly waking up from a long dream. "Did it work?" she asked through lips that felt thick and numb. She wanted to raise her hands up to wipe her eyes but her arms wouldn't move.

"Not hardly." The voice sounded like Harlan's but had a dry, mechanical quality to it. The brilliant lights turned down and Sally turned her head to look at her surroundings. She was in what could only be described as a surgical suite, although one more suited to a nightmare. Brown spatters and stains decorated the peeling walls. Rusty machines of unknown purpose, dripping with lubricant and hydraulic fluids, were bolted all around the walls and ceilings. Some of them sprouted implements that looked more appropriate for a torture chamber than a surgical suite. Others bubbled and hissed, pumping a cocktail of fluids through a yellowed plastic tube into Sally's arm. She realized she was strapped down to a gurney with stained leather belts tight over her wrists, waist, shoulders, and ankles. It wouldn't have mattered if she hadn't been restrained, for her entire body below her neck was numb and lifeless.

The figure who'd spoken came into view, and she knew at last she was once again a captive of the Ticking Lord. He was wrapped up in bilious green scrubs, fraying at the edges and stained down the front. They barely covered his bulk, and tubes and hoses emerged from beneath them to plug into ports on the walls and ceiling. No surgical mask covered his broad, greasy face, nor were his grimy hands protected by gloves. Decades of filth coated his skin, turning the underside of his fingernails black. He rubbed his face and licked his lips in anticipation of whatever atrocity he was preparing to inflict upon Sally. He lowered his hand and brushed Sally's fur back from her forehead. She couldn't shrink away from his touch and her skin felt like it was crawling with pestilence when he withdrew.

"You will become my general." His voice was soft, as if speaking to a lover. "Leading my armies across the face of this world until all of it has been reclaimed and made over in my image."

Sally spat at him. "Better people than you have tried to do that. They're dead now."

"By your hand, I suppose?"

"As a matter of fact, yes." She struggled against her bonds but the leather straps held her tight. "Cut me loose and I'll show you exactly how I did it."

The Ticking Lord laughed, carefree, like a child. "I don't think so." He turned away to retrieve something from a nearby table and Sally twisted her hands around. It was painful, but she could just reach the straps over her wrists with claws on her fingertips. She began carving away at them, trying to weaken the leather enough to tear herself free.

"I'll never fight for you."

The Ticking Lord turned back bearing an unholy combination of chainsaw and angle grinder in his sweaty hands. "Better people than you have said that."

"They're all dead now?"

"Hardly. The machines you see in my lands are all people who've come here before you. Every one of them has been . . . upgraded. Rebuilt into my troops, my servants."

"You're a monster and a murderer."

"I don't take their lives. I improve them. I give them immortality." He flicked a switch and the grinder coughed to life, belching black smoke into the air of the operating theater and dripping lubricants onto the floor. "Unlike you."

Sally couldn't take her eyes from the spinning blade as it lowered toward her. "I . . . *I invoke the Travelers' Questions Three!*" she shouted over the whine of the motor.

The grinder's motor died and the Ticking Lord looked down at her in surprise, as if she'd violated some unwritten rule. "I don't accept."

"You have to accept!"

"I do not."

Sally picked at her bonds faster. She didn't know how much time she'd buy herself with this distraction. "I didn't make the rules. It's an old game, older than you or me. You're the king here, you have to enforce the rules."

The Ticking Lord blinked, squeezing grease from the wrinkles of his crows' feet. "What kind of nonsense is that?"

"If you don't enforce the rules, then your word no longer carries any weight. Your kingdom will dissolve. You'll lose all your power. Do you really want that to happen?" Sally kept scratching, feeling tiny pieces of leather give way with each pick of her claws. As long as she kept the Ticking Lord talking, he wouldn't see her working at her bonds. She had no idea if she was honest in her assessment of what would happen should he refuse to play the game, but maybe if she believed in it hard enough, she might *Jedi mind-trick* it enough to make it come true.

His eyes narrowed and he rubbed his chin in consternation, smearing the remains of some ancient spill. "No," he said at last. "I will play your silly little game, and then I will transform you into a machine for me. Something fast, as befits your personality." He smiled, showing his rotten teeth. "Something without any skin."

"I'm ready to ask my first question." Sally felt more leather parting beneath her claws.

"Of course."

"Why did you imprison the Elephant Queen?"

The Ticking Lord looked at the power tool he held with an almost loving tenderness, perhaps contemplating the damage it could do to Sally's flesh. "For her protection. The world, you see, is a dangerous place, full of dangerous people who will harm a young girl for no reason more than it gives them a thrill. Keeping her safe has always been my top priority, and there is no safer place than here, in my tower, in my dungeon."

"Couldn't be that safe. I got her out in like a couple of hours."

"Nobody has ever tried before."

"Then you couldn't really know how safe it was. Looks like it was *not very*."

"I'll get her back. I'll put her into an ever safer, more secure location. Nobody will ever find her again, no matter how hard they try."

"See, that's where you're wrong." Sally heard a tiny creak and felt the pressure on one wrist immediately release. She knew she'd freed one hand. She made herself cough to cover up the sound. "Locking someone inside a fortress isn't how you keep them safe. That's how you keep them prisoner. You weren't protecting her, Ticky, you were holding her hostage." Sally grinned, showing her teeth. "But then, none of this is real, anyway. Do you understand that?"

"Understand what?"

Sally chuckled to cover the sound of her claws scritching against her other wrist restraint. "You're answering a question with another question. That's poor form and against the spirit of the rules, but maybe you really don't know the truth, so I'm going to enlighten you, Ticky. You're a construct existing only in the mind of a comatose patient. This tower, the Iron City, the desert in which it lies, and for that matter the entire world is nothing more than a dream. You're a jumble of random electrical activity in the subconscious level. All this only exists because many years ago a young woman named Reggie Washington was gang-raped and beaten into a coma. This Dream-world is a creation of her mind. You. Are. Not. Real."

"No! That's not true!"

Sally laughed again, her humor genuine. "At this point, I should say something like *search your feelings*, but I'm pretty damn sure you don't have any. You're a defense mechanism. You exist solely as a means to keep Reggie from seeing her family, her loved ones. She has a son, Ticky. A beautiful, tall son with skin like melted dark chocolate . . ." She paused, realizing she was going off the rails. "And, uh, she has never once held him in her arms. Or told him she loved him. Her entire pregnancy happened during her coma."

"A son . . ."

"She's got a brother, too. He's a—" How could she say Harlan was a good man, knowing the things he'd done?

How could she not?

She smiled. "He's got his heart in the right place. Everything he's done for many years has been to try to help Reggie, to bring her back, to wake her up. He cares about her the way very few people could ever lay claim to, or even understand. I get it, though. I see what drives people to do terrible things when it will save a billion lives. I've done those things, and I will do them again in my life, because I'm a goddamn superhero and that's what I do." She swallowed against a sudden lump in her throat. "And sometimes you have to do something terrible to save just one life, and it's worth it because it's a life that is beautiful and unique and there's not another thing like it anywhere in the universe or the Dream-world or anywhere else."

The Ticking Lord took a step back from the table, his greasy face twisted up in alarm. The grinder saw fell to the floor with a clatter. His mouth worked like he was trying to come up with something to add to the discussion but words seemed to have evaded him.

"The Elephant Queen isn't here any longer. I freed her. I don't know when Minerva will get her to wake up, but I'm sure it's coming soon. Once she's awake, I kind of don't think this place will exist any longer. Your purpose is no longer valid. And don't worry about Reggie. She'll have people to care for her when she awakens. People who love her. Family." Sally's voice grew hard. "She won't need you to protect her any longer, if you could even call holding her prisoner *protection*."

The Ticking Lord picked up his tool, grunting and straining as he bent to retrieve it. Oily black sweat oozed from his pores to darken his face. "I grow tired of this charade. Let us be done with it. Ask your third question so I am free of this idiotic game."

Sally grinned a predator's smile at him, all sharp teeth and slitted eyes. "What do you think I will ask?"

The Ticking Lord spluttered in disbelief. "Why, you'll . . . that is . . . you could say . . . I . . ."

"Hundreds. Thousands. Millions upon millions of possibilities." Sally pulled her arms free of the shredded straps and loosened the one around her waist. "And you have to consider each one as possibly the truth, because you yourself agreed to the rules of the game." She removed the belt over her shoulders and sat up. "You can't answer this one, because you have to tell the truth, and the truth is you don't know what I will ask, only what you think. And right now, questions you think I might ask are running through your head. Millions of them. But the one I'm going to ask is, *is it getting hot in here?*"

Even as she said it, Sally saw tendrils of smoke or steam rising from the Ticking Lord's scalp as his brain overheated, trying to deal with the infinite possibilities

Sally had described. His eyes glazed over until tears of shame ran unabated down his filthy cheeks, only to flash into steam before dripping off his chin. One of the hoses connecting him to the wall burst, spraying black goo all across the wall. A high-pitched whistle rent the air and a steam valve split apart with a cry like an Independence Day rocket.

The enormous clock of which the Ticking Lord's tower was an integral part skipped a beat. Sally had grown so used to the rhythm in the background that when it missed, it nearly jarred her off the table. With a creaking groan, a crack appeared in one wall from floor to ceiling and beyond it, something broke loose and fell with a distant crash. The Ticking Lord collapsed into full-on convulsions. Blue electricity arced across his torso and hydraulic cylinders burst in sequence, spraying scalding fluid the color of motor oil across the walls. Sally ducked to the floor to avoid one such spray and nearly sliced open her foot from toes to heel on the chainsaw grinder so recently wielded by her foe.

She wondered for a brief moment if she ought to try to help the Ticking Lord somehow, but one look at him suggested he was already beyond any assistance she might render. What of his skin remained outside all his integral appliances was blackening and curling up like paper, and so much heat radiated from his corpse that he smelled like he might catch fire any moment. She turned her attention instead to finding a way out of the operating theater.

The floor canted suddenly, sending all the spilled fluids and loose objects splashing and clattering into one corner. Sally hissed and dug her claws into the floor. She'd been in a high-rise before during a severe windstorm, and the building's swaying had unnerved her then. Now, with the Ticking Lord's tower leaning like a more famous tower in Italy, all Sally could think about was how to get to the ground without dying in the process.

Another crack appeared in the wall on the uphill slope as the floor shifted further and Sally crawled for it. Behind her, one of the crushed cars that made up the wall broke loose and fell away from the side of the tower. A second followed after it, then a third. The table upon which she'd been so recently tied went out the hole, followed by the smoldering remains of the Ticking Lord. Sally reached the split in the wall and squeezed herself through it into the corridor beyond, leaving behind several hunks of fur and bloodstains on sharp edges.

She recognized where she was: the corridor outside the Ticking Lord's throne room. She recalled the trap door in the floor down which Papio had been flung. Maybe it was a garbage chute, or maybe it led to an incinerator.

Or maybe it was a way out.

The tower twisted and swung, making Sally wonder how much further it could tilt before gravity snagged it and pulled it down into ruin. The crash of pieces falling away was more or less a constant reminder of how fragile the Ticking Lord's empire had been. She hurried up the corridor, canted so much she had to divide her path between floor and wall, and forced her way through the poorly-sealed door.

As she stepped into the throne room, a tremendous rending and tearing squeal of overstressed metal made her jam her fists into her ears. The top of the tower tipped and fell, snapping pipes and cables in its descent and opening the throne room to the sky, which had gone the color of rust with all the particles and smoke flying into the air. Lightning flashed above, painting everything bone-white for a moment before it vanished in a roar of thunder. Wind whipped all around the crumbling throne room and the tower swayed, tilting further and further until Sally realized it was going over.

She scrambled up the canted floor to the gaping hole left behind by the top of the tower when it broke away. She climbed the broken pipes and shifting automobile wrecks and found herself staring down the steep slope of the tower. It should have been perfectly vertical but as she saw it, she thought she might be able to run down it if she was fast enough and kept her balance.

"You were fast enough once," she muttered as she pulled herself onto the angled side of the tower. It was falling in slow motion, or perhaps time itself was no longer functioning properly with the destruction of the clock within the Iron City. "Run, Sally!"

She ran.

The tower collapsed behind her, as if her very footsteps were the agents of destruction. She ran faster, and faster, until the side of the tower was a blur beneath her feet. A gap appeared in the surface before her and she leaped, arms and legs pinwheeling like an Olympic long-jumper. She flew over the hole, rolled as she hit like a parkour enthusiast, and came up running at full speed. The tower began to twist as it fell and Sally realized she had to get off the tower so she could get clear before it dumped her over and then collapsed atop her. She saw a low outbuilding adjacent to the tower that hadn't yet fallen and jumped for it before she could risk second-guessing herself.

She flashed over open space for a moment before hitting the rooftop of the outbuilding. It began to collapse behind her even as she ran. It was like being in a video game, she thought as she tried to outrun the destruction. The tower finally crashed to the ground, sending a massive, choking cloud of dust racing outward. It blew across Sally, filling her eyes and lungs with the detritus of the Ticking Lord's tower. She gasped and coughed, blinded, and her forward momentum carried her right out into open air beyond the outbuilding.

Her flailing arms caught a horizontal pipe and she locked her fingers around it, not knowing how far above the ground she was. The pipe snapped and swung her around in an arc toward another building, like she was a fly and it was the windshield of an onrushing truck. She spotted a hanging cable and grabbed onto it just before the pipe smashed into the building. The cable broke loose from one mooring and she rode it down like a rope swing.

The ground rushed up toward her. With timing borne of instincts, she released the cable and clenched herself into as tight a ball as possible. She hit the metal cobbles hard, feeling bones crack with the first impact and fur and skin peel away as she bounced and rolled. At last, she struck something solid enough not to bounce away and came to a halt.

Lightning flashed all around her again, and the thunder felt like a dagger through her heart. She got to her feet, shaking from the collision with the ground, shaking from everything else around her falling to the ground. Overhead, the very sky seemed to be cracking apart and falling.

The Dream-world was ending at last, and she had a front-row seat.

Something had happened. Either Reggie had awakened from her coma, or she'd died. Whatever the cause, Sally knew she had to escape, somehow. She had to run, like she'd spent her entire life running, but when she started to take a step, she realized her foot had slipped between loose metal paving stones and she was stuck. For a moment she entertained the idea of cutting off her own foot and hobbling away, but the entire city itself was sinking. The white grains of the Burning Sands poured into the rusty Iron City, washing away the brown stink with clean purity. A wave of white sand splashed around a corner like a tsunami and rushed toward Sally, growing taller and taller until it blotted out everything else.

She closed her eyes and it crashed down upon her.

Twenty-Five

Forgiveness is not ever a debt owed. It's a gift given freely.

Lightning burst across Sally's eyes and air rushed back into her lungs like it had been long absent. She coughed and struggled against something unseen holding her down. Brightness above her like the Burning Sands at noon blinded her to all else.

A cooling hand rested itself across her forehead and a distant, familiar voice whispered "Hush, be still," to her. The tone brooked no disobedience and Sally forced herself to calm down. Her skin felt strangely denuded and as she coughed again, she raised a hand to cover her mouth out of habit and saw not white fur but pale skin.

She tried to speak but her mouth was dry as the Burning Sands. "Water," she croaked.

A tube slipped between her lips and she pulled a few soothing drops into her mouth, letting the moisture bathe her parched flesh.

"Gently. Sip slowly." The voice came from a shadow beside her, and Sally realized she was lying on a soft pad on a table, fundamentally different from the Ticking Lord's operating theater in that she was now in a place of healing instead of harming.

Her vision was still blurry, but there was no mistaking the mass of black ringlets atop the head of her companion. "Minerva?"

Sally couldn't see it, but she heard the rare smile in Minerva's voice. "Yes. Welcome back to the land of the living."

"Did it work? Did we free Reggie?"

"Yes. We'll talk more about that later, when you're feeling better." Minerva brushed her hand across Sally's forehead again and her touch was as healing as anything Sally had ever felt. "How do you feel?"

"Like ten pounds of shit in a five-pound bag." Sally sipped more water from the straw beside her. "My grandma used to say that. It always made me laugh. Why do I feel like this? Side effect of all the chemicals Washington used on me?"

"Not the chemicals he used before, to put you into Reggie's dream." Minerva sounded a little troubled and Sally concentrated upon her vision, trying to will her eyes to find a focal point. "The chemicals he used to revive you."

Land of the living, Minerva had said before. *Revive.* "Oh, shit. Was I dead?"

Minerva placed her hands on either side of Sally's head, concentrating her powers until Sally's vision cleared. "Yes."

Sally grabbed onto Minerva's wrists, not to interrupt her healing but to convey how important it was for her to know the truth. "What happened, Minerva?"

Minerva took Sally's hands in hers. "Reggie came out of her coma. We saw it on the monitors first by the change in her brain activity. The moment she did, March lost his connection with you. It was like you were trapped inside Reggie's mind. He tried to find you. He got very angry at Harlan, who wouldn't risk putting him back under again."

Sally sniffed. "So Washington was going to let me die there."

"No. He fought for you with an intensity I have rarely seen. He ran from one machine to the next, bending them to his will, making them battle for you.

He asked if you were to die whether I could bring you back or not."

"Could you have?"

"I don't know. I don't think so, though. I can cultivate life if there's the tiniest spark of it. I can bring someone back from the brink of death if I have enough time to do so. I've never been able to bring life back to the dead. It's beyond my reach."

"So he brought me back?"

"Eventually. First we had to let you die."

Sally blinked. "Excuse me?"

"It was my idea. If you are angry, direct it at me, not at Harlan. I felt that death might be the key to returning your mind back to its proper state. Kind of like a hard reboot when a computer is being glitchy." Minerva smiled again. "My sweet Ment would approve of that metaphor. Harlan argued with me. He had fought so hard to keep you alive when your body was failing because your mind was gone."

Sally couldn't wrap her mind around the idea that Harlan Washington, the man who'd been the greatest nemesis of her entire life, had been unwilling to give up on her in his moment of clear victory and success. "Arguing with you doesn't usually go well for whoever's trying it."

"No, it doesn't. I convinced him and March."

"March didn't want to let me die either?"

"No. His feelings for you are quite clear."

"Oh." Sally's own feelings were in turmoil, and her attraction to March seemed to have survived beyond the realm of the Dream-world. The idea of him fighting for her life, like some kind of modern techno-knight, held strong appeal for her. She tried to quash those feelings and fixed in her mind an image of her husband's face instead. "So you all just let me die."

"Yes. And then, Harlan used his machines and chemicals to restart your heart and bring you back to life."

Sally glanced around the room. Neither Harlan nor March was anywhere to be seen. "I guess I owe him thanks. But I don't think I owe him forgiveness."

"Forgiveness is not ever a debt owed. It's a gift given freely." Minerva brushed a soothing hand across Sally's forehead. "Are you starting to feel better?"

To Sally's surprise, she was. Perhaps the parahuman abilities that granted her super-speed and rapid healing extended to faster recuperation from being dead. She hoped she'd never have the opportunity to test it again, though. She sat up and swung her legs down off the table. A wave of dizziness washed over her and she had to clutch at Minerva for support.

"Easy does it, Sally." Minerva took Sally's head in her hands and the dizziness plaguing her vanished like smoke in a breeze. "I can only do so much. Don't hurt yourself worse by rushing it."

Sally coughed. "Rushing it is what I do best." She slid off the table and balanced herself on the floor, waiting to see if her dizziness would grow worse or subside. It felt like she'd been concussed. "Where are Harlan and March?"

"Not far away. They're with Reggie."

"I want to see her."

"Of course."

Minerva offered her arm and floated a couple inches off the floor so the gait of her longer legs wouldn't make Sally sway unnecessarily. Sally realized she was still wearing a sweat-stained singlet and briefs. "Christ, I look like a shorter, blonder Ripley."

"Who's that?"

"Really? You haven't seen *Alien*?"

Minerva smiled. "I must have missed it."

"Add it to the list of stuff we have to watch together." She looked around. "You think you could find me a robe or something a little less . . . revealing?" The cool air was making her nipples poke out against her tank top and she wasn't prepared to have March stare at them.

Minerva pulled a lab coat from a peg near the door and wrapped it around Sally. It had a strong, masculine scent about it that she found strangely comforting, like wearing one of Jason's sweatshirts on her days off. With Minerva helping her keep her balance, Sally emerged from the chamber into the hall beyond, where she found March leaning against the wall. He looked haggard and exhausted, his dreadlocks standing out in all directions. She could see faint lines of dried salt on his cheeks from evaporated tears. His head was bowed and his hands in his pockets. He looked miserable.

"March? What are you doing? Are you all right?" Sally touched his arm.

He nodded. "It's my . . . my . . . m-m . . ."

"Your mother? How's she doing?"

"Not well." Harlan appeared in the doorway of a nearby chamber. "I've done all I can for her. I don't think she's going to survive much longer."

Sally's heart sank. "What's the matter with her? I thought she was okay in her coma."

Harlan shook his head. "I don't know. I've been over the data more times than I can count. She should be improving physiologically, but instead she's growing worse. She's on life support now. I don't know what's wrong." He pounded a fist against the door frame.

A year ago—even a *week* ago—Sally would have made some sort of cutting comment to him to remind him of the horrors he'd wrought upon her friends and family over the years, but somehow to do that felt wrong after the ordeal he'd gone through to try to save his sister's life. He'd saved Sally's life too. She didn't know if she owed him after her journey through the Dream-world or if they were even, but she didn't care. He was hurting, and it was an unfamiliar emotion for him.

She embraced him. "I'm sorry, Harlan." His arms hovered uncertainly around her before settling around her in the most awkward hug she'd ever received. She knew it was awkward because it might have been the first hug he'd ever given. She looked over at March. "And I'm sorry for you too, March."

He nodded. "It's okay. I g-got to h . . . huh . . . She said she luh . . . loved me." A tear rolled down his cheek.

"She wants to see you." Harlan stepped out of Sally's arms. He looked confused, like he didn't know what to do with his hands anymore.

"Me? How does she even know about me?"

"I don't know that either. I didn't mention you to her." Harlan stepped aside to give Sally access to the room beyond. Sally glanced at March. He nodded to her. "Please . . ." The word sounded strange coming from Harlan's mouth. "Please, Sally. She doesn't have long."

"Of course." Sally took a step forward and dizziness threatened to overwhelm her. Minerva drifted down but March was there first, offering her his support. She gently brushed him off. "No, it's okay. I'm all right. Give a girl some space. After all, I was dead an hour ago." She smiled at him and he managed a faint smile in return. She wanted to reach up and brush his cheek, to feel his skin beneath hers, but instead she turned and hobbled into the room beyond.

Reggie Washington lay on one of Harlan's air mattresses, supporting her with jets of air warmed to body temperature like a puck on an air hockey table. Her gaunt body was swaddled in a thick blanket while a knit cap covered the short dark curls on her scalp. Her eyes were shut but instead of the dead-pale look of a coma, she had some color in her cheeks. The monitors around her told a different story, though. Sally had spent enough time in hospital rooms dealing with the aftereffects of her own superhero injuries or those of her teammates to know poor vital signs when she saw them. Reggie's heart was struggling to keep pushing blood through her atrophied body. A machine was quietly hissing as it pumped air through a tube that entered her chest just above her sternum. Other tubes ran into her arms, delivering a mixture of chemicals and fluids as Harlan's machines struggled to keep his sister alive and conscious.

Her eyes opened as Sally's hip brushed the corner of the bed. "There you are. Come over here, dear. Let me get a look at you." Her voice creaked like someone far older than her mid-forties, but perhaps that was a side effect of spending two decades in a coma.

Sally moved over to Reggie's side and took her hand. It was so frail in her grasp, she felt like she was holding a bundle of sticks wrapped in silk. "Hi, uh, Reggie. I'm Sally."

"Yes, dear. I know. I recognized you from the Dream-world."

"You know about it?"

"Of course I do. I created it."

"Oh." Sally felt very small for some reason, like she was addressing a goddess.

Reggie laughed softly, throwing her supporting machines into paroxysms of concern as they tried to keep her heart and lungs going. "I'll tell you what, my dear. I'm growing tired of this bed. Let's go."

"Go where?"

"Back."

Sally fell into the obsidian lake of Reggie's eyes.

Twenty-Six

The Dream-world is a separate place from the real world, but it is a real place.

The journey to the Dream-world seemed to take no time at all. One moment, Sally had been standing beside Reggie's bed and the next they were standing in a field of tall grasses, waving in a hot breeze. Sally looked down at herself and was shocked to see she was herself. In fact, she was wearing her Mustang Sally costume. The shiny red and gold suit looked out of place amid the greens and browns of the Dream-world, but somehow it felt right to her.

Reggie had gone through a much more remarkable change. Once again, she had taken on the guise of the child Sally had met in the Ticking Lord's dungeon, but this version was not the malnourished waif she'd encountered. This Reggie was still slender, but the healthy kind that came from lots of running and jumping and playing instead of too many missed meals. Her hair was untamed and puffed out in a natural afro. She wore a simple sarong-style robe of gray and was barefoot beneath it. She had a ragged stuffed elephant tucked underneath one arm while the other had pulled a tall pink and amber flower down to smell. She turned her head to smile at Sally. "Welcome to the Dream-world, Miss Sally."

Sally knelt beside her. "It seems really different than when I was here before. The colors are brighter, more vivid. The wind has a scent to it. I look like me. Hey, how come I look like me now and I didn't before?"

"I didn't know what you looked like before. It was the image you have of yourself in your subconscious mind."

Hearing the word *subconscious* pronounced by a five-year-old was one of the more amusing things Sally could recall. "Why are we back here now?"

"This is where I most feel at home. Everyone in my family is a parahuman." Reggie spoke carefully, slowing but not hesitating over the larger words. "My sister Irlene was in Just Cause, and she could change the size of things. Harlan makes his machines do whatever he wants. And I have my Dream-world, where I'm the Elephant Queen."

As she said *Elephant Queen*, her aspect changed, as if she briefly flashed into a full-blown elephant. "But why come back here now?" asked Sally. "Harlan says you're, uh, you're not doing so well. Medically speaking."

"It's okay, Miss Sally. I know I'm dying. My body is dying even as we speak here."

"But if you die, you'll be gone. And I'll be gone too, if I'm in here with you."

"No, you won't. That isn't how this works. The Dream-world is a separate place from the real world, but it is a real place."

"Like another dimension?"

Reggie smiled and touched Sally's nose like she was going to make it *beep*. "Now I know what my son sees in you. You're smart as a whip. Before, when I was a prisoner, you weren't in the true Dream-world. You were in a . . . I guess you could call it a bubble. It had edges. Boundaries." She flung her arms out and spun around. "This one is without limits."

"So you can come here whenever you want?"

"Of course I can. I created it, Miss Sally. I made everything in this world from the sky above to the blades of grass below to the elephants that walk the savannah. It's my most favorite place."

"Are we still up on the Moon, in your room?"

Reggie shook her head. "No. It's empty. I brought you here, like I brought March and Harlan. They're here too, at the same time as you. I'm talking to them too."

Sally looked around.

"Oh, you won't see them. It's like there are different channels and each of you is on one."

"That sounds really complicated."

Reggie smiled. "It is. But that's the Dream-world for you."

"Why did you bring me here?"

"To thank you. To show you where it is I will be after you leave. You worked so hard and sacrificed so much in your journey to come rescue me. I'm so glad you did, Miss Sally."

Sally bowed her head. "I didn't really have a choice. I owed your brother a favor for something he did."

"You had a choice. You always did. I'm just glad you chose to help him." Reggie sighed. "People say mean things about Harlan. They always did. They called him names like *Greasy* and worse. No wonder he hates people so much. The last time I saw him before today I was five years old and they were taking him away to jail after all the terrible things he did as Destroyer."

Sally found herself chewing on her lip. She wondered how much Reggie knew about Harlan's actions during the intervening years. It was probably better not to share them, though. The girl didn't need that kind of complication in her life. Or whatever she was going to have in her Dream-world. "Hey, so you're just going to stay here? Like, forever?"

"Yes. This is where I belong."

Sally looked around the horizon. "Well, it's a beautiful place. You enjoy it."

"And you look after my boy when you can. I didn't get much time with him, but it's for the best. He's his own man now, and I'm a stranger to him as he is to me."

"He loves you, Reggie."

"And I love him. And he knows that." She smiled. "He's very fond of you."

"I'm, uh, married."

"Of course."

The way Reggie agreed in such an off-handed way made Sally wonder what Reggie knew that she didn't. "I'll keep an eye on him. Make sure Harlan doesn't turn him into a supervillain or anything."

Reggie chuckled. "You should probably keep an eye on Harlan too. Once I'm gone, he'll need a new hobby to keep his mind occupied. Probably would be better for everyone if it was a positive direction."

Sally shivered. She knew what could happen when Harlan decided he was going to seek out revenge or lash out in anger. Body counts rose into double digits. "How do I go back? Leave the Dream-world?"

Reggie pointed past Sally. "Just keep on running that way. You'll find your path." She stepped back from Sally. "And I'll find mine." The ground rumbled as Reggie swelled up like a gray balloon. Sally jumped back in surprise as the small girl morphed into a huge elephant. Her majestic tusks shone pure white in the bright sunshine. She raised her trunk and trumpeted into the sky. A chorus of answering trumpets swirled in the air from a great distance away. Like a ship leaving its dock at the beginning of a new journey, the Elephant Queen departed through the tall grass.

Sally found her cheeks were wet with tears she didn't remember crying, but she wasn't sad. Reggie had found peace at last. No longer a prisoner, she was the embodiment of the Dream-world, and Sally couldn't think of any better hands in which to leave it.

She turned and ran.

* * *

Sally sat up suddenly, realizing she'd fallen asleep on the floor of Reggie's room in Harlan's Moonbase. She looked up at the bed and wasn't the least bit surprised to find it empty. Reggie was truly gone, body and soul, living on only in the Dream-world.

In the hallway beyond, both Harlan and March were sitting up from where they'd apparently fallen asleep on the floor. Reggie had been telling the truth when she said she was speaking to them at the same time she was with Sally. March looked despondent, his dreadlocks drooping over his face even in the low lunar gravity while tears trickled slowly down his cheeks to drip from the tip of his nose. Harlan, on the other hand, had both his fists and his teeth clenched in barely-suppressed rage. He saw Sally as she stared at him in awe of the cracks forming in his fortress of emotional equanimity. Much like the Ticking Lord's tower as it had collapsed, she could see the faltering flaws in the years of armor Harlan had built to cage his heart and keep it from ever being freed enough to show a real feeling. "Harlan . . ." She stopped, not knowing what to say.

He jumped to his feet and stalked down the corridor.

"Harlan?" She could have run after him, caught him in the space between heartbeats, made him turn around to face the truth of the world, but what would that really have accomplished?

"Let him g-go." March got to his feet and leaned against the corridor wall, looking like the weight of the world was resting on the back of his neck. "You can't help him."

"I have to try, March. It's what I do. I try."

He raised his head enough to meet her gaze. His eyes were as dark as the shadows of lunar craters, but like in the Dream-world, in his panther-form, they had starlight sparkles deep within them. Sally's mouth ran dry. "Deep down, I think we b-both knew she was guh . . . going to die."

"She's not dead!" Sally's vehemence surprised her. "How can you say that? She's a parahuman like you, March, and like both her brother and sister. How do you think you got your powers if not from her? Her powers are to create and enter into the Dream-world, and that's where she is right now."

He shook his head. "That's crazy."

Sally grabbed his hand and tugged him away from the wall. "It's not crazy, March. It's true. Come here. Look. If she was dead, her body would still be in here." She pointed at Reggie's room and the empty bed. "She didn't want to die. She didn't have to die. Staying here was killing her, though. Her body couldn't handle the stress of consciousness after being dormant so long. She went into the Dream-world to save herself. That's why she left. If anyone can find her in the Dream-world, it's you with your abilities." She turned back to him and found herself standing close to him. Very close. Closer than she'd expected.

She didn't pull away, and she knew she should have.

"Do you really believe that?"

"Yes, I—" They locked gazes, and before Sally could gather her thoughts, her lips were pressing against his. Had he bent down to kiss her or had she stretched up to meet him? She wasn't sure. She didn't remember moving but then, she couldn't think about anything except the warm glow suffusing through her from her toes and fingertips all the way up to her head. The kiss lasted an eternity and only a brief second or two before they both jumped away from each other as if scalded.

"I'm sorry," they both said at the same time.

"I, uh, n-need to go ch . . . ch . . ." March staggered away, heading toward the hangar like a drunk.

"I'll go check on Harlan." Sally's voice echoed louder than it should have in the corridor. She turned away from the direction March had gone, even though her feet wanted to pull her back, to follow him. "What are you doing, you asshole?" She whispered to herself.

"Sally, I—oh." Minerva came out of the room where Sally had been resting and stopped short. There was more surprise and more than a little judgment in that *oh* than if she'd been lectured for a solid two hours.

At first, Sally wondered how she'd known, but then realized it was *Minerva.* Of *course* she'd known. She could see the flush in Sally's cheeks, the foreign saliva on her lips. For that matter, she could probably smell Sally's arousal. "I . . . I'm sorry. It just . . . happened. Please don't tell anyone. It won't happen again."

"It's not my place to say." Minerva floated past Sally in the same direction March had gone. "We should leave soon. I'll be waiting by the hangar."

"I, uh, I won't be long." Sally fled, hoping to find a place she could be alone, gather her thoughts, and get herself back to some semblance of normalcy before rejoining March and Minerva. Minerva was right; it was well past time for them to return home. Sally needed to be far away from the Washington family, especially the tall young man with the dark eyes.

Her feet had other ideas, though, and she found herself approaching Harlan's workshop. The sounds of tinkering and muffled muttering came from within it. She nearly turned back again, but she was drawn toward the open door like she was an iron filing and it was a powerful electromagnet. She stopped in the doorway and looked in on Harlan. He was elbow-deep in his Steel Soldier recreation project, wrestling with some piece of recalcitrant technology buried deep within the machine's torso. At last, he pounded a fist on the Soldier's chest plate in frustration and hurled a wrench against the wall. Sally squeaked as it struck near her, and Harlan jumped around in furious embarrassment. "What are you doing here? Get out!"

Sally raised her hands in supplication. "Harlan, I'm sorry. I'm just . . . I don't know why I came here. I guess maybe to thank you."

He froze. "Why would you thank me?"

"I got to meet your sister, even if only for a few minutes. I got to travel through her Dream-world. It was an amazing experience, and I'll never forget it. She was—she *is* a magnificent person, and I wouldn't have met her if not for you. So yeah, thank you for that."

Harlan leaned against the workbench, for the first time looking his age. He crossed his arms tight over his chest and stared down at them. "Twenty years. And now she's gone."

Sally took a small step toward him. When he didn't respond, she took another. "But not forgotten. And not dead, Harlan. She went to the Dream-world. Not just her mind, but all of her, mind, body, and soul."

"There's no such thing as a soul. You can't quantify it. Can't measure it."

Sally realized she was standing right next to Harlan. She couldn't ever recall willingly being so close to the man who'd killed so many innocent people, who'd killed her father, and the man who might have been her father. She didn't see an enemy any longer. She saw a man who'd been obsessed, driven by his need to protect the one person who had meaning to him, a man who no longer had that motivating force to drive his actions.

He was lost.

"*There are more things in heaven and earth, Horatio, than are dreamt of in your philosophy.* Hamlet said that."

Harlan narrowed his eyes and looked at Sally for the first time. "He died."

"Okay, how about *luminous beings are we, not this crude matter.*"

"Yoda also died."

Sally stamped her foot. "You're missing the point I'm trying to make here, Harlan. They're both saying the same thing. You're a man of science, of hard numbers and ticking clocks and everything. But there's far more to the world than you can control using a machine. Look at me. Where does my super-speed *really* come from? Can you explain it? Yes, I've got the parahuman gene, but why does mine give me super-speed and yours gives you your machine telepathy or whatever it is? How do these things work without violating physics?"

"Physics? You?" Harlan snorted, a ghost of his sarcasm coming out from behind his façade of misery.

"I'm a sci-fi buff. Of course I know about physics. And I know that I violate the laws of physics every time I run fast. But I don't ask why, not because I don't want to know, but because there are more things in the universe that we don't know than things that we do. Reggie said she talked to you while she was talking with me. You must know she's not dead. She's just . . . somewhere else."

"Yes, we spoke." Harlan sighed. "It's just hard for me to believe. That's all. That, and I spent twenty years trying to achieve what I guess I finally did. I . . . I don't know what to do with myself now."

Sally embraced him. She hadn't planned on any such thing, but if there was anyone in or outside of the world, it was the man who stood before her. "You've already begun it. You spent twenty years being Destroyer. Now you're creating something instead. That's a marvelous thing, Harlan."

Harlan froze at the unexpected physical contact. He didn't pull away, but neither did he return the hug. It didn't matter to Sally. Her lifelong archenemy needed a hug, and nobody else was going to deliver it if she didn't. Maybe it wouldn't change anything.

But maybe it would.

Twenty-Seven

Maybe there's hope for all of us.

The flight home was over too soon, took way too long, and was filled with lengthy stretches of the most awkward silence Sally had ever experienced on any journey.

Harlan didn't accompany them back to the Earth. Privately, Sally thought it likely he would never again set foot on the world of his birth. He'd thanked Sally for her help and her concern, and then he'd turned his back on her like she'd never existed. She rejoined Minerva and March in the hangar and shortly thereafter, the flying van blasted off into space, leaving the Preserve behind.

Although Minerva didn't come right out and say anything to Sally about her misbehavior with March, there was a sense of cool judgment flowing from the dark-haired young woman as she watched the progress of their journey out the windows. Sally knew the best thing she could do would be to put effort into rekindling the flame with Jason. If anybody could drive March's dark eyes from her thoughts, it would be her big blond Mastiff of a husband. Even so, she knew deep down she would always have the question of *what if?* needling at her in her weakest moments. Hopefully, March would head off on his own life journey, and the two of them would chart separate paths through the remainder of their lives.

Somehow, though, Sally didn't think so.

The way Harlan's life had intertwined with hers time and time again, beginning before she'd ever been born, she suspected March would turn up many times over the years. She would just have to be strong.

The van, stealthed against detection of all kinds, descended toward a city that Sally figured was Philadelphia. As they dropped lower, she recognized the parking garage where from where they'd departed. It meant their journey really had reached its end. They'd come full circle.

The van touched down on the concrete rooftop with a slight bump. Sally's muscles protested the return of earth-normal gravity, but at the same time, she felt glad to be home. Running on the Moon had been too difficult, and she was anxious to get some miles under her feet.

The side door of the van slid open and Minerva floated out, shaking her hair loose in the breeze blowing atop the parking garage. "I'm going to fly back to New York. I need the fresh air." She picked up her bag and slung it over her shoulder. "Are you coming, Sally?"

Sally shook her head. "No, there's something I need to do first. It'll only take a couple of days at the most. I need to go talk to my mom. In person."

Minerva nodded. "I understand. I'll keep the plates spinning at home while you're gone. Don't be long."

"I won't."

Minerva's costume appeared around her as if it had always been there. Sunlight glinted off the bronze of her helmet and breastplate, and her crimson cape spread wide as she launched into the sky, heading northeast.

Sally turned to see March holding her bag up to her. "I g-guess this is goodbye."

She took the back from him. "Yes. It has to be, March. We can't do this, even though it's what we both want. It's wrong. I'm married, and I'm happy." A lump rose in her throat. She felt like a heel, saying what she was. "You'll find someone else, someone who you can love and who can love you back."

"I know." Where he stood on the roof, the sun was behind him, keeping her from seeing his eyes.

Sally thought that was for the best. "Take care of your uncle. He needs you in his life more than ever now. He needs someone to nourish that spark of goodness within him. To encourage him to become a creator instead of staying Destroyer. I can't wait to see what he might come up with."

March nodded. "I will." He turned to get back into the van but stopped at the door. "Sally . . . If things were d-different . . ."

"Oh, the hell with it." Sally dropped her bag and flashed across the space between her and March. She threw her arms around his neck and kissed him, long and hard, her perceptions accelerated so she wouldn't miss a single nuance of the experience. Their tongues danced around each other and she buried her fingers in the tangle of his dreadlocks. A tiny moan of pleasure escaped her as he pressed her to him. She knew she had to stop *right now* or there would be no stopping herself. She wanted him so badly it was making her legs shake. Unwillingly, she stepped back until she was just out of arm's reach.

"Wow." March's eyes were wide and his teeth brilliant white in the darkness of his face. "We should m-meet again sometime just so you c-c-can say goodbye like that again."

"We will, someday." Sally heard herself say the words, and realized she meant them. "Farewell, March, but not goodbye. That's forever, and that's too long." She paused. "I'll see you in my dreams."

She grabbed her bag and fled down one level of the parking garage. She paused to catch her breath for her heart was pounding like she'd run halfway across the state. After making sure nobody was around, she ducked between two parked cars, opened her bag, and changed into her Mustang Sally costume. If she was going to be doing any sort of running, it would be best if she were dressed for the occasion. As she repacked her clothes, she thought maybe she could see March one last time. She zipped back up the steps to the top level of the garage, but the van was already gone.

"Well, shit. That's probably for the best." She checked the map on her phone. Pittsburgh. Yeah, that would be a nice run. Nothing helped her clear her head like speed. She dialed a number. "Hello, Davey? It's me."

"Hi, boss. How was your conference?"

"It was . . . it was very interesting." Sally was glad her assistant wasn't standing in front of her. Davey was sharp enough that she would have picked up Sally was hiding something. "I'm going to need a couple more days though. I need to run home. Well, not *run* home. Can you book me a flight from Pittsburgh to Phoenix?"

"I thought you were in Philadelphia."

"I am. But I'll be in Pittsburgh in about an hour."

"All right. I'll email you your flight info."

Sally disconnected and looked at her phone. Was she ready to call Jason? She knew she should, but it felt as insurmountable a task as any she'd ever felt. Texting would have to do.

Hey babe I'm back.

She waited. It felt like forever before Jason replied. *Hey darlin when are you coming back to the Fort?*

Soon. I need to go home and see my mom.

Everything ok?

Yeah. I'll be home in a couple days.

Ok. Give her my love. And give yourself my love too.

I love you, Jason.

Love you too, Sally. Hurry home.

Hurrying was what she did best. She turned on her phone's navigation and set a course for Pittsburgh. *305 miles*, it told her. *4 hours 49 minutes.*

Sally grinned. She'd see about that.

She ran.

* * *

Phoenix was hotter than ever, and Sally enjoyed the feeling of the desert heat baking her bones. She sat on the pergola of her childhood home and sipped lemonade with her mom. Faith Thompson looked as she always had to Sally, bottle-blonde hair, blue eyes, bronze skin with maybe a few new wrinkles since the last time they'd gotten together. Her mom was short and slender, like her, and in recent years had given up super-speed in favor of yoga, which she said helped her maintain her figure better.

"I was surprised to get your call, but I'm glad you came by." Faith came out onto the porch from the kitchen. "I haven't got any snacks or anything. Wasn't really expecting company."

"That's okay, mom. The lemonade is fine."

Faith sat down at the table. "What brings you way out west?"

"Can't a girl visit her mom without getting grilled about it?"

Faith snorted. "Don't bullshit me, young lady. You never were any good at that."

Sally chuckled. "No, I don't guess I ever will be." She took a drink and held up her glass, watching the bits of lemon pulp swirl around. She had practiced what she was about to say during her run from Philadelphia to Pittsburgh. Then again on her flight from Pittsburgh to Phoenix. And it still wasn't getting any easier to say. "Mom . . . Was Lionheart my father?"

Faith didn't answer right away, which was as good as an admission in Sally's eyes. If she'd flatly denied it, or responded with shock and anger, Sally would have believed it. At last Faith looked up into her daughter's eyes. "How did you find out?"

"It doesn't matter, mom. Honestly. I'm not mad. I just want to know why, and why you never told me the truth."

Faith picked at a splinter on the table. "I was already married to Bobby when we joined Just Cause. He was my first love, my only love. And then one day Lionheart joined us, and there was something about him that I couldn't resist. Oh, we tried. We held each other at bay for a long, long time. Until we couldn't."

"I understand, mom. Really, I do." Sally reached across the table to squeeze her mom's hand. "So you had an affair."

"It was more than that. I . . . *loved* him. When he left for China, it broke my heart. He was gone for five years. You'd think in that time I would have gotten over my infatuation with him. But no." She shook her head. "He came back when Tornado started getting sick. It was just one night. I seduced him. He was married by that time too. And he had a little girl—Yunbao, who's on Just Cause with you now. I went to him. I wouldn't take no for an answer. I wanted to see if we still had the . . . the magnetic attraction that we'd had for so long."

"Did you?"

Faith smiled. "We did. It was amazing. And I found out I was pregnant only a few days later."

"Did dad, uh, Bobby know?"

"No. We made sure of that. We never saw each other again afterward."

"Are you sure I'm Lionheart's?"

"Yes. You have his eyes. Your hair is the exact shade of his fur. You've got his stubborn streak in you. The timing pretty much confirmed it." Faith rested her chin on her hands. "I can't imagine what you must think of me now. *My mom is a liar and a cheater.*"

"No, mom. I understand. I forgive you for not telling me, and I'm grateful that you finally did tell me the truth. Now me, I can't imagine what it must have been like to lose both Bobby and Lionheart at the same time."

Faith snarled. "Destroyer. That son of a bitch. Wherever he is, I hope he rots in hell for what he did."

Sally glanced up at the crescent Moon, pale white in the blue sky. "Someday he might, but maybe there's hope for him yet." She smiled. "Maybe there's hope for all of us."

ABOUT THE AUTHOR

Ian Thomas Healy dabbles in many different genres. He's a ten-time participant and winner of National Novel Writing Month and is also the creator of the *Writing Better Action Through Cinematic Techniques* workshop, which helps writers to improve their action scenes.

When not writing, which is rare, he enjoys watching hockey, reading comic books (and serious books, too), and living in the great state of Colorado, which he shares with his wife, children, house-pets, and approximately five million other people.

Visit www.ianthealy.com for more information.

ABOUT THE ARTIST

Jeff Hebert is the creator of the HeroMachine online character portrait creator. He lives in Durango, Colorado, where he pursues his lifetime dream of drawing superheroes all day while not wearing pants.

www.ingramcontent.com/pod-product-compliance
Lightning Source LLC
Chambersburg PA
CBHW031938240626
47153CB00003B/784

* 9 7 8 1 9 7 1 4 4 5 0 9 0 *